# Praise for the Books of J. C. E~~

"A thoroughly entertaining series deb
characters and enough plot twists—ar.
beginning to end."
>—*Booklist*, starred          _.. *Booked 4 Murder*

"Filled with clues that make you go 'Huh?' and a list of potential
subjects that range from the charming to the witty to the intense.
Readers root for Phee as she goes up against a killer who may not
stop until Phee is taken out well before her time. Enjoy this laugh-
out-loud funny mystery that will make you scream for the authors to
get busy on the next one."
>—*Suspense Magazine* on *Molded 4 Murder*

"Engaging characters and a stirring mystery kept me captivated from
the first page to the last."
>—Dollycas, Amazon Vine Voice, on *Divide and Concord*

"Well-crafted sleuth, enjoyable supporting characters. This is a series
not to be missed."
>—*Cozy Cat Reviews* on *Death, Dismay and Rosé*

"A sparkling addition to the Wine Trail Mystery series. A toast to
protagonist Norrie and Two Witches Winery, where the characters
shine and the mystery flows. This novel is a perfect blend of
suspense and fun!"
>—Carlene O'Neil, author of the Cypress Cove Mysteries,
>on *Chardonnayed to Rest*

# Books by J. C. Eaton

## The Wine Trail Mysteries

*A Riesling to Die*
*Chardonnayed to Rest*
*Pinot Red or Dead?*
*Sauvigone for Good*
*Divide and Concord*
*Death, Dismay and Rosé*
*From Port to Rigor Morte*
*Mischief, Murder and Merlot*

## The Sophie Kimball Mysteries

*Booked 4 Murder*
*Ditched 4 Murder*
*Staged 4 Murder*
*Botched 4 Murder*
*Molded 4 Murder*
*Dressed Up 4 Murder*
*Broadcast 4 Murder*
*Saddled Up 4 Murder*
*Grilled 4 Murder*

## The Marcie Rayner Mysteries

*Murder in the Crooked Eye Brewery*
*Murder at the Mystery Castle*
*Murder at Classy Kitchens*

# Grilled
## *4*
# Murder

J. C. Eaton

BEYOND THE PAGE
PUBLISHING

*Grilled 4 Murder*
J. C. Eaton
Copyright © 2022 J. C. Eaton
Cover design and illustration by Dar Albert, Wicked Smart Designs

Beyond the Page Books
are published by
Beyond the Page Publishing
www.beyondthepagepub.com

ISBN: 978-1-958384-85-5

In memory of Streetboy (Streets), our little chiweenie, who was the inspiration for Streetman in our Sophie Kimball Mysteries. We took your antics and gave them a whole new meaning in our books. Your spirit will always live on in print. And please, don't snap at anyone in Heaven! At least wait until we meet you over the Rainbow Bridge.

# ACKNOWLEDGMENTS

Wow! This is the tenth novel in our Sophie Kimball Mysteries, and if it wasn't for Susan Schwartz in Australia, who has been editing these quirky mysteries since the first one came out in 2017, we would never have gotten this far. Susan, your editing prowess continues to amaze us and we are so grateful for your time, energy, and enthusiasm!

Authors in the Cozy Mystery Crew, we are so appreciative of your time, advice, and support! Thank you, Libby Klein, Linda Reilly, Becky Clark, Esme Addison, Tina Kashian, Vicki Delany, Elizabeth Penney, Shari Reynolds, Raquel V. Reyes, Ellen Byron, and Olivia Matthews.

When it comes to technology, we are complete dunderheads, but thanks to Larry Finkelstein and Gale Leach, whose understanding of all things technical has saved us numerous times, we are exceedingly grateful.

We still shake our heads that we have such an amazing agent, Dawn Dowdle, from Blue Ridge Literary Agency. Her guidance, knowledge, and patience have carried us through this book and all of our cozy mysteries.

Cover artist Dar Albert, from Wicked Smart Designs, deserves a special kudos for the spectacular cover that really captures the essence of the story.

And to our extraordinary editor, Bill Harris, at Beyond the Page Publishing, we thank you for your sense of humor and for appreciating the weird writing world we inhabit.

# CHAPTER 1

*Williams Investigations*
*Glendale, Arizona*

"Welcome Back, Mrs. Gregory!" Augusta announced the second I walked through the door of our office. "How was the honeymoon? I already got your husband's version before he rushed off to Sun City to see a client."

"Fantastic! An entire ten days in Maui without any frantic phone calls from my mother or the book club ladies. Of course, she made up for it the minute we arrived home yesterday. How brave Streetman was during the Fourth of July and something about Herb and a barbeque cook-off. I let it waft over me."

"Her neighbor? Pinochle-playing Herb Garrett from across the street?"

"Who else? He and those wacky cronies of his are always up to something. No worries. Whatever it was, I'm sure she'll repeat it. Oh, and before I forget, I'm still keeping Kimball as my professional name. I'm now Sophie Kimball Gregory."

"Sounds like one of those trust-fund babies."

"Ha. We should be so lucky. Marshall and I will have to earn our money the old-fashioned way by working for it. Hmm, I don't hear Nate's voice. Is he out?"

"Yep. In your favorite neck of the woods, Sun City West. Had a meeting with Deputy Bowman to finalize some paperwork on prior cases. By the way, I thought I'd seen everything until your aunt Ina walked into your wedding ceremony wearing that bizarre paisley caftan with the long ropy train. Best part was when your mother's dog attacked it. Wouldn't let go of the rope."

"Aargh. Don't remind me."

"And the dog dance at the conclusion. Whoa. That was a first. Quite a wedding ceremony. Never expected anything like it in my life."

"What part? My aunt's attire or the dog? And by the way, that was one of her more subtle outfits."

Augusta widened her eyes. "I meant the dog."

"I think the staff at the Peoria City Hall are still in shock. My mother just *had* to bring him in her tote bag along with a recording of that 'Pizzicato Moonbeam' song the dog likes. At least she drove him home before the reception."

"For which the Renaissance Hotel is eternally grateful, I'm sure."

We both laughed. I grabbed a K-Cup of dark roast and put it in the Keurig. "Well, no sense putting it off," I said. "Those invoices aren't going to pay themselves. Not to mention the billing."

"Relax. You've got the entire week to get back into your routine. No earth-shattering cases going on. Only the usual stuff. Maybe the worst thing we'll have to put up with this summer is the heat."

As I opened the door to my office, I prayed Augusta was right. Ever since I arrived at my job as the bookkeeper/accountant for Williams Investigations, it was one murder after another. And all of them courtesy of my mother's senior retirement community in Sun City West.

Augusta is our office secretary and I'm Sophie (Phee) Kimball, oops, Kimball Gregory now. A former divorcée in my forties with a now-grown-up daughter, I moved out here from Mankato, Minnesota, at the beckoning of my friend, former police detective Nate Williams, who retired to start his own investigative business in Glendale, Arizona. Essentially, he made me one of those "offers you couldn't refuse," but *really* it was emotional blackmail. He reminded me of the time I kissed the icy pavement in a Target parking lot compliments of the Minnesota snow and ice.

True, Glendale is practically spitting distance from my mother's retirement community, but Nate promised we'd keep it that way. He lied. Williams Investigations got dragged into more cases out there in the past three years than Gibbs ever saw on *NCIS*. The one truly good thing to come out of it was the fact Nate hired another detective, Marshall Gregory, whom I just married eleven days ago.

Like Nate, Marshall retired from the Mankato Police Department but wasn't quite ready to quit working. As long as that work meant living in a climate where snow was optional. I later found out that Marshall took Nate up on his offer because he knew I had relocated here as well. It turned out we both had secret crushes on each other back in Mankato but never acknowledged it.

Now, settled into a comfortable rental home in the neighboring community of Vistancia, Marshall and I were coming to grips with what it was like living in a place where people referred to a hundred and three degrees as "warm."

The blue light flashed on the Keurig and within seconds I inhaled the aroma of my dark roast. "Yell if you need me," I said to Augusta and trotted off to my office. It felt good to boot up the computer and attack the small pile of bills that Augusta had thoughtfully placed next to the keyboard. *Thank you, Augusta.*

About an hour or so into my morning, I heard a familiar clarion call from the outer office. "Phee! Your mother's on the phone. Said she didn't want to monkey with your cell number. She sounded frantic."

*If she didn't sound frantic, then I would be concerned her pulse stopped.*

"Thanks." I picked up the phone. So help me, if this was about Herb's barbequing, I may have screamed.

My mother's voice did sound a bit more anxious than usual. "Phee! Thank goodness I reached you."

*I'm in the office, not trekking the Andes. Of course you reached me.*

She continued before I could utter a syllable. "Streetman grabbed something from one of those bushes they never trim a few doors down from Herb Garrett and the dog won't let go of it. I think it's some sort of animal. All I saw was dark fur. It could be anything. He ran under the bed as soon as we got inside and I can't get him out. It could be a rat or worse. Can you drive over here? We need to move the mattress and box spring from the bed. It's too heavy for me to lift and Herb's not home. He and Wayne are trying out bacon renderings at Wayne's house for the Master Grillers contest."

"Mom, I'm at work. Work! I can't stop what I'm doing and drive over there. Did you try the book club ladies?"

"It's Monday morning. Shirley went shopping with Lucinda. Cecilia has a meeting at her church, Myrna's with the bocce club and Louise isn't answering her phone."

*Good for Louise.*

"And forget about my sister. Ina's been way too wrapped up with the Phoenix Opera Company's summer schedule."

"Streetman probably found a piece of old cloth. The wind blows everything around."

"It's not an old cloth. It could be a rat. My God, Phee! The poor dog could get bitten."

"Hold on a second, will you?"

I pushed the door open wider and called out to Augusta. "Didn't you say Nate was in Sun City West with one of the sheriff's deputies?"

"Uh-huh. At the posse station. Been there awhile."

Before she could continue, I grabbed my cell phone and tapped Nate's number. "Sorry to interrupt your meeting but my mother is having some sort of catastrophe with the dog and I'm not about to drive over there, so I wondered—"

"If you could convince me to check it out?"

"Yeah. Please."

"You're in luck, kiddo. We finished up a few seconds ago and I'm about to get into my car. I'll swing over there. She's only a few blocks away."

"You're a lifesaver. Call me when you get there."

Seconds later, I resumed my conversation with my mother. "Nate's on his way over. He was at the posse station. Does Streetman sound like he's in distress?"

"It sounds like he's licking something. He could be wounded and whatever he grabbed could be running loose around here. I'm unlocking the front door so I don't have to waste time when Nate gets here."

"Okay. Sounds good. Talk to you in a bit."

"What was that all about?" Augusta asked. She was now standing in the doorway to my office.

"Don't ask. The dog found something in a bush during his walk and my mother's convinced it's alive. He wouldn't let her get near him and now he's under the bed."

"Um, what exactly is Nate going to do?"

"Move mattresses, I think. Frankly, I'm not too worried. That dog gets attached to all sorts of things, and so far they've all been inanimate."

"Hope you're right." She turned and walked back to her desk.

I pictured the dog latching on to an old piece of stinky material or someone's discarded lunch bag. Of course, my mother did say it was furry, but that didn't mean anything. Her imagination was right up there with most fantasy writers'. Not wanting to waste another second, I returned to the bills and continued working until the next phone call came in.

This time it was Nate. "Not a rat. It was a kitten."

*"Was?* Oh, how awful. Streetman killed a kitten. That's horrible."

"Oops. Wrong word choice. *Is* a kitten, but he may lick it to death. He's enamored with the little thing. And from the looks of it, the kitten likes him, too. He or she's been crawling all over that dog."

"Did you have to remove the mattress and box spring to get to him?"

"No, by the time your mother let me inside, the dog was next to the couch with the kitten at his feet. Here, I'll let you talk with your mother."

"It's a cat, Phee. A cat! What am I supposed to do with a cat? And you know how territorial that dog is, he won't let it out of his sight. I can barely get that fleece thing away from him when it needs to be washed. And now, a cat of all things. What am I going to do with a cat?"

"The same thing you do with the dog. Feed it, give it water, and get it a litter box. It's a kitten, for crying out loud, not a Bengal tiger. Besides, chances are it belongs to someone in your neighborhood and they're probably frantic to find it. Especially with all the coyotes roaming around. You said it was found a few doors down from Herb. Have him ask his neighbors when he gets back. Put Nate on. I'll call you later."

"It's fine, kiddo. I could hear your voice. Look, I've got a few minutes. I'll scout out those houses and see if anyone's lost a kitten. Catch you later."

4

In the background, I could hear my mother moaning, "A cat . . . a cat . . . what am I supposed to do with a cat?"

Miraculously, I was able to get caught up with my billing before the next interruption a couple of hours later. This time it was Nate and the knock on the doorjamb caused me to jump.

"Whoa. Didn't realize you were that engrossed. I'll make it quick. I scoped out the houses that were near the bush your mother described and all of them are locked up for the summer. Then I ran into a lady from across the street who was picking up her paper and she confirmed it. Said, and I quote, 'the tiny weeds by the sidewalk are a dead giveaway the snowbirds have flown the coup for the summer. Sissies. They didn't even wait till it hit a hundred and eight degrees. Nope. Out of here when it reached ninety-nine.'"

"Did she have any idea whose kitten it was?" I asked.

"Nope. Said two of the neighbors had 'fou-fou' dogs but no cats as far as she knew. What the heck's a 'fou-fou' dog?"

"I think the opposite of Streetman. Not size, mind you, but temperament. You know, sweet, cuddly, and neuroses-free."

"So, a small, normal dog, huh?"

I nodded.

"I stopped back at your mom's place and told her to post some signs around the neighborhood. The dog was still licking the kitten when I left."

"That's encouraging."

Nate shook his head. "Did I mention your mother was still seated with her head in her lap? All I could hear amid the groaning was, 'What am I going to do with a cat?'"

"Oh, brother."

# CHAPTER 2

At a little after four, I phoned my mother and suggested she contact one of the pet rescue places. Needless to say, I wasn't prepared for her response.

"What???" she bellowed. "You want to take Streetman's cat to a shelter? That will destroy him. Have you gone crazy?"

*Me? That gives new meaning to the expression "turn on a dime."*

"First of all, it's not Streetman's cat. Not yet anyway. Have you at least tried to put up a few posters in your neighborhood?"

"For your information, Lucinda posted it on that Sun City West pet rescue site two hours ago. I swear that woman's on Facebook before she even has her first cup of coffee. Good thing she suggested we phrase it 'call to describe' because there are a lot of nutcases out there. Between you and me, I hope no one sees the announcement. I can't imagine what this would do to the dog."

"I'm sure he'll get over it. Buy him a new chewy toy or something."

"Shirley already did. I asked her to do me a favor and pick up some cat food and a few supplies while she was at Costco. That's how I wound up talking with Lucinda."

"Supplies? I hope you didn't go overboard."

"No. Not really. Just two different varieties of canned kitten food, a litter box, the deluxe litter scooper, two varieties of litter, two bowls—although the kitten's been drinking from Streetman's bowl—a small cat bed, a scratching post, a cat carrier, and, oh, a toy mouse that's large enough so the dog won't choke on it."

*In other words, another dog toy.*

"Can you tell if the kitten is male or female?"

"No. I thought maybe you and Marshall could take a good look after work."

"We won't be able to tell either. Besides, it'll have to wait until another night. Marshall has a meeting tonight with clients who are driving in from Gold Canyon, outside of Apache Junction, and I thought I'd take a nice swim. Look, don't get too attached to that cat. Its owner will most likely be checking the pet rescue site. In fact, they may have posted a lost kitten announcement already."

"No, they didn't. Lucinda checked. I wish you could see them, Phee. They're both sound asleep on the couch. The kitten is snuggled under Streetman's chin."

6

*I don't want to be around when she has to extricate it in order to return it to its owner.*

"That's wonderful. Absolutely wonderful. Look, I've got work to do. Talk to you tomorrow."

I rolled my neck a few times and stretched my arms before getting back to the computer screen. By ten minutes to five, I had finished the last of the invoices and handed Augusta the bills to be mailed.

"There'll be hell to pay if someone comes forth to claim that kitten," I said. "Thanks to the Costco pet department, that cat has more worldly possessions than most lottery winners."

Augusta's grin couldn't have been any bigger. "Yep. Saw that disaster coming the minute you told me about it. You think the dog's neurotic? Wait till the cat grows up. Harrumph. Like I said, too bad it wasn't a kangaroo rat or a raccoon."

Just then, the office phone rang and Augusta picked up. "It's Marshall. For you. He's in Sun City with another client. Do you want me to transfer it to your office or just hand it to you?"

I reached for the phone. "It's Marshall. Not the Secret Service."

The call was a quick one. Marshall let me know he had no idea when his meeting tonight with the couple from Gold Canyon would end. "Don't worry about dinner, hon. We'll figure something out."

"I wasn't going to prepare anything that exciting," I said. "Ham steak and veggies. We can always nuke a frozen meal instead."

"Sounds good. Hope this won't be too long. They want us to track down some relatives they've lost contact with. Since they don't have children, they figured they'd leave their inheritance with the family."

"Wow. Someone's going to get a heck of a surprise. Unlike us. We'll wind up with Streetman. And a garage full of his stuff. My mother better live well into her late nineties and then some."

"For sure. Go enjoy an evening swim and we'll chat when I get home. I don't care if I have to eat cottage cheese and crackers."

"Ugh. I think we can do better than that. Catch you tonight."

A short while later, Augusta and I turned off the lights, locked up, and headed out for the day. Since Marshall wouldn't be home for quite a while, I called my friend Lyndy to see if she wanted to meet me at our neighborhood pool. Like me, as soon as the temperature got above eighty, she was in the water.

"It's your first day back from your honeymoon," she said the second I got her on the phone. "Don't you want to spend it with your husband?"

"Of course, but he's with clients. At least it's not a meeting with Bowman and Ranston."

"The MCSO deputies? I keep getting them mixed up."

"Bowman's the one who looks like a grizzly bear and Ranston has an uncanny resemblance to a Sonoran desert toad. Good grief. I can't believe I'm being so catty."

Lyndy laughed. "Relax. I don't think anyone's tapping your phone. Are you still at work?"

"No. I'm about to start the car. I need to be quick. I'm melting from the heat already. So, is it a go?"

"Sure. Meet me in forty minutes. I'm just getting out of work."

"Thanks, Lyndy."

Lyndy Ellsworth worked for a medical billing company and lived in my neighborhood. Like me, she was a transplant from another state who couldn't get enough of the water. "I'm making up for lost time," she once said. "I spent the first forty years back East and the only time I got to swim was once a year when I came out West to visit my loony aunt. Now I can swim all the time but I'm also stuck contending with my aunt every other day. Go figure."

I met Lyndy's aunt on a few occasions and I had to agree with her. The woman was right up there with my mother's book club ladies, but fortunately their paths didn't cross. According to Lyndy, her aunt spent most of her time unofficially patrolling her street and reporting violations to the Covenants, Conditions and Restrictions committee, better known as the CC & R police.

An hour later, I paddled around Vistancia's pool with Lyndy. We stuck to the deep end so as not to be bothered by families with small children.

"My gosh," I said to her. "I'm really becoming an old stick-in-the-mud, swimming way over here in order to avoid those kids."

"You're not the only one. I don't want to be splashed either. Silly, huh? Considering we're already in the water. So, catch me up on the latest Williams Investigations intel and any new Sun City West gossip I haven't heard from my aunt."

I grabbed a water noodle from the edge of the pool, tossed one to Lyndy, and then drifted over toward her. "You won't believe this one. Streetman found a kitten while he and my mother were out walking today. He latched on to it like nobody's business and thinks he's its mother. All but licked the fur off of it."

"And your mother's okay with this?"

"I wouldn't exactly say 'okay' but she bought enough feline paraphernalia to last all nine lives that the cat may have."

"What if its owner shows up?"

"Then she'll have to figure out a way to extricate Streetman's teeth from the owner's legs or arms when he or she tries to remove the cat."

"Oh, my gosh. You're serious."

"Oh, yeah. Just pray she doesn't decide to name the thing."

"Whoa. Bet you wish you and Marshall were back in Hawaii, huh?"

"Actually, if my mother keeps the cat, she and that neurotic chiweenie of hers will wind up doting over the thing. Either that or throwing themselves into fits of despair should the owner come forth."

"Hey, before I forget, I really enjoyed meeting your daughter and the rest of the family at the wedding."

"Yeah, I miss Kalese already. She and my niece Ramona were able to extend their stay and drive to the Grand Canyon. Ramona's in the Navy and just got reassigned from Qatar to San Diego. Maybe she'll be able to visit us once in a while, especially if it can coincide with the holidays when Kalese's school is on break."

"Your cousin Kirk is quite a riot. Your aunt Ina's son, right?"

"Uh-huh. We're all surprised he turned out so normal considering his upbringing. Frankly, I was surprised he and his wife flew in. After my aunt's bizarre nuptials, I figured he and Judy wouldn't dare come back here. She says she still has nightmares about sleeping at the Cactus Wren."

Lyndy let out a chuckle. We continued our swim for a few more minutes before calling it a night and agreed to get together for an evening swim in the next few days. The forecast called for temps above a hundred and three and our only salvation was the pool.

Once home, I changed into shorts and a T-shirt and set the table, figuring I'd nuke something as soon as Marshall got in. Minutes later, I heard the familiar key in the door.

His voice all but resounded, "Boy, it's good to be home. And it'll be even better once I give you a hug. But the hug will have to wait until I get these salads into the kitchen. I decided to stop and pick up chicken Caesar salads. Beats the alternatives. Interesting couple, by the way. He's a retired commercial pilot and she recently retired from a major software company in the the valley. They're intent on putting their affairs in order so that they can enjoy their retirement."

"Think it will be difficult tracking down their relatives?"

Marshall shrugged. "Hard to say, but I've got some decent info to work with. Geez, I've been so busy all day I never got a chance to catch up with Nate."

"My mother did. This morning."

"Huh?"

"I wanted to tell you earlier but there wasn't time. Streetman found a small dark gray kitten in a bush a few doors down from Herb Garrett's house and latched on to it. Refused to give it up and ran into the house with it. My mother was convinced it was a rat so I had Nate check it out."

"I'm afraid to ask."

"No worries. The dog didn't do anything awful to the poor little thing. In fact, he adores it. Licked it and everything. *That's* the problem. When the kitten's owner is found, the dog will go berserk. You know how territorial he is. Nearly bit that woman's arm off at that bogus garage sale a while back when she reached for a fleece blanket he'd nabbed."

"So I take it your mother's okay about owning a cat?"

"If it would make the dog happy, she'd own a rhinoceros."

By the time we finished our salads, we collapsed on the couch and turned on the TV. Marshall put his arm around my shoulder and sighed. "Should be a pretty normal week. Nothing out of the ordinary."

It was the sentence that tempted fate, because everything afterward was anything but ordinary.

# CHAPTER 3

I was two steps behind Marshall as we raced out of the house to get to the office the next morning. That's when the landline rang. "You go ahead," I said. "I'll grab the call and see you over there." Normally, I'd let the answering machine pick up, but in the back of my mind I had a sneaky suspicion it was my mother with the latest catastrophe. *Cat* being the key part of the word.

"Phee! Thank goodness I didn't miss you. This is a nightmare. Someone just called because they think Essie might be their neighbor's cat. The neighbors are in Vegas for the week and the caller is watching the house."

"Essie? You named the kitten?"

"I didn't. The dog did. Essie is the sound of the initials *S* and *C*. They stand for Streetman's cat. I can't very well go around calling, 'Streetman's cat, Streetman's cat.' So, I shortened it to Essie."

"Mom, I told you not to get too attached."

"The person is going to be here any minute. Oh, no. The bell. That's them. I'll call you back."

"Call me at the office. I'm on my way out."

"I knew this was going to happen," I said to Augusta when I got to work a few minutes later. "I can only pray the dog didn't go berserk along with my mother."

"You can relax. They didn't. Your mother left a detailed message on our phone. It was the first message I played when I got in. Here, you can listen for yourself."

Augusta pushed the Play button on the phone and I took a breath as my mother's voice permeated the room. "This is Harriet Plunkett. Phee, are you there? We can all breathe easy. Essie isn't the neighbor's cat. Very nice woman, by the way. Name's Velda Hochberg and she lives on the street behind Herb. Turns out her neighbors own a solid gray Russian Blue kitten and Essie has one white paw so it's not that cat. Also, the Russian Blue cat isn't missing after all. He was hiding in the linen closet. So, there's no need for you to rush over here. I'll talk to you later."

My jaw dropped and it took me a minute to gather my thoughts. "I wasn't planning on rushing over there but good golly, if my mother gets another call from anyone claiming to own that cat, I'm afraid she'll go off the deep end. Preceded only by Streetman."

"Someone probably dumped that cat off in her neighborhood. Used to happen to us all the time. Of course, you can never have too many barn cats on a Wisconsin dairy farm."

"Sun City West is hardly a dairy farm but you may be right. For all of our sakes, I certainly hope so."

At midmorning my mother called back. This time to tell me she made an appointment with the vet this week to find out if the cat was male or female and "go from there." Then something about Shirley making matching vests for it and Streetman. I all but gagged. I was about to tell her that my lunch break was over and I needed to get back to work when she dropped the latest bombshell.

"Chopped Grill Masters from the Food Network will be judging that competition Herb and the pinochle crew are in. They made the qualifying rounds last month, then the finals a few weeks ago. Now it's down to two teams. The competition takes place in a few weeks. Right here at the Rec Center on RH Johnson Boulevard. In addition to the contest, there'll be lots of food trucks serving up all sorts of grilled specialties, and the Sun City West Square Dance Club will be performing. I completely forgot to tell you, what with Streetman finding Essie and all."

"Um, that's nice. It will give Herb something to do." *Other than gossip.*

"Herb? Who cares about Herb? Myrna, Paul, and I were asked to MC the event. Phee, are you still on the line? Phee?"

I struggled for words to form in my mouth but the only thing I succeeded in doing was to clear my throat while my mother continued to talk.

"This is national television, not some rinky-dink local show. And they're sending three judges. Famous grill masters. Too bad it's not a baked brisket competition or we could use your Alte Tante Rosie's recipe from the old country. I only hope Paul can get through the event without mentioning fish but I suppose that's impossible."

My mother and Myrna had a weekly cozy mystery book talk show on KSCW, the local radio station, while Paul Schmidt had a radio show of his own, *Lake Fishing with Paul*, at the same station. Apparently Myrna and my mother got the schedule mixed up a while back and the three of them went on the air at once. It was a verbal melee complete with pointers about bait mixed in with all sorts of references to cozy mysteries. And while Augusta and I were stunned listening to it, apparently the Sun City West audience couldn't have been more delighted. As a result, Myrna, my mother and Paul now hosted a monthly *Fiction and Fish Talk* show.

"Please, Mom, don't tell me that you need Marshall and me to babysit your menagerie while you MC that event."

"Of course not. But I promised Herb that you and Marshall would taste his team's latest sauce tomorrow night after you get out of work. It should only take a few minutes."

"At Herb's house?"

"Yes. He's right across the street."

"And he wants us to taste marinating sauce? Ew."

"Don't be silly. Not by itself. On the ribs he plans to marinate tonight. They need at least twenty-four hours."

"Why us? Can't the book club ladies taste the sauce?"

"Honestly, Phee. Myrna and Louise have to smother everything in salt, Cecilia doesn't like any sort of condiment, Lucinda doesn't believe anything is cooked unless it's dripping in salsa, and don't get me started on your aunt Ina's seasoning preferences. They're worse than her book choices."

"What about Shirley?"

"She told Herb she'd be there but he'd really appreciate it if you and Marshall came. Something about younger taste buds."

"Fine. But only for a few minutes. I suppose I could talk Marshall into it." *And owe him big-time.*

"Wonderful. I'll meet you over there tomorrow."

I pictured a quick run in, taste the sauce, tell Herb it was great, and get the heck out of there, but in retrospect, I should have known better.

We took one car to work the following day since I was pretty much tethered to the office and Marshall didn't have any late meetings. Nate, on the other hand, was just warming up for a long night of possible infidelity surveillance in Goodyear.

"This should be a short night for me," he said as we headed out the door. "The party in question lives in Robson Ranch, a senior community. If he *is* cheating on the wife, I guarantee he'll be in before midnight."

Augusta gave him a quick look and locked the door behind us. "I wouldn't be so sure about that, Mr. Williams. Some of those men tank up on those male potency pills and next thing you know they're all but swinging from the rafters."

Nate nearly choked. "This Tarzan better get all his swinging done at a reasonable hour. I've got a full day ahead of me tomorrow."

"At least you didn't get suckered in to tasting Herb's marinating sauce," I said. "I really hate commenting on other people's cooking." Then I turned to Augusta. "What if it's really horrible?"

"Even if it's bad enough to take the finish off a car, tell him it's very interesting. Use the word *interesting*. Can't go wrong with that."

All of us laughed and headed to our respective vehicles. A half hour later Marshall turned onto my mother's street and pointed to the left. "It's the house diagonal from your mom's, right?"

"Uh-huh. They're all assorted shades of beige but Herb's is the one with the Zuni design on the front security door. Besides, that's Shirley's enormous Buick parked in front, and if I'm not mistaken, that looks like Kenny's Toyota across the street."

Just then, a Chevy Equinox pulled behind the Toyota and I watched as Wayne, Bill, and Kevin got out. "Yep, the gang's all here. If we're lucky, Herb won't make a production out of this and we can all be on our way. I took a quiche Lorraine out of the freezer this morning."

"Hey, honeymooners!" Wayne shouted. "How was Hawaii? Did you go to any luaus? Eat any poi? Heard that stuff was awful."

By now, the men had crossed the street and we were a few feet from Herb's door.

"No poi, but we did have pork and butterfish wrapped in luau leaves," Marshall said. "Not bad."

"It won't come close to the sauce we've been cooking. Wait till you try it. It's a shoo-in for that contest. I've already spent my share of the prize money on a new power drill."

"Lucky you," Kevin muttered. "The wife will have my share spent at that beauty parlor of hers. I practically have to re-mortgage the house every time she schedules a manicure."

Before I could say anything, Bill rang the bell adjacent to the security door. Within seconds, Herb opened it. "Harriet and Shirley are already out back. Count your lucky stars. She left the little ankle biter at home." Then he looked at me. "Shh. Sorry about that."

"Oh, you don't have to apologize to me about your description of Streetman. I've called him much worse."

Herb's house was the exact same model as my mother's but the floor plan was reversed. Kalese referred to the style as the yenta special, since it had front kitchen windows that faced three sides of the street along with a side window from another front room that caught the action that the other windows missed.

Surprisingly, the place was fairly neat but without any specific style or décor. It also appeared to be larger than my mother's house but I attributed that to the fact it was missing a conglomeration of tchotchkes and there were no photos of dogs on the refrigerator door, only a notice from the electric company about the rate schedule.

"Got plenty of chairs set up on the back patio," Herb said. "And I've got a bucket with cold beers and sodas. Help yourselves."

We walked through his living room and out the sliding glass doors to where my mother and Shirley were seated. The pungent aroma of barbequed beef hit my nostrils the second I walked outside and I all but salivated. Herb must have noticed because he immediately took me by the elbow and walked me to the grill. Meanwhile, Marshall and the pinochle crew dug into the ice bucket with the drinks.

"It's that extra dab of oyster sauce that gives it its kick," Herb said. "And not that crappy stuff you buy in the supermarkets. I drive all the way over to the Asian market on Forty-third and Union Hills for the good stuff."

"What else is in the marinade?"

"The usual: soy sauce, lemon, garlic, honey, olive oil, pepper, basil, parsley, and a nip of Worcestershire sauce. But it's all in the ratios. One screwup and you might as well buy a bottle of premade marinade from the store."

"When are we going to taste this stuff, Herb?" Bill asked. "I want to catch the Diamondbacks tonight."

"Hold your horses. Let me grab some paper plates. Got a pile of plastic forks next to the napkins on the patio table."

While Herb rummaged around for plastic cutlery and plates, I moseyed over to where my mother and Shirley were seated. They were so engrossed with something on my mother's cell phone that I wasn't sure they paid attention to our arrival. As I got closer, my mother looked up.

"I was about to say hello, but Herb ushered you off to the grill. Frankly, I wasn't sure what to expect, but if the meat tastes as good as it smells, Herb may have a winner."

"I'm sure his—"

"And speaking of winners, would you look at these marvelous dog and cat clothing outfits?"

She thrust the cell phone at me before I could finish my thought. But it didn't matter. My mother kept on talking.

"I'm having Shirley put together an entire ensemble for Streetman and Essie. Of course, we'll have to wait until Essie reaches full size and we find out if it's a he or she, but in the meantime, Shirley can start off with some simpler gender-neutral kitten outfits."

Suddenly, Marshall broke in. "Did you want a beer, hon, or a soda?"

"The first choice." *And there's not enough alcohol in the world to save me from this calamity.*

# CHAPTER 4

J ust then, Bill handed a folded newspaper to Herb. "I grabbed your weekly paper when I came in the door and stuck it in the kitchen. Then I figured you wouldn't notice, so here it is. Must be your block gets the Thursday paper a day early, huh?"

Herb took the paper from Bill and removed the rubber band. "Only if the delivery guy's got something going on Thursday mornings. Otherwise we get it by noon. Wonder what the local scuttlebutt's got in store for us this week." He glanced at the front page and I swore I saw his face turn red. "You have *got* to be kidding me. Is this some kind of a joke?"

He shoved the paper at Bill, who widened his eyes right before waving the front page at all of us. "Who elects these idiotic morons to the county planning commission?"

I glanced at Marshall and refrained from commenting while Bill continued his tirade. "Listen to this. 'Cosmo Pruett, chairman of the Maricopa County Planning Commission, has just announced a proposal to build a waste transfer station on county property adjacent to Sun City West on the northwest corridor, directly across from Sun City Grand in Surprise.'"

"Give me that," my mother said before extracting the paper from Bill's hand. "I don't believe this. Those imbeciles want to put a garbage dump in our backyards? A garbage dump!"

I bit my lip and tried not to grimace. "It's not a dump. It's a transfer station. Not like a landfill."

"It's the same thing," my mother said. "Except the refuse is above ground. And don't tell me the garbage is only there temporarily because garbage is garbage and no matter what you do, it will smell."

Shirley looked up from the cell phone and put a palm over her cheek. "Lordy, Harriet's right. Why do you think they make all those scented garbage bags? I'll tell you this much, no one's going to be deodorizing that transfer station. And odors linger. Imagine what it will smell like in monsoon season with all that wind."

"When's the public hearing?" Kenny asked. "They're supposed to hold public hearings."

My mother scanned the article and looked up. "Next Tuesday. At seven. They're holding it at our social hall since it can accommodate this community and Sun City Grand. Ha! I've got news for them. They think only a handful of people will turn out. Well, we'll see about that."

I caught Marshall's eye roll and turned away so I wouldn't laugh.

Then Herb snatched the paper from my mother's grip. "Cosmo Pruett. Why does that name sound familiar? I've seen it before. Hmm, give me a minute." Herb paced back and forth while Shirley went back to whatever cat and dog costume site she and my mother had pulled up on the phone. Then, Herb slammed his hand on the patio table. "Hell's bells! I know where I saw that name. Hold on everyone. I'll be right back."

"This better not take too long," Bill said. "Those Diamondbacks aren't going to wait forever."

"Here it is!" Herb announced when he returned from the house. "Right here in last week's *Sun City West Independent*. He's on the other finalist team for the Master Grillers contest. I knew I saw that name somewhere. Hard to miss. Cosmo Pruett. It's got to be the same guy because how many people can have that name? What was I saying? Oh, yeah, I'll read it to you. 'Cosmo Pruett, along with Clinton Badger and Therm Whittaker, are finalists along with Herb Garrett, Kenny—"

"We know who we are," Bill said.

Herb put the paper down. "Cosmo, huh? Must mean the jerk lives somewhere in Sun City West."

Within seconds it was utter bedlam as everyone, with the exception of Marshall and me, spoke at once.

"Google him!"

"Pull him up on Facebook!"

"Where's your Sun City West directory, Herb?"

"Does anyone have Cindy Dolton's phone number? She'll know."

Then Herb's voice. "Let me finish, will you? I think the contest organizers sent us everyone's phone number and address. It must be in the same drawer where I keep the extra pinochle deck. Give me another minute."

A collective series of groans followed as Herb headed back into the house. Two seconds later we heard his voice. "No surprise there. That turncoat lives in the expansion district by Corte Bella. The ritzy area. On the opposite side of where they want to put the transfer station. Someone must have paid him off."

By now Herb was back on the patio and fuming, along with everyone else.

"Look," Wayne said, "not much we can do about it now, but Tuesday night will be another story. What do you say we taste those ribs and see if our sauce cuts the mustard?"

And like that, Herb put the papers down and charged over to the grill. "Get your plates, everyone. And you may need extra napkins."

He didn't have to ask twice. Shirley and my mother were at the grill in a flash, followed by Bill, Wayne, Kevin, and Kenny. It was like watching kids at a popcorn stand. Finally Marshall and I made our way over and helped ourselves to one of the tantalizing-looking ribs. I'd eaten foods before that looked scrumptious but tasted awful. I prayed this wouldn't be the case.

"Well?" Herb asked. "What do you think?"

If ecstasy could be described as devouring a mouthwatering beef rib, this was it. I couldn't get enough of the taste and all but bit into the bone. "This is amazing. Frankly, I never expected the ribs to be so extraordinary."

"So we've got a winner on our hands, huh?" Kevin said.

Marshall grabbed a napkin and wiped the sides of his mouth. "You've got my vote."

Wayne scratched his head and took another bit of his rib. "You think we ought to crank it up a notch and add some Jack Daniel's to it?"

"I think it's fine the way it is," Shirley said. "All alcohol does is leave an aftertaste when you're done tasting what you should be tasting."

My mother glanced at the men and sighed. "She's right. Once you start messing with a good thing, you only make it worse. Like the time my sister decided to cut her son's hair when he was seven. Kept trying to even out the bangs. The poor boy looked as if he'd run into a buzz saw."

I turned to Marshall and whispered, "My cousin Kirk still has a phobia about going into a barbershop and those are run by trained professionals." Then I walked over to where Herb stood. "No need to change a thing. It's perfect. Well, thanks for inviting us but we really should get going. Lots to do at home."

"Wait!" my mother said. "We can't leave this transfer station nightmare up in the air."

"Huh? I thought you folks said something about Tuesday's public hearing."

"Oh, that goes without saying, but you should know by now how those public hearings work. They give everyone lip service and then do whatever they want. In this case they want to infiltrate our air with noxious fumes."

Wayne reached for another rib and eyeballed my mother. "What are you suggesting, Harriet?"

"We find out all we can about this Cosmo fellow and discover what's really behind the commission's horrific idea. In fact, Phee should see what Cindy Dolton has to say at the dog park."

*Or not. Cindy has lots to say and it's always at six in the morning with Streetman making amorous advances at anything with four legs.*

I tossed my paper plate in Herb's trash and shook my head. "I've got a busy schedule this week."

"I'll tell you what Cosmo's up to," Kenny said. "He wants to get all of us so distracted that he can breeze in and nab the Master Grillers competition. Well, I've got news for him. We belong on the Food Network right up there with Guy Fieri, Bobby Flay, and the rest of them. Even the woman with the gourmet dog food."

"Rachael Ray?"

Kenny looked at me and shrugged. "If you say so."

"Lordy!" Shirley gasped. "None of you said anything about being on the Food Network. Is that part of the prize?"

My mother bolted out of her seat and thundered over to Herb. "Why didn't you tell Shirley the winners would be on the Food Network?"

"I figured you'd beat me to it."

I immediately grabbed my mother by the elbow and tried to keep my voice low. "The winners, not the KSCW radio hosts, so don't get Myrna and Paul in a tizzy."

"That's the last thing I'm worried about. We've got to stop this Cosmo what's-his-name from turning our community into a landfill and upstaging Herb's pinochle crew. I'm calling the book club ladies the minute I get home so we can come up with a plan."

"I've got them all on speed dial," Shirley announced as she waved her phone in the air. "Who should I call first? When do we want to meet? I imagine at Bagels 'n More." Then she pointed at the men. "And don't think you can afford to sit on your duffs while we do all the work. Or worse yet, guzzle beer at Curley's while some self-serving honcho gives you the double whammy."

Marshall muttered "Oh, brother," but I don't think anyone heard him. Then he walked toward Herb and reached to shake his hand. "Terrific sauce. A definite winner. Don't change a thing. Good grief, it's getting late and I've got an early start tomorrow. Keep us posted on your progress."

"Not so fast," my mother said. "Maybe you and Nate can do one of those background checks on Cosmo. For all we know, he could be a wanted fugitive."

"Mom! Marshall and Nate don't have time for your wild-goose chases. They have a backload of work. Go one step at a time, beginning with the public hearing on Tuesday. Maybe the planning commission will be more receptive than you think. A well-thought-out statement articulating the community concerns is the way to begin."

My mother crossed her arms and looked at Marshall. "You agree with that?"

"It makes more sense than jumping into the deep end right away."

"Fine. We'll see you on Tuesday then. I'll make sure to save you seats if you get out of work late."

Marshall barely got the next syllable out of his mouth when my mother hustled back to her seat and took out her phone. "Shirley, I want you to take a look at these cat and dog outfits on Pinterest."

I took Marshall's wrist and gave it a squeeze. "Forget it."

"I don't even know what happened. One minute I tasted barbequed ribs and the next I was commandeered into attending a public hearing."

"Welcome to the family."

# CHAPTER 5

"**M**r. Williams will be in late this morning," Augusta announced when I walked into the office the following morning. Marshall was already in but I lagged a few minutes behind. "Can't say I didn't warn him about a long night. He didn't get home until after three. Seems our senior citizen lothario and his consort spent the night at the Hilton Gardens in Phoenix."

"That's good news, I suppose. In a way. I mean, at least Nate got the evidence he needed to finalize that investigation."

"Oh, he got the evidence all right. But it took some doing. He had to pay off someone from room service so he could impersonate the guy."

"Whoa. That's one for the books." I turned on the Keurig and stood for a moment as I waited for the blue lights to turn on before plunking in a K-Cup.

"Maybe his next surveillance detail can be done from behind the wheel of his car. According to my calendar, he's working on another similar case."

"Senior citizens?"

"Let's put it this way—they reached the age of consent when Eisenhower took office."

"Yeesh. Say, did Marshall mention anything to you about our fun-filled evening at Herb's yesterday?"

"Said the ribs were damn good and if I wanted more information to check with you. Then said something about a planning commission meeting and moaned. I figured that has to do with an upcoming case of his."

"Not exactly."

I removed my coffee from the machine, added creamer and sugar, and then proceeded to tell Augusta about the transfer station proposal. She listened intently before shaking her head.

"This is going to spell trouble, you know. Especially when those women mention 'a plan.' The last ones they concocted belonged in a Marx Brothers movie."

"Don't remind me. I'm hoping the kitten Streetman found will keep my mother's mind off the transfer station. At least until everyone clears the air at that meeting this Tuesday."

"From the sound of things, you and Marshall will be clearing the air there as well."

"Only breathing it. Ugh. Well, I've got more invoices staring me in the face and a ton of other stuff. Catch you later."

Marshall was out of the office and on his latest case while I focused on billing and accounts receivable. At a little before noon my cell phone rang and I took the call without bothering to check the caller. I was reasonably certain it wasn't my mother since she preferred "a real phone without all that voicemail nonsense."

When I heard my cousin Kirk's voice at the other end, I panicked. He didn't even start with "Hi, Phee" when I broke in. "Did something happen to Aunt Ina and you couldn't reach my mother?"

"No, not at all. Sorry to scare you like that. Especially during the day when you're working, but I've got to go out of town for business and wanted to get a reality check from you. Especially when it involves my mother. By the way, Judy and I loved the wedding ceremony. That dog was too much. Anyway, I got a frantic call from my mother this morning about the county putting in a garbage dump across from her development."

"Not a dump. A transfer station."

"In her mind it's the same thing. She went on and on about Louis's delicate nostrils and how the odors would be an assault to his senses. Good grief! The man played with a jazz band on cruise ships most of his life when he wasn't gambling. He should be used to all the odors from those casinos: cigarette and cigar smoke, heavy perfume, greasy foods from the adjacent buffets . . . I could go on all day."

"Did she call you to complain or did she have something else in mind?"

"She wants me to fly out there and threaten your county's planning commission with a lawsuit. I told her that was *not* about to happen and that I'd speak with her later when she regained her faculties. Needless to say she didn't take it well."

"Don't worry. Marshall and I got roped into attending that meeting. I'll keep you posted. I've got to admit, I don't like the idea of a nearby transfer station either, but if enough community members voice their objections, the commission will have to rethink their idea. Besides, there's lots of county property in the desert for that sort of thing."

For the next few minutes we chatted about family stuff and how much Kalese and Ramona enjoyed seeing each other. I sent my love to Judy and stepped into the front office to see if Augusta felt like calling out for lunch. True, we had plenty of peanut butter, jelly, and bread in the break room but I really wanted to bite into something with more substance.

One Italian sub later, I was back to work trying desperately to put the whole transfer station dilemma on the proverbial back burner. Unfortunately, that wasn't about to happen. My mother called at a little before four to inform me she had made an appointment with the vet for tomorrow morning and that Shirley would be joining her so that she could manage the dog and the cat.

"I didn't know the dog had an appointment, too," I said.

"He doesn't, but you don't expect me to leave him home alone and take Essie. He'll be panic-stricken thinking we deserted him."

I played a mental song in my head while she went on and on about Streetman's anxieties. Then, thank goodness, she shifted gears and mentioned meeting with Herb's crew and the book club ladies to work on their plans. To escape any involvement in *that* disaster, I told her I'd "poke around and see what I could find out about Cosmo Pruett." That seemed to placate her and I was able to get back to work.

It wasn't until the next morning when my mother delivered more news than the *New York Times*. The clock at the bottom of my computer screen read 9:50 a.m. and she had just gotten back from the vet.

"Essie's a girl. A girl! No wonder Streetman is smitten. The vet thought she was about seven or eight weeks old and in good health. I scheduled vaccinations for next week. It's been over four days and no one has come forth so I think it's safe to say we have another Plunkett in the family."

*Exactly what we need.*

Then my mother catapulted to the part of her call that made the hairs on the back of my neck stand up. "If you and Marshall have fish for dinner between now and Tuesday, freeze the remains and drop them off at Herb's house."

For a minute I was positive I misunderstood, but no, that's exactly what she said. And it got worse. "We've got everything except fish. And fish can be especially noxious. I was going to ask Paul but I didn't want to listen to any of his fishing lectures."

"I'm not sure I follow. This can't be for the cat."

"The cat? Whatever gave you that idea? Essie has to eat mushed foods. It's for Tuesday night's public hearing. Sometimes the only way to get a point across is to demonstrate it. And that's exactly what we have planned."

"Have what planned?"

"We intend to get to that meeting before it starts and fill the trash containers with—"

"Oh no you don't! That's the worst plan ever. Ever!"

"I'm telling you, Phee, no amount of talking will change their minds once they've decided on a course of action. We have to take a stronger stance. And what's stronger than—"

"Making people gag in their seats?"

"Yes, if that's what it takes."

"Well, count us out. Marshall and I are not bringing over fish entrails, or any entrails, for that matter. Come up with a new plan. One that doesn't involve garbage. I'll talk to you later."

When I got off the phone, I felt beads of sweat on my neck and my hand shook as I reached for the computer mouse. Thankfully the remainder of the day went smoothly, allowing me to use my break time to see what I could glean about Cosmo Pruett. Not because of my mother and Herb, but because I wanted to save my cousin the anguish of having to fly out here to placate my aunt.

Having grown up in the same neighborhood, coupled with being only children, Kirk and I were more like brother and sister than cousins. We were also close in age and shared many of the same friends. Family holidays were always celebrated together along with some vacations that the both of us would rather forget. If I could spare him the agony of dealing with Sun City West's latest catastrophe, it would be well worth the time.

Cosmo Pruett all but bounced out of the social media pages, making my search easy. A graduate of the Thunderbird School of Global Management with a focus on financial metrics, Cosmo worked for an equity company in Philadelphia before retiring to Arizona. He was divorced with no children and enjoyed golfing and travel. With a past history of serving utility commissions in Pennsylvania, it was no wonder he got elected to the Maricopa County Planning Commission.

I hoped to uncover some tidbit that would give me greater insight into the guy but no such luck. Not yet anyway. His photos were fairly nondescript, making it tough to draw any conclusions about his habits or personal tastes. Mostly golf courses and scenes of European landmarks. Cosmo's only profile picture had to have been taken years ago given his full head of light brown hair, no discernible crow's feet or wrinkles and a perfect smile. Then again, this area was known for Botox, dental implants, skin rejuvenation, and all kinds of restorative treatments meant to make seventy the new fifty.

My luck held as far as the weekend was concerned. No dire emergencies. No frantic calls. Only delightful swims, a long early-morning hike on Sunday with Marshall, and a weather forecast that couldn't be beat. Even my mother's phone calls were benign, mostly anecdotes about Streetman and Essie and a few reminders about the public hearing. I kept my fingers crossed she and her friends wouldn't do anything outrageous, but who was I kidding? I should have known better. Much better.

# CHAPTER 6

W ith a successful relative search underway regarding the couple from Gold Canyon, Marshall was feeling pretty confident he'd finalize that case by the weekend. We left my car at the office and took his to Sun City West after work on Tuesday with a quick stop at the Wildflower Bread Company for dinner.

With the summer heat gradually rising, salads and homemade breads made for the perfect meal. With twenty minutes to spare before the public hearing was to take place, Marshall approached the turn-in for Sun City West's Rec Center complex on RH Johnson Boulevard and gasped.

Two fire trucks, along with official vehicles from the sheriff's office, Epcor Water, and Southwest Gas lined the front of the building. In addition, three or four posse cars were also on scene. The parking lot was packed and people were milling all over. Mostly small clusters that seemed to break up with members joining other clusters.

Marshall took the closest parking space and turned off the engine. "What the heck? Doesn't look like a fire and there are no ambulances. What do you suppose is going on?"

"Beats me. Whatever it is, my mother and Herb will most likely give us the rundown. They've got to be around here somewhere. Might as well start looking."

"Do you think someone sent the commission a death threat? That's been known to happen. Maybe they're scouring the area to make sure no one left anything suspicious."

"At this rate the hearing won't even get started for another hour. Aargh. This is going to be a long night. Glad we ate before driving over here."

We got out of the car and walked toward the building. As we got closer I swore I caught a whiff of sulfur gas. "I bet it's a gas leak. Can you smell that?"

"Barely. Yeah, now that you mention it, the odor's getting stronger."

Up ahead, Sun City West PRIDES volunteers began to place orange hazard cones along the front of the building while posse members directed the growing crowd to stay put. We continued to scan the area for my mother and the book club ladies but it was impossible. The small clusters of people grew into widening clumps that resembled unbaked loaves of bread as the yeast rose.

To make matters worse, they were boisterous as well and blocked all the available space between the cars. It took a Herculean effort on

Marshall's part and mine to elbow our way through them in search of our own cluster of busybodies.

"Look!" Marshall exclaimed. "Way over there on the right! It's Herb, and if I'm not mistaken, isn't that Paul Schmidt next to him? Come on, maybe those two know what's going on."

We started in the direction where Marshall spotted Herb but we were quickly engulfed by a crowd of people who brandished signs reading "Transfer Cosmo out of here!" and "No Dumping in Sun City West!"

The combination of large placards and an even larger throng prevented us from budging more than a few feet. By that time Marshall had lost sight of Herb and I thought we'd never escape the parking lot.

"Does anyone know what's happening?" Marshall shouted into the crowd.

"I think they've got a sewage leak in the social hall," someone shouted back.

"Not sewage. Gas!" someone else yelled.

"Only one way to find out," Marshall said as he took me by the elbow. "Work your way through the smaller mob by those jeeps and I'll muscle in right next to you."

I took a deep breath and did more traversing than most seasoned skiers. Five or six minutes later we emerged a few yards from the orange cones that blocked the entrance to the social hall.

"This area is off-limits," a gray-haired posse volunteer said. He held up his palms and motioned for Marshall and me to step back.

"What's going on?"

At that instant, the doors to the social hall flew open and the most god-awful stench permeated the air. The posse volunteer covered his mouth with a bandana he pulled from his pocket and said, "Gas or sewage leak. Got all utility crews working on it."

"Thank goodness it's a gas or sewage leak," I whispered to Marshall as we stepped away from the volunteer. "Don't get me wrong, but at least it's something mechanical and not anything my mother and her looney friends came up with. They wanted to douse the area with fish entrails to make a point about odors from transfer stations. I was going to mention it to you but I put it in the back of my mind and didn't think about it until now."

Marshall laughed. "Thanks for sparing me."

"My mother and her friends have *got* to be somewhere in this crowd. Maybe if we stand off to the side they'll see us and make their way over. Especially if Myrna leads the way. Between those power-move classes of hers and all that bocce practice, she's in pretty good shape."

We skirted off to the edge of the building and stood on the curb where a driveway separated the social hall from a large supermarket.

"It's after seven," I said. "They can't possibly be thinking of still holding that public hearing."

Marshall crossed his arms and leaned back. "Listen to that crowd. They're holding their own meeting. Or should I say, rally. And if I were Cosmo Pruett, I'd hightail it to the nearest safe space and stay there."

I stood still and tried to take in the voices amid the cacophony. No surprises. They reiterated what they had printed on those signs, only in this case with expletives that could make paint peel off a wall.

A few minutes passed and no sign of the book club ladies or Herb's pinochle crew. I don't know why I didn't think of it, or why Marshall didn't, for that matter, but I took my cell phone from my bag and started to phone my mother when all of a sudden someone with a handheld megaphone stood in front of the social hall and announced, "Tonight's public hearing is canceled and will be rescheduled. Repeat—Tonight's public hearing is canceled and will be rescheduled."

No sooner did that announcement end when I heard a man's voice coming from behind where we stood. "This is all we need. A damn post-ponement. I need to get things moving. *We* need to get things moving. If we're lucky, it'll be a week. Worse case, two. By then the entire municipality will be out for blood. Listen to them."

Then another voice, fast approaching. "Calm down, Cosmo. Let them blow off steam. We're the ones voting, not the Tower of Babel out there."

*Cosmo? Voting?*

I scooched close to Marshall and kept my voice low. "That's Cosmo Pruett behind us. Do you hear him?"

"Uh-huh. That's why I stopped talking." He immediately took out his phone and pretended to show me something on it as the two men behind us crossed the driveway and walked toward the supermarket.

"They're smart," I said. "Blending in with the shoppers."

Meanwhile the crowd in front of the social hall all but erupted with shouts.

"You did this on purpose!"

"Probably just a stink bomb!"

"Cowards!"

"Cosmo can keep his garbage!"

And those were the nice comments. It went on like that for at least ten minutes while the man with the megaphone interrupted now and again to reiterate that the meeting had been canceled. So as not to get swept up in a sea of humanity, Marshall and I held our own off to the side of the building, hoping for the crowd to disperse.

Little by little, the clusters grew smaller and cars began to exit the parking lot.

"We may have a fighting chance to find your mother," Marshall said. "Give it another minute or two and we can move about."

"Uh, that won't be necessary. There's Herb catty-corner from us. And he's not alone. Bill, Kevin, Kenny, Wayne and Paul are over there, too. Wait. Isn't that Cecilia thundering over to him with Lucinda at her heels?"

Marshall squinted into the sunset and nodded. "Yep. Sure looks like it. Reminds me of Sally Fields in *The Flying Nun*, only in this case it's Cecilia moving like a windstorm and Lucinda getting caught up in the draft."

"Yikes. You're getting as bad as I am. And Lucinda always looks like that."

Then, out of nowhere, my mother's voice. Booming and unmistakable. She was now with Herb's growing entourage and motioned for us to get over there. "Hurry up. Phee! We need to get out of here. It's a gas leak and this building could go up in flames at any minute."

I seriously doubted it was a gas leak because the odor smelled more like raw sewage than propane gas or natural gas with the infused warning odor. Besides, the fire department and Southwest Gas would have evacuated the area by now. My money was on putrid waste, and while it was disgusting beyond measure, it wasn't about to cause an explosion.

Nope, that came when two Maricopa County sheriff's deputies charged over to where my mother and her friends stood. All we could see were hands flailing in the air, and I wondered what prompted law enforcement to select that particular cluster for a discussion.

Then, in a flash, the Southwest Gas vehicles exited out of the parking lot followed by the Epcor Water vehicles. Moments later, three restoration services trucks took their place.

"Good grief," I said to Marshall. "What do you suppose is going on?"

"Only one way to find out—straight to the horses' mouths. All of them."

As we raced over to where they stood, my mother yelled, "The building isn't going to explode after all. It wasn't a gas leak."

"That's what I thought all along," I said to Marshall. "It has to be raw sewage. But why did Epcor leave?"

By now we had joined the ever-growing clump of busybodies, along with Myrna, Shirley, and Louise. I feared Aunt Ina wouldn't be too far behind and I was right. With her long braids wrapped around her head with a glimmering green floral fairy headpiece in front, I could have sworn she invaded a Shakespearean costume room and found the box marked *A Midsummer Night's Dream*. Her flowing gauze caftan completed the outfit, but it paled against the headpiece. My uncle Louis stood behind her in a white short-sleeved shirt and dark pants. If it wasn't for the gold plaid ascot that encompassed most of his chest, he would've faded into the crowd.

We couldn't discern what the deputies were saying but Paul's response was loud and clear, "It was an accident. You think I'd pour an entire bottle of moose urine in the room? How was I supposed to know this klutz would bump into me?"

Then Herb responded, "I saw you bending over and thought you were choking. I tried to give you the Heimlich maneuver."

"Couldn't you see I was dabbing something on a cotton ball?"

At that moment I was genuinely sorry I nixed my mother's fish entrails idea. A restoration company wouldn't have been needed for the cleanup.

# CHAPTER 7

"It was moose urine!" my mother shouted as she waved Marshall and me toward her.

I waited until we were a few feet away and responded, "Yeah, we heard."

Meanwhile, the deputies continued to question Paul and Herb, who had now relocated off to the group's side.

"Think those two are going to be arrested?" Myrna asked. "We're going to have to chip in to post bail."

Marshall turned his attention to the deputies and then back to us. "I don't think so. I just overheard one of them saying it was a Rec Center issue."

"That's good news," I said. "Either they'll revoke their activity privileges for a few months, fine them, or put them on probation like they do with Streetman all the time."

"It's not all the time, Phee." My mother literally jumped all over me. "Only when he gets too amorous."

I did a mental eye roll and watched as one of the deputies appeared to send a text to someone. At the same time, the posse volunteer with the megaphone made another announcement. "This is a nonhazardous environmental issue and will be resolved. The public hearing is canceled for tonight. I repeat, this is a nonhazardous environmental issue and will be resolved. The public hearing is canceled for tonight."

A few more people started to exit the parking lot, including the two deputies. Unfortunately, they didn't get very far. Cosmo Pruett, donning a peachy pink long-sleeved shirt and tan khakis, thundered toward them with a short, stocky man lagging behind. If I thought my mother's voice was loud, it was soft and delicate compared to the explosion that emanated from Cosmo's lungs. "What do you mean the building was sabotaged? Your text said the cause of the odor was environmental interference. Is that another name for sabotage?"

One of the deputies raised his palms and motioned for Cosmo to calm down. "Our office thought the planning commission needed to be informed of the reason your meeting had to be canceled. The county may need to post additional security at the next public hearing."

"Way to go, Paul!" Kevin exclaimed. "Like blowing a giant fart in a cubbyhole."

"It wouldn't have been a giant fart if Herb minded his own business."

Herb shook his shoulders and then straightened his back. "Like I told you earlier, how was I supposed to know you had moose urine with you? It's not something most people carry around, like a Kleenex or cough drop."

"Moose urine?" Cosmo turned away from the deputies and gave Herb a slight push. "That was you with the moose urine?"

"Hey, watch who you're shoving. And it was an accident. My buddy over here wanted to make a point about odors from a transfer station with a tiny dab of that stuff on a cotton ball."

Cosmo's nostrils all but flared and I couldn't get the image of a charging bull out of my head.

"Okay, enough is enough," one of the deputies said. "Break it up and go home. Nothing more to be done at this point."

"That's what you think," Cosmo said. He pointed a finger at Herb and then at Paul. "Let's get one thing straight. Nothing is going to slow down the planning commission. Nothing!"

"Forget it, Herb." Bill gave Herb's shoulder a bump. "We've got other, more pressing issues. Like the Master Grillers contest."

"Isn't that the one you're in?" the short stocky man asked Cosmo. He pulled out a blue bandana from his pocket and wiped his brow and neck before sticking the bandana back in his pocket. "You've been talking about your special sauce for months."

Then Cosmo eyeballed Herb as if he was a piece of lint on someone's jacket. "Herb, huh? Don't tell me you're one of the contenders."

Herb sucked in his stomach and lifted his head. "I most certainly am, along with my pinochle crew over here." He extended an arm and all but knocked Wayne in the mouth.

"I'd stick to melding if I were you," Cosmo said. "I have no intention of losing that contest or you'll be—"

"We got to get going." The stocky man elbowed Cosmo, but not before shooting all of us a dirty look. Had it ended there, things might have been different. But oh no, Herb just *had* to have the last word.

"You threatening me? Because if you are, it will be the last threat you make."

The older of the two deputies stepped between Herb and Cosmo. "Do we need to discuss this at the posse station?"

Both men shook their heads. "Good," the deputy said. "Go on home and work on your sauces or your melds. We've got to clear out this parking lot."

Cosmo and his cohort took off without another word, but it was only when Bill said the word *Curley's* that the men decided a cold beer was in order. Even my uncle Louis decided to join them once Cecilia mentioned getting pies at the Homey Hut. "Who wants to join me?" she asked. She might have been better off asking who *didn't* because everyone spoke at once.

"Count me in."

"It's Tuesday. The banana cream special."

"Bananas make me constipated."

"Order the blueberry. That will flush you out."

I grabbed Marshall by the wrist and whispered, "You may be better off at Curley's. Unless of course you'd prefer saturated fats and conversations about digestive issues." I didn't have to convince him that Curley's was the better choice.

"How about I pick you up at your mother's in an hour or so? Text me."

By the time we left the parking lot, most of the cars had cleared out. My mother was more than thrilled to drive me to the Homey Hut, especially since she wanted "to run a few more ideas through my head regarding a new plan to stop the dreadful transfer station."

While Marshall and Louis continued to nurse their beers at Curley's, according to the text Marshall sent me, my mother's entourage had grown to include her former neighbor, Gloria Wong, and two of Gloria's friends from the flower arranging club. Together with the book club ladies, they spewed more gossip than the dog park and Bagels 'n More combined.

Gloria had heard Cosmo had a major renovation project going at his house and counted on monies from a joint business venture with someone else on the planning commission, but that person backed out, leaving Cosmo high and dry.

"That lowlife is getting paid off from someone to ramrod that transfer station down our throats," Gloria said. She patted her sleek black hair down and reached for her coffee cup. "I wouldn't be at all surprised if someone gets even."

Then my mother told her about the moose urine incident and she almost spat out the coffee she had just sipped. "So that's what it was. Moose urine. Of all things."

A half hour later Marshall sent me another text. One that consisted of full sentences: "I'll be late. The sheriff's office sent a deputy to bring in Herb and Paul for questioning. Not the moose urine this time."

"What's the matter?" my mother asked. "Did Louis get involved in a card game at Curley's?"

My aunt Ina immediately jumped to attention. "I'm not waiting around while he plays cards all night. I need my beauty sleep."

I looked at her and then at the women around the table. "No, not Louis. But for some reason the sheriff's office decided to question Herb and Paul about something. They had to go to the posse station and Marshall went as well."

"It's probably nothing," Myrna said. "Maybe some new and ugly rumor is circulating around. You know how those men can gossip."

I glanced at my cell phone to avoid bursting out laughing. "Well, Mom, guess I'll be keeping you and Streetman company for a bit longer tonight."

"And Essie. Don't forget Essie."

Gloria turned to my mother and tilted her head. "Who's Essie?"

For the next five or six minutes, we were all subjected to various cell phone photos of the little gray cat and the neurotic dog that found her. Somewhere in between my mother waved around a few photos from my wedding ceremony but they were mostly of Streetman doing his dance.

After what seemed like more endless chitchat, Louis walked in to pick up my aunt. For a man in his late seventies, he always appeared chipper and wide-awake no matter what time it was. I imagined it was because he was used to playing that saxophone of his at all sorts of venues, no matter the hour.

"Hi, ladies! How was the banana pie?"

"Scrumptious!" Cecilia said. "Absolutely decadent."

"I suppose you got Marshall's message," he said to me. "Seems someone tampered with Cosmo's car, and given the moose urine incident, the sheriff's office wanted to question Herb and Paul."

"Huh?" I was dumbfounded. "Car tampering? That doesn't make sense."

Louis pulled up a chair and plunked himself down. "The deputy said Cosmo had parked his car between the social hall and the supermarket. When he went near it, he detected a slight fishy odor but dismissed it. Then he turned on the ignition and the odor of dead fish filled the interior to the point where he gagged and turned off the engine. That's when he called the sheriff's office."

I widened my eyes and looked at my mother. "Please don't tell me Paul put a dead fish under the hood of the car."

"Don't be ridiculous. What good would that do? Besides, how would he even know what kind of car Cosmo drove?"

"Hmm, that's a good point. However, given the prior idiocy those two managed to pull off, I doubt the sheriff's office will be very understanding. Geez, I hope poor Marshall doesn't wind up there for hours while they question the men." Then I looked my mother right in the eye. "Now aren't you glad you didn't bring those fish entrails to the social hall? It could have been you they questioned."

"It didn't have to be fish entrails," Louise said. "Old chopped liver works just as well."

"And yogurt. Spoiled yogurt," Lucinda added. "Nothing clears out a room like rotten yogurt."

Gloria nodded and leaned into the table. "Really old egg foo yung will do the trick, too. I once forgot I had some in my fridge and found it two weeks later behind a large bottle of V-8. And all that time I thought the odor was left over from some spoiled cottage cheese."

*And I worry about milk past its expiration date.*

"Did the deputy mention what kind of fish it was?" Myrna asked.

Shirley picked up a napkin and dabbed the side of her lips, leaving a dark mauve residue on the paper. "Lordy, what difference does that make?"

"If it was store-bought, it would probably be headless and tailless. If it was something Paul caught, then the whole kit and caboodle would be in the engine. I'd find out if it was a lake trout. Paul's passion is lake trout fishing."

"Ugh. Don't we know," my mother said. Then she looked at her watch. "Heavens. We've been here forever. I'd better get home to my precious little bundles of fur."

If I could have heaved at that moment, I would have. Instead, I stood and said my good nights to the ladies and my uncle. Then something dawned on me. "Louis," I asked, "how did the deputy know where to find Herb and Paul?"

"Said their office was tipped off."

*Either someone knows Herb's habits or it was a pretty good guess.*

# CHAPTER 8

Bad news for Paul. The fish was indeed a lake trout, but that didn't mean it was his catch. According to Marshall, the men adamantly denied having anything whatsoever to do with putting a dead trout in Cosmo's manifold.

The deputy on duty took their statements and told them that the office would be looking into the matter and to refrain from having any further contact with Cosmo or anyone else on the planning commission or the Master Grillers contest.

In spite of the fact that I was exhausted from a long day and even longer night, I hung on to Marshall's every word as he described the interaction that took place at the posse station.

"I think it's a widening circle of loonies if you ask me," Marshall said. "Those folks are so riled up about the transfer station, they'll do anything to derail it."

*Derail.* I didn't realize what an interesting choice of words it was until the next morning, when my mother phoned to tell us not to take Grand Avenue if we needed to get into Sun City West.

"I wanted to save Nate and Marshall some time if they're working on any cases here."

I sighed. "They're not."

"Good, because the only ways in and out are from El Mirage or Bell Road. The railroad flashers are up on both entrances: Meeker Boulevard and RH Johnson. Some train must have derailed or something. Louise called me first thing because she found out about the commotion from her neighbor who goes jogging at some obscene hour."

"Okay. Thanks for letting us know. Marshall and I have to get to work. I'll catch up later."

"I'm driving over to Louise's and we're going to check it out."

"Seriously? You actually want to see a train wreck?"

"Not the train wreck. We want to see who's there. It's a good way to catch up with people we never see."

I rolled my eyes at least a half dozen times and stopped from saying something I'd regret. "All right, then. Have a nice day."

If nice day could be described as sharing the gory details of what actually took place on the railroad tracks behind the hospital, then my mother had a splendid day. Her intel was delivered to our office in waves beginning at nine thirty.

"Someone got run over by a train."

Then at ten fifteen: "It was a man. I found out from Cecilia, who still volunteers at the hospital, that it was a man."

Then at a little past noon: "The rumors are circulating like crazy, Phee. They think it might have been that awful Cosmo Pruett from the planning commission. According to an eyewitness, the man they found mangled on the tracks wore a pinkish shirt just like the one Cosmo wore when he was last seen in the parking lot by the social hall. And trust me, lots of people saw him there."

"Don't go adding to rumors, Mom. For all we know, the poor victim could have been one of those homeless people who walk by the railroad tracks."

"I turned on the news but all they said was that someone had apparently fallen under a train. How does someone fall under a train? It's like falling under a couch. Or a chair. Who falls under a train?"

"I don't know. Maybe they'll have more details later. Listen, I've got to get back to work."

"Have Nate or Marshall find out, will you? They're pretty chummy with those deputies."

"They're both out on their own cases. Most likely this was a terrible accident. And peach or pink are popular colors in men's attire these days. It doesn't mean anything. Besides, the shirt might not have been pink. It could have been off-white and only looked pink in the sunlight."

"Pink, white, it doesn't matter. Everyone I've talked to thinks the man in the shirt was Cosmo. And it wouldn't surprise me if someone pushed him right into the train. You saw that crowd yesterday. They were vicious."

"That may be the case, but until the sheriff's office releases an official statement regarding the identity of the victim, please don't say anything."

"Fine. But mark my words, the Sun City West rumors are rarely wrong."

*And the seats on the rumormongering train are selling fast.*

"I don't know about you, Augusta," I said when I stepped in the front office, "but I'm starving and I didn't pack a lunch."

She looked up from her computer screen. "You never pack a lunch. Well, practically never. Can't say I blame you. I don't either. It's too much work in the morning. So, what do you feel like this time? Tacos? Subs? Gyros? Pizza? I'm game for most anything."

"We haven't had gyros in a long time and the pita place is just down the block. I'll be happy to pick them up."

Augusta laughed. "You just want to get out of here before your mother calls again. I have to admit, it's better than watching a soap opera. It moves quicker."

"Not quick enough. If a positive identification isn't made on that victim by the end of the day, I'm afraid my mother and her friends will trounce over to the hospital morgue and make it for them. Like I mentioned when we got her third call, she's convinced it's Cosmo Pruett."

"How on earth would he have wound up on the railroad tracks?"

I shrugged. "Beats me. Last I heard, he registered a complaint with the sheriff's office about someone putting a dead fish on his car's manifold. Herb and Paul were dragged out of Curley's for questioning last night, but according to Marshall, who accompanied them, they left the posse station and went home."

"Don't worry about it. It probably wasn't Cosmo. Most likely some poor vagrant who staggered onto the tracks. And frankly, Herb and Paul better hope I'm right."

"Why?"

"Because if it does turn out to be Cosmo, those two clowns could become prime suspects. Face it, by now everyone knows they ended a public hearing before it started and exchanged not-so-pleasant words with the guy in the parking lot. Oh, and let's not forget they're still not off the hook for the fish-in-the-engine deal."

"Ouch."

Again, another choice expression—*off the hook*. Herb and Paul were on that hook by the time the four p.m. news came on the air. Channel 3 was all over it and my mother wasted no time delivering it to Augusta and me secondhand. I happened to be at the Keurig and pushed Speakerphone as soon as her call came in.

"They made a positive identification and notified next of kin. Must have set a new record for expediency. It *was* Cosmo after all. The TV anchor said the man had his driver's license and insurance cards in his wallet, which they found on the scene. No mention of a cell phone or car keys, but I suppose if he did have them in his pocket, all that would be left would be bloody shards of glass from the phone and twisted pieces of metal from the keys."

"Ew. Did the anchors speculate on what might have happened?"

"No. They said they'd have a full report on the six o'clock news. We'll have to wait. Oh my gosh, you don't suppose they'll arrest Herb and Paul, do you? Everyone heard that confrontation in the parking lot yesterday."

"Following the preliminary autopsy, the coroner will have to issue a time of death."

"The coroner?" my mother practically shrieked. "Why the coroner? Get the time of death from the train conductor who ran over him. What do Nate and Marshall have to say about this?"

"I don't know. They're still out on cases. And the coroner is only the first step. It moves to the medical examiner, a certified pathologist."

My mother let out an audible huff. "Begs the question, Phee. Was Cosmo dead when he landed on those tracks or did someone give him a good shove? And don't tell me he stumbled into the train."

"That's a distinct possibility if he was impaired."

"You saw how uptight that man was yesterday. Didn't strike me at all as the type who'd go out drinking, or smoking marijuana, for that matter."

"Once the preliminary toxicology report comes back, the authorities will have a better idea of what might have caused his death."

"Not *what*, Phee, *who*. And no toxicology test is going to tell you that. If you want my two cents, he was murdered."

"Look, before you start sharing your two cents with everyone in creation, hold off until the facts are in. If it's a suspicious death, the sheriff's office will conduct a complete investigation."

"Since when? They'll take the nearest shortcut and stay there. I've got to call Herb. Talk to you later."

"Mom—"

It was too late. She got off the phone and most likely speed dialed Herb. I was left literally holding the phone and staring at Augusta.

"Want me to hang up the receiver for you or do you think you can manage?"

"Very funny. My mother will get Herb so unnerved who knows what he'll do."

"I know what I'd do. Find a good attorney and plunk down a retainer fee."

I sincerely hoped Augusta and my mother were wrong, but for the first time since I moved out here, the two of them were right on the money. Only Herb didn't call an attorney. He called Nate. And not because of my mother's phone call.

It was a little before five and Marshall was still out. Nate had just stepped in the office from what he called an easy surveillance when Herb's call came in. Augusta wasted no time rushing into my office while Nate was on Augusta's phone with him.

"How much you want to bet Herb Garrett is our next client? I'll put five dollars down."

"I'm not betting, Augusta, because you're probably right. But I think everyone is jumping the gun. For all we know, Cosmo could have been out walking and suffered a seizure."

"That's what I like about you, Phee. You're such an optimist."

I followed Augusta back to her desk so that I could hear what Nate had to say, but before I could ask, Paul came rushing in. He was out of breath and panting as if he'd been followed by an angry mob.

"I think Herb and I are being framed for murder."

# CHAPTER 9

That was the only coherent and full sentence he uttered. Paul grabbed his chest, took a series of deep breaths and spewed out a series of words consisting of, but not limited to, *finger-pointing*, *setup*, and *murder*.

Nate, whose call with Herb had ended, pulled out a chair for Paul, leaned a palm against Paul's shoulder, and pretty much shoved him into the seat. Augusta opened the mini-fridge by her desk and handed him a bottle of water. "Drink it slowly," she said. "Don't need you choking to death."

"Death," Paul stammered. "Cosmo Pruett is dead and someone thinks I did it. Found it by my front door. Here, see for yourself." With that, he reached into a plastic grocery bag and pulled out a small, dead fish. It had a pin stuck to its gills with a note that read, "You'll get caught for murder just like this tasty little fellow."

Augusta peered over at the fish. "Is it still fresh? We can stick it in the fridge and grill it later. Hate to see a good fish go to waste."

Nate shot her a look and she replied, "Never mind."

"Did you call the posse?" Nate asked.

Paul nodded. "They told me they thought it was a prank but they'd pass the info along to the MCSO deputies. Said to drop off the note at their station and email them a photo of the fish. Told me not to worry. Yeah, right. Herb got a similar prize only it wasn't a fish."

"I know," Nate said. "I spoke with him a few minutes ago."

I looked at Nate and gasped, "What prize? What horrible thing did someone leave on Herb's doorstep?"

"Not horrible. It was a deck of pinochle cards with a Post-it attached. The note said, 'The trick in your case will be to get out of jail free.' And before you ask, Herb called the posse, too. Got the same answer. He's on his way to the posse station to deliver the cards and the note."

Paul took a giant gulp of water and tried not to burp. "You see? You see what I'm saying? Someone is setting us up. We need your help. You've got to find out how Cosmo landed on those train tracks before we land in the Fourth Avenue Jail."

"Not that I'm refusing to take your case, but I think you may be rushing things a bit. The official reports have not come in and cause of death is speculative at best. Tell you what. Let me see what I can find out from the two sheriff's deputies that we've worked closely with on prior cases— Bowman and Ranston."

At the mention of those names, I all but recoiled. It was the same reaction Laverne and Shirley had at the mention of Lenny and Squiggy, only those two had some redeeming features, unlike a large, heavy mammal or a well-fed warty amphibian.

Nate's response seemed to placate Paul, who agreed to drive back to Sun City West and deliver the note, sans fish, to the posse volunteers. Once he left, Nate all but burst out laughing. "I know it's not funny, but all I could think of when Paul showed us the trout was that quote from *The Godfather.* You know, the one about Luca Brasi sleeping with the fishes."

"At least it wasn't a horse's head," Augusta chimed in.

"Aargh. Both of you are creeping me out. Enough with *The Godfather.*" Then I looked at Nate. "Think Bowman and Ranston will take this seriously?"

"Considering the fact they've got an unexplained death on their hands, I do."

"I hope the medical examiner's office works fast," I said. "They'll need to in order to stay one step ahead of the rumor mill."

Marshall returned a few minutes later from Avondale. It was another surveillance situation, only this one wasn't about infidelity. Parents of an eighteen-year-old were convinced their son was involved in all sorts of nefarious activities and needed our firm to find out for sure. Our official office hours had ended and Augusta turned off her computer, the copy machine, and the Keurig.

"I'm on my way out," she announced. "Someone tell Mr. Gregory what's going on because I don't want to be late for canasta."

"No problem," I said as I stepped into the front office. Like Augusta, I, too, had shut down my computer and was ready to head home.

Marshall glanced at Augusta as she made her way out the door and then looked at me. "Tell me what? What did I miss? I haven't checked my news app all day. Too busy keeping up with a hyperactive teen."

From Cosmo's positive ID to Herb and Paul's puzzling notes, Marshall got the full story from me. Well, almost full. Nate managed to get ahold of Ranston on the phone and was able to get his take on the situation.

"Can you believe it? The sheriff's office thinks Herb and Paul concocted those notes themselves to take any suspicion off of them regarding Cosmo's death. But like I told Paul, it's way too early in the case to reach any conclusions. Ranston said they'll take action once the full autopsy and the preliminary toxicology reports are in."

"So now what do we do?" I asked him.

"We go about our business, kiddo. And mine is to get home and grill a good steak. Too bad I didn't ask Herb for his marinade recipe."

"You don't suppose someone murdered Cosmo over a marinade recipe and not the transfer station issue, do you?"

"I'm not ruling anything out. But right now, it's an unexplained death. And until it's deemed a homicide, that's where it stands."

• • •

As things turned out, Cosmo's unexplained death didn't stand unexplained for long. It was officially deemed a homicide a week later. A week, mind you, that was filled with speculating, gossiping, tattletale-ing, and yenta-ing. That all came to an end at six in the morning on a Wednesday, when my mother turned on KPHO's channel 5 to learn that the "official cause of death for Maricopa County Planning Commission chairman Cosmo Pruett was a blow behind the head resulting in trauma that most likely rendered the victim unconscious, thus explaining his unfortunate fall onto the railroad tracks." I doubted the news anchor finished his or her statement before my mother rushed to share the information with me.

"Unfortunate fall?" my mother all but shouted. "Why don't they come right out and admit someone pushed his comatose body onto the tracks? Do they think we're too old and senile in our retirement community to deduce that for ourselves?"

"Huh? What?" It took a minute to process what was going on. And Marshall was no help since I could hear the water running in the shower. Unlike me, he tended to get up with the sun, not with a high-powered caffeine fix.

"Cosmo Pruett, Phee. It was murder." Then she repeated everything she said before. Only louder.

"Um, okay. Thanks for letting me know. I'll turn on the news."

"Is that all you're going to do?"

"No, not all. I have to shower, grab breakfast and get to work."

"You know what I mean. Let your boss and your husband know that Herb and Paul's days as we know them may be numbered. They need to get on this."

"Stop with the drama queen stuff. The sheriff's office is in charge. Our firm is not on the case."

"Ha! We'll see how long that lasts. Call me when you get a break. Oh, goodness, Streetman and Essie are cuddling under the covers. If you hold on, I can get my phone and take a picture for you."

"That's okay. I've got to get going. And whatever you do, don't get Herb or Paul any more worked up than they probably are."

"Honestly, Phee. It wasn't as if I was about to call them. Well, not until eight at least."

"Aargh. I'll catch up with you later."

Marshall wasn't surprised to learn Cosmo's death was a homicide, only that it was blunt force trauma. He slathered cream cheese on a toasted bagel while he spoke. "It seemed a no-brainer that the guy was murdered. I mean, even if he'd been out on a bender, he wouldn't have ventured down the railroad tracks. Too far away from the bars. I figured someone drugged him and drove him there. If anyone saw anything at the time, it would have appeared as if Cosmo was drunk, not drugged. But trauma to the head is different."

"I don't understand." I reached for the tub of shmear.

"Unlike slipping something into someone's drink, which isn't all that noticeable, hitting someone over the head is. Anyway, I'm sure Nate and I will learn more from Bowman and Ranston. They're the lead detectives for that sort of thing."

"They may be the lead detectives but you and Nate always seem to close the cases."

"That's because we've got you and that quirky book club of your mother's."

"Yeah, speaking of which, do you plan to contend with them at the next public hearing for the transfer station? It should be coming up soon. They can't postpone it indefinitely."

"I don't think I have much choice. One bit of good news, though. Now that Streetman found that kitten, your mother won't be dragging him everywhere in that giant floral tote bag of hers."

"The Vera Bradley. Don't remind me. If the designer saw what her creation was being used for, she'd find a new line of work."

"At least we won't be looking over our shoulders at that hearing wondering if the dog will make an escape."

Talk about jinxing things. Marshall should have bitten his tongue because that's exactly what happened the following Tuesday. Only worse. It seemed to follow a pattern of things going wrong.

The preceding week hadn't gotten Bowman or Ranston any closer to solving Cosmo's murder, and they exhausted their interviews with the other members of the planning commission, according to Nate, who had a quick conversation with Bowman on another matter—how to retrieve lost cell phone data. It seemed Bowman's notes from those interviews were on his cell phone and it crashed.

Nate was able to contact our cyber-sleuth, Rolo Barnes, who resolved Bowman's data issue in less time than it took me to prepare a cup of coffee. Rolo was the IT specialist when Nate, Marshall, and I worked for the Mankato Police Department before branching out on his own. He was positively brilliant when it came to encryptions and hacking into overseas banking accounts. He was also as looney as they came. He refused to accept certain numbers on payroll checks and considered sugar to be a lethal poison, right up there with cyanide. In addition, Rolo was always on some new fad diet that promised him Richard Roundtree's physique, but as far as I was concerned, he resembled a black Jerry Garcia sans the guitar.

When he worked on cases for our firm, he preferred to be paid with kitchen gadgetry. Expensive kitchen gadgetry. I imagined IKEA had a plaque in his honor somewhere in their corporate office.

Bowman and Ranston also hit a roadblock when it came to the timeline. The last contact anyone had with Cosmo was when he notified the sheriff's office about the dead fish in his engine. After that, it was as if he vanished into thin air, only to be found the following morning at the junction of Meeker Boulevard and Grand Avenue.

And even when Bowman was able to retrieve his missing interviews, they didn't offer him much. That meant a broader search, hence the next public hearing. The deputies thought perhaps they'd be able to glean more information from the high-profile members of the community who were opposed to the transfer station.

Needless to say, Nate and Marshall were asked to assist with that detail. When Tuesday evening rolled around, not only was my mother's Booked 4 Murder book club on the scene along with Herb's pinochle crew, but the four investigators were there as well.

The venue, however, had changed from the social hall to the Stardust Theater on RH Johnson Boulevard because the Sun City West Square Dance Club had reserved the social hall well in advance. Too bad they didn't ask to commandeer the Stardust Theater's stage, because that would have saved everyone from the chaos that ensued.

# CHAPTER 10

It was hotter than usual that following Tuesday in July with evening temps in the low hundreds. I made sure to take a bottle of iced water with me since that theater could get stuffy in spite of the air-conditioning. Marshall and Nate took their own cars directly from work in case they got tied up and I drove mine. Since this wasn't our first rodeo with Sun City West meetings, we phoned in an order for pizza and ate it before taking off for the Stardust Theater.

Lyndy, who was forced to attend the hearing in order to accompany her cantankerous aunt, met me in the small courtyard in front of the theater so we could have a few minutes to chat before I had to find my mother and the book club ladies.

"Where's your aunt?" I asked.

Lyndy pointed to a petite gray-haired woman directly behind us. "Getting caught up on some gossip with a few of her neighbors. Can you believe this crowd? It's total bedlam. And I thought the social hall parking lot was bad two weeks ago. What'd they do? Bus in people from Wickenburg?"

I looked around. "Yeah, it does look larger. We'd better get inside before there are no seats left. My mother said she'd be down in front so I'd better go look. What do you say we get caught up at the pool this week?"

"For sure."

I hustled off to find my mother and nab a seat. The aisles were packed and I had to press my elbows against my sides to get through. Sure enough, I spotted Myrna down front and knew my mother had to be there as well. Aunt Ina and Uncle Louis were seated at the far end of the front row all the way to the right. Donning a raspberry sundress with matching ribbons in her braids, my aunt was hard to miss. Next to her was Shirley and next to Shirley, Lucinda. As I got closer, I spotted my mother at the opposite end of the row from my aunt and uncle. Apparently she had been bent over so that's why I didn't see her at first.

Cecilia and Louise were in the second row along with Paul, Herb, and Herb's cronies. Ringling Brothers couldn't have asked for a better turnout.

"Hey, cutie!" Herb shouted the second he saw me. "Has your office figured out who axed Cosmo?"

I moved closer and kept my voice low. "Not yet. It's very early in the investigation."

Then Paul stood and gave Herb a nudge. "Isn't that one of the deputies over there? Midway up the aisle on the left. They're casing the joint, aren't they?"

I bent down and motioned for Paul to sit. "They're trying to find out who the major players are regarding the opposition to the transfer station. It's part of the process. Don't muck it up."

My mother must have heard my voice because she stood, spun around and pointed to the seat next to her. "Here. I saved a seat for you." I started toward her and stopped dead in my tracks. I could have sworn my mother's peach-colored shirt had some sort of a papoose in front. *Dear Lord, do not tell me she brought Streetman in that thing.*

"Is that some sort of a hoodie you've got on? With a pouch for the dog? Is Streetman in that pouch?" I narrowed my eyes to get a better look.

"Don't be ridiculous. Streetman is right here in his little tote." She leaned over and held up the multicolored floral Vera Bradley bag. "Essie is in the Kitty-Meow-Roo shirt. I got it on Amazon this week. Comes in all sorts of colors. The turquoise one is hanging in my closet."

Sure enough, I spied the little dark gray kitten behind the meshing on the pouch. "You brought both animals here? What were you thinking?"

"I couldn't leave them home alone at night and take the chance they could be traumatized."

"They weren't traumatized the last time. They were asleep when you got home."

"Every time is different, Phee. Hurry up and sit down, looks like the hearing is about to start."

There were ten members on the planning committee, representing five different districts with two members per district. Cosmo was the chairman and a man by the name of Neville Lindblossom was the vice chair. He was also the same stocky man who was present during the unfortunate verbal altercation between Cosmo and Herb in the social hall parking lot.

At tonight's meeting, nine seats were lined up on stage for the remaining members of the planning commission. And while I noted racial equity, the same could not be said for gender. Only two women and seven men. Cosmo would have made it eight.

Each member had a large placard on the table in front of them, with their name spelled out in large block letters. In addition, they each had their own microphone.

Neville approached the podium in front and said a few poignant words about their former chairman. Then he spelled out the rules for the public hearing and called upon a guest speaker from the waste management department to explain why the county needed to add another transfer station to the area.

I was surprised to find out that the transfer station was to be privately owned and managed, and not a part of the county resources. Given that tidbit, I seriously wondered if Cosmo had been paid off to ramrod the process through and something went array.

When the waste management speaker finished up his spiel, Neville returned to the podium and explained the process for public input. "There's one microphone down in front. Members of the community are invited to approach the mic and address the commission. Comments are limited to three minutes. First come, first speak. This is not a free-for-all and the audience is reminded to show courtesy to the speakers."

I'm not sure who the first resident was, but the man appeared to be in his late fifties or early sixties. He wasted no time lambasting the commission for their "ill-conceived and idiotic idea." He was followed by a fragile-looking elderly woman who had to be escorted to the microphone by another octogenarian. She echoed the prior sentiments and then began to cry. Something about noxious odors interfering with the delightful honeysuckle that surrounded her house.

On and on it went. Complaints, threats to sue the county, and passionate pleas to "take the damn transfer station and transfer it the hell out of Sun City West." I caught a glimpse of Bowman to the left of me. He stood against the wall and took notes. Shifting around in my seat, I tried to find Ranston as well as Nate and Marshall, but no luck.

The procession to the microphone continued and I swore I heard someone snoring in the row behind me. Then, without warning, a voice belonging to one of the two women on the commission came over her microphone loud and clear. Apparently she didn't realize she had accidently turned it on. "For heaven's sake. You'd think we were installing a nuclear waste site."

Unfortunately, her comment came across to some members in the audience as "We're installing a nuclear waste site." In seconds, the atmosphere turned explosive. People stood, waved their hands in the air and shouted. It was a cacophony of voices and expletives, all with the same message.

"No plutonium in our backyard!"

"Send the commission packing!"

"The commission's on the take!"

"Stop the commission before it's too late!"

And finally, the one comment that sent Bowman charging up to the mic—"Cosmo knew too much. That's what got him killed."

Ranston was three or four yards behind Bowman and moving as fast as he could. Bowman picked up the microphone and bellowed into the audience. It was a double sound whammy and I had to cover my ears. "Who said that? Whoever you are, you can't withhold information from the sheriff's office. Who said 'Cosmo knew too much'?"

Suddenly, everyone quieted down. Not a single comment, cough, or sneeze. Dead silence. Neville wasted no time rushing to the podium on stage. "Forgive that slight indiscretion from the commission. All table mics should be turned off. Allow me to clarify. The county is proposing a waste disposal transfer site. Household waste. Not industrial waste. And certainly not nuclear waste. I repeat, household waste."

My mother poked me in the elbow and whispered, "That man looks like he's about to have a stroke."

I rolled my eyes and hoped she didn't notice. "Wouldn't anyone given that fiasco?"

Bowman retreated back to the audience with Ranston at his heels. "Do you think this will last much longer?" I asked my mother.

"Not sure. The audience needs a minute to regroup."

"Regroup?"

"You know, go back to their original complaints now that the nuclear waste site is off the table."

"It was never *on* the table."

"Shh. Someone's approaching the mic."

The someone turned out to be Ricky DeLong from Ricky DeLong Realty. He went on and on about decreasing property values and people's nest eggs being wiped out. That, sad to say, started another maelstrom.

By the time that wave of complaints echoed the theater, I was ready to sell all my worldly possessions for a fast-acting aspirin. Instead, I mustered through like everyone else. Then, for some inexplicable reason, my mother decided to throw in her two words. Only she never got the chance.

She stood and marched to the microphone when the same woman who started the nuclear waste fracas left the stage and raced toward my mother. "Aha! I thought that was a cat in your shirt. You can't bring a pet in here. Pet dander is highly toxic."

"It's not toxic, Enid," one of the men on the commission said. "It's an allergen. Big difference. Now sit down, will you? We need to get this over with."

Enid straightened her shoulders and pointed a finger directly at Essie. "I don't like cats." And while I'm sure the little kitten didn't understand the words, she must have sensed something because she let out a "me"- yowl that was intensified by the microphone.

I felt something bump against my leg, but by the time I realized it was Streetman, who had extricated himself from the tote bag, it was too late. He charged to the front of the stage as if he was leading a cavalry—growling, snarling, and barking. Then, to everyone's horror, he latched on to Enid's pant leg and peed.

Herb, along with Wayne, Kevin, Kenny, Bill, and Paul, stood and applauded. "Way to go, Streetman," Herb shouted. "You tell her."

My mother snatched the dog from the floor, tucked him under her arm, and announced, "I believe that's the final word on this transfer station hearing."

Neville must have agreed because he promptly concluded the hearing and told the audience the board would render its decision "in time."

"Lordy, we'd better hurry out of here," Shirley said, "before the theater puts that dog on probation again, or worse yet, fines your mother."

I gulped. *What else is new?*

# CHAPTER 11

As the grumbling, disgruntled crowd exited the Stardust Theater, I looked around to see if I could spot Marshall or Nate. No luck. However, Lyndy managed to elbow her way to me and gave my shoulder a shake as we approached the exits.

"You're not going to believe what I overheard. The man seated next to my aunt told the person he was with that Cosmo got stiffed by someone on the commission."

"Yeah, that's the same thing Gloria Wong said at the Homey Hut. Gloria's another one of my mother's friends. She used to live on the same block but moved to a larger house when her daughter moved in. Guess that setup works for some people. Kalese couldn't wait to get out of the house, and if I could have crawled out a window back in junior high, I would have done so."

Lyndy laughed, then spun around. "Good, my aunt is still talking to someone. Did Gloria happen to have the details about what happened with Cosmo?"

"A bad business deal or something. Guess he lost out on money he needed for his home renovation so speculation had it he entered into some nefarious payback scheme to get that transfer station up and running. *Speculation* being the key word."

"The men next to us didn't talk about that but I don't think it was a business deal gone wrong. More like a romance that fizzled out. Cosmo got dumped by one of the women on that commission. At least according to their conversation."

"Not that Enid woman who accosted my mother? It has to be the other one. Darn it, I couldn't read those placards. Now I'll have to dredge up the county website and plod through it when I get home."

"Think she had something to do with his murder?" Lyndy glanced behind her shoulder again and sighed. "My aunt's still yakking."

"If she was the one who dropped him, I doubt she'd kill him. Unless he had something on her and tried to blackmail her. Dear Lord. I'm sounding more and more like my mother every day. Anyway, it's all rumor and innuendo."

"Are you heading home or going back to your mom's?"

"Home. And not fast enough. I bolted out ahead of her and the book club ladies so I could track down Marshall."

Lyndy pointed to a cluster of people off to our right. "If I'm not mistaken, isn't that him with that group of men?"

"Yeah. That's Marshall all right. With Deputy Bowman. And take a closer look, four of the men are the ones from the planning commission."

"Maybe you should go over and see what's going on."

Before I could respond, Deputy Ranston ran past us, huffing as if he was about to keel over.

"Think there's a problem?" Lyndy asked.

"Oh, hell. There's always a problem. But last thing Marshall needs is to have me interfere. I'll grab a seat on one of those empty benches and text him."

"Wish I could stick around but I've got to get my aunt home before the witching hour."

This time it was my turn to laugh. "Good luck. Catch you later."

The crowd had thinned and I had the whole bench to myself. I reached in my bag for my cell phone when Nate took the seat next to me. "Quite a night, huh, kiddo?"

"I'll say. I wish my mother would leave that dog home. And now she's carting around the cat."

"Have to admit, when Streetman lifted his leg on Enid, I was sorry I didn't take a picture."

"She'll probably track down my mother and send her a dry-cleaning bill for those pants. Tell me, how come you're not with that huddle over there? Do you know what's going on?"

"Uh-huh. Four men on the planning commission arrived to the hearing with jackets. They put those jackets over their seats, and when they went to leave, they all found a single playing card in one of the pockets. Neville waved Bowman over to tell him, and since Marshall was in close proximity, Bowman told him."

"What about you and Ranston?"

"Marshall shot me a text and Bowman did the same with his partner."

"So how come you're not over there?"

"I was on my way when I saw you. I figured I fill you in. This could be a long night."

"Hmm, I take it you and Marshall are officially on the Cosmo Pruett murder case."

"No. We were asked to do some crowd surveillance in order to identify high-profile suspects. You'd be surprised how people slip up and reveal more than they should at these public venues."

"Were any threats written on those cards?"

"That's what I'm about to find out."

"Do me a favor and tell Marshall I'm heading home and will wait up for him."

Nate gave my shoulder a squeeze. "You're a good wife, kiddo."

Thankfully it wasn't as long a night as Nate anticipated. Marshall got home about forty minutes after I did and gave me the rundown on those cards. "Not exactly a threat written on those cards but a strong suggestion."

"What suggestion? What did they say?"

Marshall opened the fridge and took out a Coke before plopping himself in the nearest kitchen chair. "Two jacks of diamonds and two queens of spades. That's a double pinochle. And get this, they all said 'Don't play games. Nix the transfer station.' Bowman collected the cards for prints but I doubt the lab will be able to pull anything up."

"Double pinochle? Come on. It can't be more obvious than that. Someone's setting up Herb to take the fall for Cosmo's death."

"Probably easier than pointing a finger at Paul. They'd have to get a can of sardines and put one of those in each pocket."

"I'd laugh if it wasn't so scary. Honestly, I don't think those two deputies can look past the obvious and I'm afraid Herb and Paul are the only ones on their radar. Then again, Lyndy overheard something tonight that may change everything."

I told Marshall about the woman on the commission who may or may not have given Cosmo the boot. He pulled out a list of names that he'd written down and read off the women's names, saving me from going to the planning commission's website.

Enid Flox represented District 2 in the Scottsdale area along with Neville, while Abigail McFadden represented our district, District 4, along with the late Cosmo Pruett.

"I'll let the deputies know," he said. "Given that choice tidbit, one of them should have a more in-depth conversation with Abigail. All of the commission members were interviewed but I imagine it was cursory at best."

"Nate mentioned tonight's foray into the world of snooping. Were either of you, or Bowman and Ranston, for that matter, successful in identifying high-profile players?"

Marshall shook his head. "Not really. Seemed the entire audience held the same amount of animosity toward that commission. At least Lyndy was able to home in on something."

I nodded and helped myself to a Coke as well before joining him at the table. "I realize it's only been a day or so, but was the medical examiner's office able to ascertain what kind of blunt object found its way to the back of Cosmo's head?"

"Something large and possibly round. No sharp edges but heavy. Lots of river rocks around those railroad tracks. Could have been a crime of opportunity, which makes this even more puzzling."

"How so?"

"If it was an act of revenge, then the perpetrator would have planned ahead and carried his or her own weapon. Like a small hammer. Not rely on finding just the right rock. On the other hand, if it was done in anger, that could explain it. But in either situation, it begs the question—'What were they doing by the railroad tracks?'"

"Guess Bowman and Ranston will need to get that sorted out, huh?"

"They'll have to. Unless things get complicated. Then—"

"I know. Williams Investigations to the rescue."

"They'll have to take a number. Tonight's escapade was a favor. Nate and I picked up a major case in one of Verrado's fifty-five-plus gated communities. We met with their manager last week, who wasn't sure whether or not his board wanted to hire private investigators, as opposed to relying on the county sheriff's office. Apparently they met tonight and rendered their decision. It's a go for us."

"That's a gorgeous area and a pretty neat master-planned community."

"Yep, a genuine bedroom community for Phoenix. That's for sure."

"What's the problem? Why do they need investigators?"

"For the past two months, there's been a series of break-ins. It started out small but it's escalating. The developer wanted to keep it hush-hush since more dwellings are being built, but the residents have had enough."

"You said gated. That would imply an inside job, wouldn't it?"

"Not necessarily. They've got a public restaurant and all sorts of landscapers and home improvement companies are in and out of there."

"How many incidents have there been?"

"Given the one two days ago, seventeen in all. That's a high number for such a small community. Nate and I will have to meet with those victims and review any home surveillance they may have. We'll need to study patterns and get a handle on the stolen goods. Needless to say, Bowman and Ranston will be on their own as far as finding Cosmo's killer."

"That's not very encouraging."

"They'll follow protocol and begin with the timeline. Too bad Cosmo's cell phone was destroyed by the train. Reduced to smithereens. The information on it could have helped them. Right now, all they know is that Cosmo was last seen at his car pitching a fit over the dead fish in his engine. After that, no one knows where he went or with whom."

"Well, maybe Lyndy's scuttlebutt about Abigail McFadden will point them in a new direction."

• • •

Lamentably, it didn't. My mother phoned our office at a little before ten the next morning to insist Nate and Marshall drop everything and rush to

Herb's defense. Augusta, who had taken the call, held out the phone so I could hear my mother. I stood a few feet away at the Keurig and grimaced. Of all the times to make a second cup of coffee. Then again, Augusta would have simply transferred the call to my office.

My mother sounded like a TV commentator high on energy drinks. "Herb Garrett was just informed that he is a person of interest in the death of Cosmo Pruett. He was told not to leave the country. Or the state, for that matter. I guess they don't know Herb. He rarely leaves the county. Anyway, one of those miserable deputies knocked on his door at a little past nine to discuss some pinochle cards. I don't have all the details. How soon can Nate or Marshall get here?"

Augusta put her hand over the receiver and whispered, "You want to tell her or should I?"

I took the phone from her and mouthed, "You owe me."

"I could hear you on the phone, Mom, so I took the receiver from Augusta. Nate and Marshall aren't in the office and won't be all day. They're working on a major case they picked up, not to mention the smaller ones that need their attention, too."

"I saw them last night at the Stardust Theater. In fact, I told the book club ladies that they must be working with the sheriff's office on Cosmo's murder."

"That just goes to show you have to check things out first. They were only helping Bowman and Ranston as a favor."

"Well, maybe they could help Herb as a favor, too."

I tried not to moan. "They can't. First of all, they haven't been hired as consultants, and I already mentioned the second reason."

"What kind of favor were they doing for those deputies last night?"

"Trying to home in on any conversations from high-profile individuals who objected to the transfer station."

"And?"

"Everyone objected and everyone was boisterous."

There was silence at my mother's end of the line but it only lasted a second or two before she spoke. "That's why it's best to garner information from reliable sources who have their noses firmly planted in the rumblings of the community."

I knew immediately where this was going and there was no stopping it. My mother was about to mention Cindy Dolton and the dog park. Like a fish at the end of a hook, I had no place to go.

# CHAPTER 12

"Fine. What time do you want me to pick up the crowned prince tomorrow? I want to get this over with as soon as possible."

"You'll be doing Herb a tremendous favor. And Paul, too, I'm sure. I haven't heard from him but I can pretty much guarantee that if Herb is a person of interest, then Paul can't be far behind. After all, he was the one with the moose urine."

"Don't remind me."

"I'll have Streetman ready at six. That should give you plenty of time."

*Yep. Plenty of time and one less hour of sleep.*

When Marshall and I caught up that evening, I told him about Herb's recent status and my willingness to placate my mother by snooping around the dog park. He was exhausted from a full day at Verrado with another such day in store tomorrow.

"I'll be up at the crack of dawn anyway so we'll be on the same schedule—comatose."

I had heated up a frozen veggie lasagna that I'd made a few weeks ago and made a mental note to plan ahead with some Crock-Pot meals that could be frozen. Marshall had offered to barbeque something but that meant standing outside in the sweltering heat. Once May rolls around, it's impossible to use the stove top or the oven. As my mother pointed out, "Why heat the kitchen only to spend money having the air conditioner cool it down?" No doubt, tonight was a perfect example. It was over a hundred and three degrees and both of us were wiped out.

"I'm not surprised Herb's been tagged as a person of interest," Marshall continued. "Probably Paul, too. When I get a moment, I'll touch base with Bowman or Ranston and see if they've shifted gears for a closer look at Abigail. At least she had a real motive for murder."

"I really wish you and Nate were asked to consult on this one. It's so personal, considering my mother's friends are at stake."

"The investigation's in its preliminary stages. Don't worry. Nate and I will be monitoring it from the sidelines."

Marshall's words were comforting, but I didn't want to share them with my mother. Instead, I took on the role of amateur sleuth once again as I set foot into the dog park the following day.

As planned, the little chiweenie was "at the ready" by five fifty-five. Leashed and at the door, he bounded down the walkway and jumped into the passenger seat of my car without any fuss whatsoever. Meanwhile, Essie had a few minutes to herself playing with a catnip mouse that Shirley had sewn for her. Most likely at my mother's insistence, since she had purchased fresh-dried catnip at Sprouts a few days ago.

A handful of dog owners were seated on the benches under the large yellow canopy when I walked in. Off to the right, Cindy was at her usual spot by the fence and Bundles, her cute little white dog, was a few feet away.

She hailed me over the second she saw me. "I tried to catch up with you Tuesday night at the Stardust Theater but it was total bedlam. By the way, I laughed myself silly when Streetman peed on that obnoxious woman."

"I'm trying to forget." Instinctively, I turned to see what the dog was up to, and thankfully he was only sniffing around. "As you can guess, I'm hoping you might have some insights into Cosmo's murder, because right now Herb and Paul are the only ones on the radar screen."

Cindy nodded. "So I've heard. Word gets around fast. Frankly, I'd be looking at Clinton Badger and Therm Whittaker if I was one of those deputies."

"Wait a sec. I recognize those names. Aren't they Cosmo's team members for that Master Grillers contest?"

"You bet your life they are. And the buzz is that they had something to do with his death."

I looked around to make sure no one was in earshot. "What do you mean? What have you heard?"

"The winners aren't merely going to be on the Food Network. There's a mega money prize as well. With Cosmo out of the way, Clinton and Therm would split the money. People in the park have been talking about that for days."

"Talk or something more credible?"

"You didn't hear this from me, but . . . Therm is really, really behind with his Rec Center dues. I know because my neighbor works in their billing department and blabs all the time. And Clinton's been after some fancy-dancy lady who lives in Sun City Grand and has been spending all sorts of money trying to impress her."

"From the mouth of your neighbor?"

Cindy shook her head, "No, from Clinton's ex-wife. She's my hair-dresser."

"Wow. That's a lot of information to digest first thing in the morning."

"If you want to digest more, I can give you her name and the location of her salon."

I gave my hair a quick fluff and bit my lower lip. "Hmm, it may be time to get my highlights touched up. I held off since my beautician moved to Texas."

"The salon is Angel Hair in Sun City. Be sure to ask for Bernice. She's open every day except Sundays and Wednesdays."

Streetman was still sniffing around and I wondered if he'd ever get down to business. I was about to put him back on a leash and take him for a walk around the park when he finally located the perfect spot and saved me the time.

"Thanks, Cindy. I really appreciate—"

And then, the infamous shout-out from the canopy. "Poop alert! Poop alert! Small brown dog! Poop alert!"

"That's my cue," I said and laughed. "Have a great morning."

My mother must have been looking out the window because she opened the front door before I even pulled into her driveway. "Hurry up, Phee. It's getting hot out already."

Streetman immediately raced into the house and zeroed in on Essie, who must have tired from playing with her mouse and was now sleeping on the coffee table. He gave her a nuzzle and then proceeded to lean over and lick her.

"I thank my lucky stars each day," my mother said, "that no one's come around to claim her. As far as I'm concerned, the time limit's up. Next month she'll be fixed and that will be that."

"Yeah, I'd say she's all yours. Best hope the dog doesn't bring anything else home."

My mother winced. "Did you have any luck with Cindy?"

"Maybe. She thinks Cosmo's partners in that Master Grillers contest might have had a reason to do him in. Apparently the prize money is quite substantial. I may be able to learn more because Clinton Badger's ex-wife is Cindy's beautician and Cindy thinks the woman may be willing to dish the dirt on him."

My mother took a step back and stared at me. "What are you waiting for? Make an appointment. Your stylist took off weeks ago. Time to get a move on or your hair will get so long you'll look like your aunt Ina."

"I'm one step ahead of you. I got the info from Cindy, and once I get to work and check my calendar, I'll call the woman. Her salon is in Sun City on the four corners by CVS and Jack in the Box."

"Good. You can get your hair done, shop, and eat all in the same trip. No sense wasting time. Get to your office before her schedule books up."

Usually my mother asks if I'd like a cup of coffee, but this time she couldn't rush me out of there fast enough. At least I was spared day-old reheated coffee.

"By the way, Streetman did everything he should have. And no problems with other dogs."

My mother called him over to her and showered him with kisses.

"Mommy's precious little man. Mommy's little kissy-poo. Come, I'll give you a treat." Then to me, "You can let yourself out, Phee. I'll talk to you later."

*Good, because I might upchuck right here on the spot.*

Seconds later, I started up the car, turned on the AC, and took off for Williams Investigations. With a quick stop at Dunkin', I grabbed a coffee and muffin for myself and two donuts for Augusta.

"Mr. Williams and Mr. Gregory don't expect to be in until four or four thirty," Augusta said when I handed her the bag of donuts. "Donuts? You've made my morning. That dry fiber cereal is beginning to get on my nerves. Thanks."

"My pleasure." I then told her about my conversation with Cindy at the park and my next unofficial step in the Sophie Kimball Gregory amateur investigation.

Her response was pretty typical. "A beauty parlor, huh? Nothing like touching up roots for a long process. That should give you plenty of time to get that beautician talking."

"They're not roots, they're highlights. Well, disappearing highlights that have grown out."

"Roots."

I chuckled. "I need to find out how besotted her ex-husband might be in order for him to murder for money."

Augusta plopped her elbow on her desk and rested her head in the closed fist she made. "Depends. How old's the tootsie from Sun City Grand? A lot of these old coots will do anything for a young piece of the pie."

"Honestly, Augusta."

"Motive's motive in my book."

"Aargh. I'll see if I can book an appointment this week and I'll let you know. Meanwhile, I've got some accounts to reconcile. Off I go."

At a little before eleven, when I finally came up for air and a coffee break, I called Bernice at Angel Hair. Her voice was deep and raspy and I could have sworn she had a cigarette in her free hand. She informed me she was booked solid for the next two weeks but that someone had called a few minutes ago to cancel their five fifteen appointment. Something about gastrointestinal issues. Only a minute or so on the phone and it was like picking up gossip from the book club ladies.

When she asked if I wanted to take that slot, I couldn't say yes fast enough. If my sixty seconds with her was any indication of the conversation I could expect later in the day, I was one step closer to solving Cosmo's murder. Or so I thought.

# CHAPTER 13

I texted Marshall explaining I wouldn't be home until at least seven and that we'd have to take our chances with whatever could be defrosted quickly. He responded with four words—*No worries. Pizza delivery.*

That being accomplished, I cut my lunch hour short and focused on my spreadsheets and invoices for the remainder of the day before taking off for Angel Hair. Given the worst-case scenario in which Bernice refused to talk about her ex, I rationalized I was still one step ahead as far as personal grooming went. Last thing I needed was to have dowdy-looking hair.

Angel Hair was a small storefront operation in a strip mall behind the CVS store in Sun City. It was flanked by a Chinese take-out place and EJ's Reptiles. Ew! I prayed nothing from EJ's would get loose and make its way into the salon.

Pink and mauve tones greeted me the moment I stepped inside the place and for a brief second it was like I was back in the 1980s. The only person in the salon was Bernice, even though there were two visible stations. In the corner by one of the stations was a fold-up wheelchair that I imagined was used for customers who needed curbside assistance into the salon. Not uncommon in these senior communities. Its wheels had caked-on sand and it made me wonder why so many of these developments and strip malls still used sandy pathways rather than opt for concrete.

"You must be Phee Kimball Gregory," the lanky red-haired woman said when I entered. She appeared to be in her late fifties or maybe even early sixties. Long eyelashes that might have been fake and bright red lipstick. "Tell Cindy thanks for the referral. I've been doing her hair for years. That's how I know what's going on in Sun City West. I live in Sun City myself, on West Hutton off of Del Webb. Stone's throw from her neck of the woods."

"My mother lives in Sun City West and I'm in Vistancia, not too far from where I work in Glendale. I'm the bookkeeper/accountant for Williams Investigations."

"Hmm, seems to me I've heard that name. Too bad they weren't around when I needed a private eye to catch my worm of an ex-husband dallying around."

*Oh my gosh. I'm not even in the chair and she mentioned Clinton. I better talk fast.*

"Anyway," she continued, "take a seat right here and let's see what you've got going."

Bernice slipped a vinyl covering over me and ran a brush through my hair. "Whoever did your hair before did a good job. If you don't mind my asking, why aren't you staying with him or her?"

"It's a her and she moved to Texas."

"That'll do it. Can't very well commute to Texas. So, I take it you want the same-colored highlights and maybe a trim?"

"Uh-huh."

"I do foiling. Easy and less painful than pulling hair through a rubber cap."

"Great. That was the process my prior beautician used."

"Fine. I'll mix the hair color and we'll get started right away."

I watched through the mirror as Bernice took out a small bowl and proceeded to add packets of hair color and who-knows-what-else to the mix. She reached into one of the drawers in the cabinet behind her and pulled out a stack of square-shaped foil pieces. It was a process I was familiar with and one that would require a decent amount of time.

"I imagine everything worked out for you," I said, "about your ex-husband."

"If I know Cindy, she's probably given you all the details."

"Actually, no. When I do see her, it's usually about a recent murder in the area."

"Cosmo Pruett. *That* murder. What have you heard? And believe me, if there was ever a time I was grateful not to be married to that conniving weasel of a husband I had, it's now. Cosmo and Clinton were like Tweedledee and Tweedledumber. Throw in Therm Whittaker and you've got the Three Stooges. When I divorced Clinton, I divorced the other two as well."

Bernice slipped the end of a comb through a strand of my hair and then used a brush to apply the color mixture. She continued the procedure as she spoke. "Their latest enterprise is that Master Grillers contest in Sun City West. Someone on that rec center board sure knows how to work the media. Don't know what they did to get the community noticed by the Food Network, but whatever it was, it worked. They were selected over thousands of communities for the next hometown contest location. When I found out Clinton and those other two were qualifiers I all but fainted. He couldn't grill a hamburger if his life depended on it."

"With Cosmo out of the picture, it's just Therm and Clinton. Maybe Therm's the marinade mastermind."

"Must be, because the only thing Cosmo masterminded was how to put one over on his own ex-wife. Too bad Clinton followed suit. Frankly, I still blame Cosmo for ruining my marriage even though he wasn't the one stepping out on me. He was the one who taught Clinton how to do it."

"Ew. I'm sorry to hear that. You don't suppose Therm or your ex had anything to do with Cosmo's death, do you?"

Bernice gave the bowl of color mix another stir before dipping the brush in it. "I hate to say it, but I wouldn't put it past either of them. Especially if money was involved. I heard through the grapevine that Clinton's latest floozy has real expensive tastes. Got to find the money somewhere."

"You think Cosmo was killed over money?"

"*That* or the transfer station fiasco. Who wants garbage in their backyard even if it's only temporary? But if you ask me, I wonder if Clinton's trollop didn't pressure him to do something drastic to ensure a bigger cut of the prize money."

I think Cindy may have had a similar thought in the back of her mind and that's why she mentioned her beautician. Bernice continued with my hair and the conversation gradually shifted to the usual stuff—restaurant reputations and good summer cooling-off spots. I left well enough alone as far as probing into her ex. No sense trying too hard because that kind of thing has a way of backfiring. Besides, I could always return for a shorter haircut.

When Bernice finished, I was ecstatic. My hair had golden highlights that made me look years younger even though I was in my late forties. I thanked her and added a generous tip to the bill, letting her know I'd be back as a continuing customer. Then it was a race to get home and find out how Marshall's day went.

"You look amazing," he said when I walked into our living room. "Not that you weren't stunning before, but—"

"Say no more. Bernice at Angel Hair is a keeper. In more ways than one. She has no love lost for Cosmo, whom she blames for her divorce, and wouldn't put it past her ex-husband to have done the dirty deed in order to keep his latest love interest in baubles and finery."

"Baubles and finery. That's a mouthful. Tell me over dinner. I'm pushing the pizzeria app as we speak. Pepperoni and mushroom?"

"Perfect."

Marshall agreed to pass on my latest Cosmo intel to Bowman and Ranston. "Not that I think they'll pursue it," he said, "but they'll have it on a back burner if their focus on Herb and Paul fizzles."

"It won't fizzle. That's what has my mother so worried. You know how those two deputies latch on to something and put blinders on regarding everything else."

"They can latch on, hon, but right now all they have is circumstantial evidence. Which, by the way, is more than what Nate and I have regarding that mess up in Verrado. We were able to work with their maintenance department to plant cameras in some of the larger palm trees. The few home surveillance videos we watched that weren't blurry showed the back end of individuals who could have been men or women. Not much to go on."

"You mentioned break-ins. What did they take?"

"No heavy items like TVs or artwork. And no desktop computers. No surprise there. What they did manage to abscond with was jewelry and money. One would think people with pricey jewels or large sums of cash would lock those things in a wall safe or even a fire safe. But no. In some cases, money was left on dressers and jewelry in drawers or boxes. Fine for that costume stuff but we're talking platinum, diamonds, and other rare stones."

"Maybe it's an inside job, like the proverbial cleaning lady? Or maybe it was conjured up by a circle of friends who thought they could dupe their insurance companies."

"Harrumph. Nate and I shared similar thoughts and trust me, we'll pursue all of them. I've got a few things to work on in the morning, mostly data-driven investigations, and then I'll take off for Verrado to meet up with Nate."

"You know where I'll be. Six yards from Augusta and one phone call away from my mother."

I thought I was being facetious with that comment, but as it turned out, my ten thirty break time the next day was disrupted by my mom's need to tell me she and the book club ladies came up with a "reasonable and safe" plan to flush out Cosmo's killer. Myrna apparently came up with the general idea sometime between midnight and two and shared it via an impromptu Zoom meeting with the ladies sometime between seven and eight a.m.

"There's nothing reasonable or safe about that plan," I said to my mother. "In fact, it could cause worse problems."

"How could it be worse? The man is already dead. This coming Tuesday when our Booked 4 Murder radio show is on the air, we'll casually mention an eyewitness who, up until this point, remained silent but who has now decided to come forth and share what he or she saw with the deputies. We'll tell our audience that we learned from a very reliable source who wished to remain anonymous that the witness planned to meet secretly with investigators at the Crowing Rooster Restaurant at noon. Our book club will already be there and we can see who shows up to spy on the witness."

"How can they be meeting secretly if you and the whole world know about it?"

"That's the point, Phee. No one knows. We're flushing out the real culprit."

"It's a horrible plan. Like I said, it's bound to backfire. Last thing you need are Bowman and Ranston on your backs."

"Maybe we can be a bit more subtle with the phrasing when we're on the air. In fact, you've given me a terrific idea. I've got to go. Streetman's begging for a treat and I think he taught Essie how to meow for food."

"Don't say I didn't warn you."

I placed the receiver back on the phone and closed my eyes. If ever I needed a session in meditation, now was the time. Instead, I marched to the Keurig and prepared my third cup of coffee. Unfortunately, I was so worked up I forgot to put my mug on the drip tray base. In seconds, hot coffee filled the overflow tray below and started to flow onto the counter.

"Oh my gosh!" I announced. "The coffee!"

I shoved my mug onto the base and grabbed a handful of napkins. "It's finally happened, Augusta. I've lost my mind."

# CHAPTER 14

From surveillance tape reviews to interviews with theft victims and their neighbors, Marshall and Nate were kept hopping all weekend in Verrado. And when they weren't doing that, they finished up their prior cases and tackled smaller ones like finding birth parents or lost property. Meanwhile, I worked an easy half day on Saturday to do some billing and prepare for quarterly taxes.

No major breaks in the Cosmo Pruett murder as far as any official news went. The full toxicology report hadn't come in, but given the preliminary tox screen, the deputies were confident blunt force trauma was the cause. The rumor mill was active as ever churning out the latest scuttlebutt, including the possibility that the murderer had been identified at Putters Paradise on Saturday night since Deputies Bowman and Ranston were seen going in there. It turned out they went there for the Saturday cheeseburger special and not to make an arrest.

According to my mother, Herb and his crew did another test run for the barbeque sauce because Wayne was still insistent it needed the kind of kick that only some Jack Daniel's could deliver.

"They might as well work on perfecting that marinade while they can," she said when she called me Sunday morning to ask if I wanted to join her and Myrna at Bagels 'n More. She knew Marshall was in Verrado and was worried I might be bored or hungry. I thanked her and assured her I was neither. Then, I broached the subject of her radio talk show scheduled for Tuesday.

"Please tell me you dropped the idea about an eyewitness," I said.

"Not exactly, but it will be subtle. *Very* subtle."

*Subtle. The one word that cannot possibly apply to anyone in my family.*

"Okay. Augusta and I will try to tune in during our break." *Or for damage control.* "Paul's not going to be on the show, is he?"

"Heavens, no. The mystery and fish show is the following week. Paul's clamoring to talk about hatcheries and Myrna thinks we can work it into mysteries than involve caviar."

I rolled my eyes. "Wonderful."

• • •

When Marshall and I sank into bed on Monday night, we were relieved Herb and Paul were still persons of interest and not official suspects.

"The deputies made a quick pivot to interview Clinton and Therm a second time," he said, "along with Clinton's new love interest. I imagine that's why they haven't pressed too hard on Herb or Paul but that won't last forever. Public altercations have a way of standing out when it comes to these kinds of things."

"I take it the investigation isn't moving as quickly as one would hope."

"I don't think it's moving at all and that's worrisome."

"Oh, it'll be moving all right. I'm terrified my mother and Myrna will see to that tomorrow morning."

"Not the *Booked 4 Murder Mystery Hour?*"

"I'm afraid so. The only mystery will be how long they can stay on the air before creating a real hullabaloo."

Regrettably, it wasn't long.

Augusta couldn't wait to get to the break room at ten the next day. "There's a phone in here so I can grab it if a call comes in," she said. "And, with the break room door open, we'll know if anyone walks in. I have to admit, I'm getting addicted to that quirky radio show."

*Addicted* wasn't the word I'd use. *Frightened* would be more like it. The comments coming out of my mother and Myrna's mouths were enough to keep a libel, slander and defamation attorney on speed dial. I clenched my fists, turned on the radio, and took a seat at the table next to Augusta. "Pray to the gods they stick to cozy mysteries," I said.

"And ruin the fun?"

"Shh. It's starting."

My mother's voice seemed louder than usual. "Good morning and welcome to the *Booked 4 Murder Mystery Hour*. I'm Harriet Plunkett and with me is Myrna Mittleson. Today we'll discuss the difference between circumstantial and eyewitness evidence via a few of our favorite cozy mysteries."

"Yes," Myrna added. "As most of you know, circumstantial evidence relies on inference. For example, if a woman's favorite scarf was found around the neck of her philandering boyfriend's corpse, that would be considered circumstantial, as opposed to a witness catching the woman in the act of strangling the no-goodnik."

"So far, so good," Augusta whispered.

"Give it time."

"Take that wonderful food blogger novel by Debra Sennefelder—*The Uninvited Corpse*. An awful real estate agent is found dead on the floor with her head bashed in by a rock," my mother said. "Now that's circumstantial and it's—"

"Just like the recent murder in Sun City West. Wasn't that man's head bashed in with a rock, too? Or something that could have been a rock. Of course, the body in the Sennefelder book was found in someone's house on a nice carpeted floor, whereas the body in our community was sprawled all over the railroad tracks." Myrna continued talking but my brain flat out refused to process anything more. It wasn't until Augusta gave me a nudge and grimaced that I snapped to attention and resumed listening.

I thought the conversation between my mother and Myrna couldn't get any worse when all of a sudden my mother said, "At least the eyewitness in Sun City West isn't a cat like the one in Patricia Fry's delightful caper *Cat-Eye Witness: A Klepto Cat Mystery.* You can't very well interview a cat."

Augusta pushed herself back from the table. "Did she just say there was an eyewitness to Cosmo's murder?"

"Uh-huh." I sat perfectly still. Eyes fixed to the radio.

*Subtle. What happened to subtle? This is about as subtle as a sledgehammer banging on a concrete wall.*

"As long as they don't bring up the subject of Cosmo again, the listeners might gloss over it."

It was wishful thinking. Seconds later Myrna took the subject to a whole new level. "You know what's bad about eyewitnesses? The murderer always tries to bump them off."

"Are you implying we could have another murder here in Sun City West?" It was as if my mother had completely forgotten she was on the air and not at Bagels 'n More.

"Dear Lord," I said to Augusta. "If ever I wanted Paul Schmidt to make an appearance on that show and start talking about fish, this is the time."

Then Myrna jumped back into the fire. "I don't think so, Harriet. Not if the eyewitness meets with the sheriff's deputies and asks for protection, like they always do on the Hallmark Channel. In fact, if I were the eyewitness, I'd want to meet someplace with just the right amount of privacy and good food. Like the Crowing Rooster Restaurant on RH Johnson Boulevard. And I'd do it at noon on a Wednesday when they weren't so crowded."

My hand hit the table and Augusta jumped. "Can you believe it? Those two pretty much told the whole world that there's an eyewitness who may be meeting with sheriff's deputies tomorrow."

"It could be worse."

"How so?"

"They could ask you to join them when they show up to keep track of who walks in."

"My mother and Myrna are on their own with this fiasco."

Miraculously, Myrna managed to move the topic of evidence back to fictional cozies. I slipped out of the break room and into my office but not before asking Augusta to call me if my mother did anything to compromise a crime investigation more than she already had.

"I think you're safe," Augusta called out when I walked across the room. "They're talking about someone named Emily Pollifax. Another book club lady?"

"Nope. An amateur sleuth in the Dorothy Gilman novels. She's a senior citizen who works for the CIA and— Oh no. This could be worse than I originally thought."

"You think your mother or one of those ladies will go incognito and pretend to be a spy of sorts?"

"It's possible. Anything's possible. If we're lucky, they'll have a nice quiet lunch tomorrow at the Crowing Rooster and take notes on who comes and goes. And if we're not lucky, well—Holy mackerel—I don't even want to think what could happen. As soon as her radio show is off the air, I'll call her and use my best powers of persuasion to keep her at bay."

• • •

At a little after four, Nate and Marshall returned to the office looking as if they'd hiked Camelback Mountain. I don't know which one of them moved slower.

"Do you have any idea how many companies work in that Verrado community? Not to mention the individual contractors and landscapers. It's mind-boggling. We're knee-deep in interviews. Heck, we haven't even reached the part in our investigation where it feels as if we're treading water," Nate said.

"Yep, that'll be something to look forward to." Marshall twisted the cap off the bottle of iced tea he'd brought in and took a long gulp. "The heat's not much help, either. Anyway, how are things going in the office?"

"The office is wonderful, Mr. Gregory," Augusta said, "but I'm not so sure the same thing can be said for the Crowing Rooster tomorrow at noon."

"Is that something like 'the crow flies at midnight'? Because I'm way too tired to decipher a code."

Nate plopped himself in the nearest chair and leaned back. "Don't look at me. I can barely think straight."

"It's a fairly new restaurant in Sun City West that my mother's book club intends to stake out tomorrow in the hopes of catching the person who murdered Cosmo."

Nate and Marshall exchanged looks as if they'd missed the first act of a play.

"It's a convoluted plan they cooked up and announced on their radio show," I groaned. "Thankfully I'll be here in the office so I won't be privy to watching it unfold."

Augusta didn't waste a second spewing out all the details she'd heard over the air. When she was done, the men were expressionless.

Nate stood and gave his head a shake. "The mess in Verrado is looking better and better."

# CHAPTER 15

"Have you heard anything?" Augusta asked me the next day. She stood in the doorway to my office and leaned in. "It's twelve thirty already. No calls into this office from your mother but I figured she might have tried your cell phone."

"Nope. And I hope it stays that way. I'm ducking out to pick up something to eat. What's your pleasure?"

"A club sandwich from the deli. That'll take care of my veggie intake for the week. I tend to be a meat and potato person myself."

"No kidding."

Fifteen minutes later, having phoned in our orders, I was back at the office. Augusta waved a paper in the air as I handed her the sandwich. "Got a message for you. And I quote, 'Tell Phee the zymurgy club decided to have a luncheon today at the Crowing Rooster. Do you have any idea how many wine and beer drinkers we have in Sun City West? The restaurant was packed and the book club ladies had to cram into a corner. Impossible to see who came and went. We're going over to Shirley's to work on a new plan.'"

"That's a relief," I said. "I pictured someone in that book club making a citizen's arrest or causing some sort of ruckus. Now maybe we can enjoy a peaceful day."

Augusta unwrapped her sandwich and took a bite. "Unless the new plan is worse."

"Bite your tongue."

My mother and the book club ladies never worked on the new plan. That's because someone had gotten into Herb's house that afternoon by using one of those universal garage door openers and then prying open the utility room door. Possibly with a crowbar. Herb, who was at the Home Depot, phoned my mother when he got a call from the posse volunteer who noticed his garage door up when she made her regular drive-through in the neighborhood.

The minute she notified him, Herb speed dialed my mother to see if she had seen or heard anything. My mother informed Herb that if she *had* seen anything suspicious, which she did not, since she was at Shirley's house, she would have called the sheriff's office pronto.

My ear was practically glued to the phone as I took in every word my mother said. It was a little past two and for some reason she called my cell phone to inform me she and the ladies were on their way over to Herb's house to "access the damages."

"It was a break-in," I said. "The deputies aren't going to let you in there. Last thing they need is Cecilia clutching her rosary, Shirley muttering 'Oh Lordy,' Myrna stomping her feet, Lucinda sputtering in Spanish, and Louise doing heaven-knows-what."

"Herb needs our moral support."

*Or a beer with the guys at Curley's.*

"The deputies don't need your interference."

"Say what you want, Phee, but I'm headed over there. We all are. After Myrna calls Wayne and Bill. They can let the other men know. I'll call your office as soon as I find out what horrible damage was done to Herb's house. I hate calling that cell phone of yours but the office line has busy signals."

"That's because we're a place of business."

"I'm anxious to find out what those thieves absconded with. It wouldn't surprise me at all if Herb puts in a security system. Thank goodness I have Streetman *and* a security system. And Essie. Cats can claw and hiss, you know."

*Terrific. Essie is now the only eight-week-old attack cat on record.*

"Fine. Keep me posted but please stay out of the way. Okay?"

"Stop worrying. Oh my goodness. I forgot to call your aunt. She and Louis are in Scottsdale at the Poisoned Pen. Some author book talk. Bye."

"Trouble in paradise?" Augusta asked when I stepped out of my office and sat in the chair next to her desk.

"You could say that. Herb's house was broken into. I don't know what disturbed my mother more, the fact that she got a busy signal on our office phone and had to call my cell, or that someone burglarized her neighbor's house. I won't know anything more until she calls back later. Terrific. Just what we need, more drama."

"Senior citizen communities are notorious for that sort of thing. Crooks and ne'er-do-wells think we're an easy mark. Well, not this lady. I've got Smith and Wesson tucked away and ready to make their move if they have to."

"Very reassuring. I'll fill in the rest of the soap opera when my mother calls back. And believe me, she will."

I enjoyed uninterrupted work time for the next two and a half hours before I heard from my mother again. Thank goodness it was on the office line.

"You won't believe this, Phee. Not in a million years."

"What? How bad? What was stolen? Anything vandalized?"

"Nothing was stolen. Well, not *nothing*, but nothing that anyone would expect."

"Huh?"

"First of all, those two Neanderthals were at the scene. Shirley and I knocked on the door and that dreadful Deputy Bowman opened it a crack and do you know what he said?"

"Um, er . . . ." I know what I would have said—Please leave this crime scene. "No, what did he say?"

"He asked if I had Streetman with me. And not in an endearing manner. Then Herb came to the door and asked if we'd wait on the patio outside with the pinochle men because a forensic crew was inside dusting for prints in his kitchen."

"The kitchen? Only the kitchen?"

"That's the only place where anything was missing. The big-screen TV was still there with all the other electronic stuff Herb has. And Herb's fire safe was untouched as well."

"What'd they take from the kitchen? His blender? His coffee maker?"

"His recipe for that barbeque marinade. It was written on a file card that was tucked inside an old Betty Crocker cookbook that he left on the counter. The cookbook and the file card were missing."

"That's it? Did they root through his kitchen cabinets and leave a mess anywhere?"

"That's the unsetting thing about the break-in. There was no mess. In fact, whoever was in there washed the dishes Herb had in the sink, wiped his kitchen table, including some sticky jam that he'd meant to clean, and took out his trash. Took out his trash! Can you imagine? What kind of a sicko does something like that?"

*One I'd like to see show up in my house and do some serious cleaning.*

"And it gets worse," my mother continued. "The book club ladies and I sat on the patio, elbow to elbow with the men, while those deputies were still inside the house. Then Herb came outside and announced that one of the deputies thought whoever broke in had to be a woman on account of the tidying up in the kitchen. Shirley went ballistic about stereotypes and gender roles. All but chewed their heads off when they stepped outside."

"Do the deputies realize that whoever broke in most likely had something to do with that Master Grillers contest? That's where I would start. Maybe one of the competitors. Like Cosmo's team. Cindy's beautician told me she wouldn't put it past her ex-husband, who's on that team, to have murdered Cosmo for a bigger share of the prize money."

"You didn't mention all of that. All you said was that you were going to check it out."

"That's because you got me so turned around with that cockamamie idea about creating the fake eyewitness. I never got the chance."

"Never mind about that. How was Cindy's beautician? Please tell me she touched up those fading highlights of yours."

"She did. And she's quite good. I'm keeping her. Look, where are you now? Still at Herb's?"

"No, I'm back home. Wayne's fixing Herb's utility room door and then the men are going over to Curley's for their Friday fish fry and beer. More like the other way around if you ask me. I'm joining Shirley and Lucinda at the Homey Hut for their chicken special and you're more than welcome to come if Marshall's going to be working late."

"Uh, thanks for the offer but I made plans *(or will)* for an evening swim with Lyndy."

"That's all right. The really important meeting is tomorrow at Bagels 'n More. At ten thirty. If I'm not mistaken, it's one of your Saturdays off. And before you say no, digest this—those deputies will be lollygagging around with that murder investigation until the cows come home. Suppose for a minute that whoever murdered Cosmo was after *his* marinade recipe and poor Herb could be next."

"He won't be next. They already have his recipe. And the Betty Crocker cookbook. Most likely Cosmo's killer was someone involved in the transfer station deal or, well, yeah, the Master Grillers contest."

"You see? You're already spouting theories, which is more than I can say for those deputies. Herb needs your help, Phee. He's dangling from a very thin rope, and don't get me started on your aunt Ina."

"Aunt Ina? What does this have to do with Aunt Ina?"

"She's gotten herself worked into a tizzy about the transfer station. Who knows what that woman will come up with? Last thing we need is to have her turn out to be a suspect in Cosmo's murder. Ten thirty tomorrow, Phee. Lives are at stake."

"Aargh."

# CHAPTER 16

aturday morning came way too soon after a deep sleep. Nate and
Marshall had a full day of interviewing planned in Verrado. This time
with some of the landscape and construction companies that had been
hired by the unfortunate folks whose homes were burglarized.

"The toughie will be to get answers from those folks without sounding
accusatory," Marshall said over coffee. "Basically, we'll be looking for
patterns. Timing and that sort of thing."

"Sounds better than the deal I've got going."

Marshall chuckled. "Someone needs to keep a semblance of order
when that crew gets together. Too bad we don't own a gavel."

"Forget the gavel. Earplugs would be a boon. By the way, what's your
take on that break-in at Herb's? I meant to ask you last night but we were
so exhausted I could barely think straight."

"Seems like a no-brainer. Someone knew he had a winning marinade
recipe and wanted it. It's got to be one of those Master Grillers competitors.
Either that or someone who wanted to make it appear that way to throw
everyone off course."

"If it's the grillers, that would leave Therm Whittaker and Clinton
Badger. I'm pretty sure Bowman and Ranston have spoken with them by
now. And if those forensic techs can pull up decent prints, then it will be a
fait accompli. But if it's something more diabolical, I'd say those deputies
better get moving."

"Yeah, well, you know those things take time."

"Tell that to my mother. Heaven save us from whatever new scheme
those women have in mind."

"Like I said, someone needs to be the voice of reason."

"I thought it was semblance of order."

"That, too."

I stood, walked over to where he sat and planted a kiss on his forehead.
"It's good to be appreciated."

"Listen, what do you say we give ourselves a break and eat at Twisted
Italian tonight?"

"Consider it a done deal."

• • •

The management at Bagels 'n More had to add another table to the
large center one in order to accommodate the book club ladies, the pinochle

men, and Paul Schmidt, who felt it was his obligation to "solve the damn murder so that we can get on talking fish."

My aunt Ina, who was seated next to Paul, immediately launched into a discourse about pickled, creamed, and poached herring, to which he replied, "Can you do that with trout?"

I was seated on the other side of my aunt with my mother's chair all but butting up against mine. Another fun Saturday morning at gossip's epicenter. "We're not meeting to talk about fish. Cooked or otherwise. Once that waitress takes our food orders, we need to get down to business on our murder investigation," my mother said.

I turned my head so fast in her direction I all but got a kink in my neck. "Your *what*?"

"You heard me, Phee. Shirley and I got to talking last night and we thought our tried-and-true method of infiltrating the clubs or activities that the victim was in would be our best bet."

I picked up my coffee cup and took a large swallow. "What clubs? What activities? I've already checked his social media profile. The man was on a county planning commission and you can't infiltrate that. And besides, other than Abigail, the ex-girlfriend from District 4, there's no one intimately involved with him."

Wayne, who was seated across from us, leaned forward. "Forget the bedroom intimacy. What about a business involvement? Like making a deal for some payola from the transfer company. Kind of like 'you scratch my back and I'll scratch yours.' Then something goes wrong, and boom! Next thing you know, the guy's lying facedown on a railroad track."

Lucinda gasped. "He was facedown? How do you know that? I didn't read that in the paper."

Wayne rubbed his temples. "I don't know. I was only *saying*."

Thankfully, our waitress arrived at that very moment, causing everyone to forget about Cosmo's demise and instead interrogate the one person who stood between our orders and the cook. They flung questions at her before she had a chance to take out her pad and pen.

"What's in the frittata of the day?"

"Can I substitute cottage cheese for the pickles?"

"Is it real mayo or that new stuff with the olive oil in it?"

"It just says ham. Is it Black Forest ham or honey ham? I don't want it if it's that smoked stuff."

I smiled sheepishly at the poor woman and kept my order simple—a BLT on white toast. And I didn't care what kind of mayo it came with.

When she finally retreated to the kitchen, Wayne continued where he'd left off. "Had to be a deal gone bad with the planning commission or an out-and-out attempt on the part of his barbeque partners for a bigger piece of the pie."

Then, out of nowhere, my aunt exclaimed, "Not according to what my Louis found out. Write down this name everyone. We'll need it—Enid Flox."

"Enid Flox?" My mother glowered. "That miserable kitten-hating woman from the planning commission?"

"District 2," my aunt said. "And I've got all the sordid details from Louis."

I suppose given the two venues where my saxophone-playing uncle spent most of his time, namely gambling casinos and entertainment hot spots, it wasn't all that unusual to find out he'd gleaned quite a bit of gossip.

"What details, Aunt Ina?"

My aunt puffed out her chest to deliver her exposé. "Louis was asked to fill in for another saxophone player at the Omni Resort in Scottsdale a few nights ago. A fundraiser for a local charity. Anyway, you know how musicians can talk. During one of their breaks, Enid's name came up. She was seen handing over a tidy sum of money to Cosmo in the coatroom at the Palomino Library in Scottsdale following an informational meeting about a proposed development in the area."

"A payoff for his vote?" Wayne asked.

"Or his services," Bill said and chuckled, seconds before someone kicked him under the table, causing him to let out an audible moan.

I shook my head. "How can anyone be sure it was a substantial sum of money? It could have been anything. Maybe they ordered out food and she had to ante up her share. Besides, if it was a payoff, like Wayne said, no one's *that* idiotic to be seen doing it in a public place like a library."

"That's not all," my aunt continued. "According to Louis, the clarinet player said that Enid was overheard telling Cosmo that it better be the last of it if he knew what was good for him."

My mother took a sip of her coffee and then reached to the center of the table for another sugar packet. "Doesn't sound like a payoff to me. More like a bribe. Or one of those offers you can't refuse."

*Thank you, Mario Puzo.*

Then she turned to me. "Put Enid Flox on your suspect list, Phee. What kind of person talks about doing business with someone in a dark cloakroom?"

"A dark cloakroom? It was a public library, for goodness sake, not a Gothic castle."

"I'm not done," my aunt said. "Did you know Enid used to live in the house behind Cosmo's but moved out of Sun City West when her husband died some years ago? Louis found that out, too."

I bit my lower lip. "The clarinet player?"

"No, two female flutists. When the clarinet player told Louis what he had heard, the flutists were a few feet away. Seems they met Enid when she moved to Scottsdale and got on the planning commission for that district. Enid told them Cosmo was a former neighbor."

I thought my head couldn't spin any faster. "Was that all they said?"

My aunt repositioned one of her long braids so it was now dangling on her chest. "Goodness. You can't expect my poor Louis to find out everything for you."

"Never mind, Ina," my mother said. "We finally have our starting point. We find out what kind of business that miserable bat was up to and if that's what got Cosmo killed. If she was a former neighbor, she might have dug up some dirt on him. Of course, that doesn't explain why *she* paid *him*."

"Like I told you, Mom, she probably owed him money for something inconsequential."

"Forget *probably* and figure it out. This should be right up your alley considering you work for a detective agency."

"As their bookkeeper/accountant. We've been through this before. I'm not an investigator."

My aunt Ina grabbed me by the wrist and shook it. "Face it, you're the only one at this table who can make sense of all those social media sites. Except for maybe Shirley, who knows her way around Pinterest."

Shirley acknowledged my aunt's comment with a nod and a smile just as the waitress arrived with our food. The men dove into their sandwiches like an Anglo-Saxon hoard after doing battle with the Britons. I was resigned to perusing a few internet sites in order to learn more about Enid when Paul made a suggestion that made every hair on my body stand.

"We find out where she lives and sneak around her house after dark. If she's up to something iffy, it'll be after dark. It's always after dark when it comes to criminal activity."

"Huh? What?" I dropped the half of my BLT on my plate and widened my eyes. "Who says she's up to criminal activity? And you're talking about stalking her. *That's* criminal activity and it will get us arrested. Look, I'll delve into her online profile and go from there. Okay?"

My mother gave my hand a pat. "I knew you'd come through. How soon can you get the information?"

"I, um, er . . ."

"And don't forget about the other suspects," Myrna added. "There's the ex-girlfriend, too. Jilted lovers are known to go crazy."

I held up my hand like a stop sign. "She wasn't jilted. Gloria Wong said she heard the girlfriend was the one who broke it off with Cosmo."

*Oh my gosh. I'm quoting gossip from Gloria Wong. I'm worse than all of them.*

Louise gave the table a quick rap with her fist. "Forget the jilted lover deal. They're not as crazy as people who are desperate for money. Like Therm and Clinton. Check them out as well, Phee, while you're at it."

"Listen, I—"

"Lordy, will all of you give the poor girl a break? We'll divide up the names and do our own sleuthing. What possible harm can there be in that?"

I was about to respond to Shirley's suggestion but never got the chance. That's because Cecilia let out a loud gasp as Deputies Bowman and Ranston marched directly to our table.

"Did you invite them?" my mother whispered.

"What? No. Of course not." *Like I would need more indigestion.*

Then Kenny tossed a business card on the table. "It's a local bail bondsman. Just in case."

# CHAPTER 17

"Shh, put that card away," I said. "They're probably here to give Herb an update on those fingerprints they found in his kitchen."

"Sorry to interrupt your brunch, Mr. Garrett," Deputy Bowman said, "but we need a word with you. We tried your house and some woman who was walking her dog at the time shouted that you're at Bagels 'n More. Hmm, didn't realize your street had a Neighborhood Watch Program going. We'll have to add it to the list."

My mother leaned into my ear. "Some Neighborhood Watch. It's the woman next door to Herb. The one with the labradoodle Streetman likes."

Herb stood and walked out of earshot from our table. He, along with Bowman and Ranston, wedged themselves against a wall on the far side of the restaurant.

"Wonder what that's about?" Bill asked. "If they were going to arrest him, they would have done it already."

"Hush!" Shirley put a finger to her lips. "No sense all of us staring at them. Might as well finish our meals."

A few minutes later, Herb returned to the table and Bowman and Ranston were out the door. That's when the barrage of questions began.

"What'd they want?"

"Do you need a lawyer?"

"Do the fingerprints belong to some psycho?"

"Did they get your marinade recipe back?"

"What about the cookbook?"

Herb pulled out his chair and plunked himself in it. "Hold on, all of you. They stopped by to tell me I wasn't the only one who had a cookbook stolen. They think the same nutcase broke into Therm's place and took a file card box off of the counter by his stove. One of those recipe boxes, according to Therm. He told them it was avocado and had small dancing chickens on it."

"Give me a break," Kevin said. "There are only two finalist teams and we're one of them. Therm probably made the whole thing up so as to remove any suspicions anyone might have about who broke into Herb's house."

Herb took a loud, deep breath. "Oh, it gets better. They told me I originally thought *I* concocted the whole thing to take any suspicions off of me. Then, when Therm called their office, they had second thoughts about my culpability as far as the theft went."

A chorus of "Oh brothers" and a few groans followed.

"Did the deputies say how the perpetrator got in?" I asked Herb.

"Same way, according to what Therm showed them."

Kevin crossed his arms and nearly knocked over his coffee in the process. "Doesn't mean he didn't do it himself."

My mother held her hands in front of her and waved them. "Doesn't matter. What does matter is that Herb isn't going to be in the Fourth Avenue Jail tonight. And Phee is going to get the lowdown on Enid. Best of all, thanks to my brother-in-law Louis, I know exactly where she can begin."

I held my breath and let it out slowly. "Where?"

"At Enid and Cosmo's block. She was his backyard neighbor before moving to the East Valley. I guarantee the other neighbors will know if any kind of business was going on between her and Cosmo."

"That was years ago."

Lucinda, who'd been pretty quiet up until now, cleared her throat. "People don't move that fast around here. They usually arrive in their fifties and stay until their eighties, when they decide it's time for resort-style senior living."

"You see," my mother said, "chances are someone's bound to know something."

"As I mentioned previously, I'll start with an internet search. I mean, I can't very well start knocking on doors and asking all kinds of questions. It's not as if I'm law enforcement or a licensed professional."

My aunt rubbed the underside of her chin and hummed. "Phee's right. She'll need a premise. A solid, believable premise. Give me a minute to think. Oh, and pass that dessert menu, will you? Why they only put one copy on the table is beyond me."

While my aunt perused desserts and thought about premises, I thought about motive. I'd always believed that killing someone involved a really strong motive but I'd been proved wrong countless times. Could it really boil down to that Master Grillers competition and money? Or was it something more sinister, as Wayne suggested?

"Phee, are you listening?"

"Huh?"

My aunt gave me a nudge. "I may have an idea for you. Give me a second. I need to flag down the waitress."

Once my aunt ordered apple pie à la mode, other dessert orders dribbled in. Pies, cakes, puddings, and something called the molten lava plate, a combination of hot fudge, chocolate cake, and chocolate ice cream. I did a mental eye roll and wondered if our table would need a hoist to remove the patrons.

"I don't know why I didn't think of this before," my aunt said. "We kill two birds with one stone. We start petitions against that dreadful transfer station and when Phee knocks on doors, that will be her premise."

"Whoa! I am not committing to going door to door with a petition. I do have a job, you know."

My aunt patted my shoulder and went on. "You only have to knock on a few doors. The ones next door to Cosmo's house and the ones behind it. We'll take care of the rest."

"You're saying you, my mother and the rest of the crew will be going door to door?"

At that point, Bill all but flung himself across the table so that he could be closer to my aunt. "I'm not going door to door like the Fuller Brush Man. It was bad enough when Red Skelton did it in that 1948 movie. And if I'm not mistaken, he becomes a murder suspect in that film."

*Wonderful. Decades before I was born.*

"None of us will be going door to door. We'll set up tables in front of the local supermarkets with our anti–transfer station petitions. They always have tables set up for that sort of thing."

I shook my head. "No, the political parties have tables set up for signatures when someone wants to run for office. And other than the Girl Scouts when they're selling cookies, I never see tables set up."

"Guess you will now," Wayne said.

Then Cecilia jumped in. "We can write letters, too. I can get a campaign going at my church. And Lucinda can do the same with the clay club, and Myrna with bocce, and—"

"We get it, we get it," my mother said. "For once you stumbled on a decent idea, Ina."

Paul elbowed the guys next to him. "And I've got an ever better one. You know how the gas company always mails us these little scratch and sniff papers to remind us what natural gas smells like with the sulfur additive? Well, I've got a buddy in a fish distribution company who can—"

A resounding chorus of *no*s immediately followed before Paul could finish his sentence.

Thankfully the desserts got to our table before anyone else came up with an idea.

"Look," I said, "I like the idea of incorporating the amateur fact-finding regarding Cosmo's death with the transfer station petitions. And I have no problem with delving into social media regarding Enid Flox. However, I'd hardly know how to segue into a conversation about her when I'm asking someone to sign a petition regarding rubbish disposal."

In retrospect, I never should have said that because my aunt immediately offered to rehearse my conversational skills. "I've had years in the theater," she said.

"What years?" My mother all but jumped down her throat. "First-row seats on opening nights?"

"For your information, Harriet, I was no stranger to the Shakespearean performances our high school held."

"If anyone knows the theater, it's Myrna and me. We starred in that Agatha Christie play not too long ago."

I knew where that conversation was going and I had to act fast. "No problem. It won't be a problem. I'll do it. Okay. I'll talk with a few of the neighbors."

The midmorning meal to save Herb had turned into a growing to-do list for me. Still, with Marshall tied up in Verrado and my workload at the office all caught up, I figured I might as well snoop around and see if Enid did indeed have a motive to murder her former neighbor and fellow planning commission member. I promised my mother and the crew that I'd let them know what I was able to find out. They, in turn, promised to craft a compelling petition and circulate it around Sun City West.

"If the supermarkets turn us down," Myrna said, "we can always set up a table in front of KSCW at the Men's Club. But we'll need to do it before the end of next week. That's when a giant heat wave is expected. A hundred and ten for starters and it could get as high as one fourteen."

Lucinda grabbed a spoon and tapped it on her glass. "I say we form a writing committee for the petition. Who wants to be on it?"

Suddenly the men all had places to go or things they had to do. In less than a nanosecond, they vacated the table, leaving only the women to discuss letter writing and committees.

"I've got to go, too," I announced. I stood and shoved my chair into the table. "Looks like you've got this covered. Great seeing everyone."

My mother turned and made eye contact with me. "Call me later."

I was at the cash register and out the door, careful not to turn around for fear of being hailed back to the table.

# Chapter 18

A few hours later, when I told Lyndy what had happened, all she could say was, "At least you don't have to take the dog with you."

"You won't believe this," I said while we grabbed a quick dip in Vistancia's pool. "I really tried not to get suckered into anything but for once, that wacky book club of my mother's might have the right idea."

"About Enid?"

"Uh-huh. I've heard how those neighbors talk about each other. If Enid was up to something underhanded, I wager one of them will know."

"And when do you plan to begin your investigation, Miss Marple?"

"Um, I was actually going to ask you."

"Me?" Lyndy stopped treading water and leaned against the side of the pool. "It was fine when I tracked down stuff in the library with you, but this is, well, you know, more upfront and personal."

"Come on. You always say how mundane your life is. This will spice it up."

Lyndy crinkled her nose. "Nice way of saying 'on the border of getting us arrested for impersonation.'"

"It's not impersonation. I *do* work for Williams Investigations, only not in investigating per se."

"Tell me exactly what you have in mind."

"I'll tell them that I work for a detective agency and that some information has come to light regarding Enid Flox as it pertains to the matter of Cosmo Pruett's death. That's about as noncommittal a statement as one can make. Then I'll go on to say that a concerned party has reached out to us to see if we can learn more about Enid's relationship with her former neighbor."

"Boy, you're getting pretty good with subterfuge."

"Lots of practice. I'll leave things as nebulous as can be and see what they have to say. If those folks living behind or next to Cosmo are half as chatty as my mother's crew, I might be able to pick up an important clue."

Lyndy pushed herself off the pool side and did a quick spin around. "What about the transfer station petition?"

"I'm not touching that with a ten-foot pole. Even if my aunt thought it was a great premise. One venture is enough. So, care to join me?"

"When?"

"Tomorrow afternoon. We need to do it before that heat wave kicks in."

"You mean before Marshall gets back from Verrado."

"Yeah, that too. But he'll be on board with it. It's not all that different from picking up gossip at the dog park."

"What am I supposed to do while you try to coax these people into talking about Enid? I can't very well go off on my own, even though it might save us some time. I work for a medical insurance company. Last thing I want to do is mention that."

"I'll introduce us by name and tell them you're helping me out with note-taking. That sort of thing. It's only five houses. One on either side of Cosmo's and the three in back. Plus, the one directly behind his is the one where Enid used to live. The person or persons who bought her house might have an interesting perspective."

"Think the original neighbors are still there?"

My mother's friend Lucinda seemed to think so.

"Fine. How about we meet for lunch first and then make the trek?"

"I'll do one better. Lunch will be on me. It's the least I can do."

"This plan's sounding better by the minute."

• • •

I was right in my assumption that Marshall wouldn't balk at the idea of me doing some serious door-to-door snooping. Then again, he was so dog-tired when he came home shortly before seven that whatever I said probably didn't register. I all but had to remind him to chew the greens in his salad and open his eyes.

The next morning was different. Our usual slow Sunday was a fast mover with Marshall up and out before nine and me scurrying around to tackle laundry and some light cleaning before hustling off to pick up Lyndy and drive to Haymaker's on Lake Pleasant Parkway.

We both ordered the California omelet and fortified ourselves with enough coffee to stay awake for days. By the time we rolled into Sun City West we were anxious, energized, and determined to find out what dealings Enid might have had with her former neighbors.

Cosmo's house was in the expansion district, the last building phase of the Sun City West community. With its newer homes that boasted granite countertops, stainless steel appliances, enormous master suites and built-in entertainment centers, it was a coveted location that made up for the fact that these homes paid school taxes, unlike the homes in the earlier building phases.

"Which one's his house?" Lyndy asked as I pulled on to West San Pablo Drive.

"According to the assessor's office, it's the third one from the corner."

"It's huge. A two-car garage and a golf cart garage, not to mention the gated courtyard and regal-looking entryway. Looks like whoever's managing his estate has the place locked down. The closed plantation shutters are a dead giveaway. Oops. No pun intended. Tell me, where do you want to start?"

I eyeballed the street and shrugged. "It doesn't matter. I'll park in front of Cosmo's place and we can take the house on the right."

Walking briskly so as not to lose my nerve, I was at the door in a matter of seconds. Unfortunately, Lyndy and I were out of there just as fast.

"Well, that was a total bust," she said.

"I guess it happens. Lucinda forgot to mention that some of these folks move back East or up north to live with their extended families when they can no longer manage on their own. Better than assisted living or a nursing home, I suppose. Anyway, the new owners seemed nice. For what it's worth."

"Maybe we'll have better luck with the other neighbor."

I knocked on the door to a house that was fairly similar to Cosmo's, only instead of a gated courtyard it had a pony wall surrounding a beautifully paved lanai. Lyndy stood a foot or two behind me and both of us held our breath. Finally, a woman who appeared to be my mother's age answered the door. "Yes, can I help you?"

"I'm sorry to disturb you on a Sunday afternoon, but I'm with Williams Investigations in Glendale and, on behalf of a client, we're looking into the death of Cosmo Pruett, your next-door neighbor."

I held out my business card and was about to explain that I was the bookkeeper and was only helping out when she stuck her head out the door and looked up and down the street. "Anything I say is strictly off the record. Do you understand?"

I nodded.

"Come inside then. No sense standing out here in the heat."

She motioned for Lyndy and me to take a seat at a corner bistro table near the door and sat between us.

"I'm Phee and this is Lyndy. We won't take up much of your time. Can you tell us how long you were neighbors with Mr. Pruett?"

"Long enough. Not to speak ill of the dead, but that man was insufferable. Complained to the CC & R committee that my oleanders were two inches above regulation. And heaven forbid if we got any rain because he'd be on the phone with them complaining about burgeoning weeds by the sidewalk. I probably shouldn't have told you that because the last thing I need is to be added to a list of suspects, but honestly, if it was murder, like the news says, then Cosmo had it coming."

Lyndy and I exchanged glances and the woman continued.

"I was here when the wife left him, you know. No loud fights, arguments or anything of that sort. Not that I could hear. Most likely the poor woman got tired of having to fold his clothes up perfectly when they came out of the dryer. Heard she moved to California."

"I see. Um, given our information, we'd like to learn more about his relationship with another neighbor of yours—the lady who lived directly behind his house. Enid Flox."

"That old goat? Now there's a story for you. Come on over here and look out past the patio to the right."

Lyndy and I did as the woman said and walked toward her sliding glass door.

"Notice the block fence behind her former house? After her husband died unexpectedly, she had it built and told everyone she did it because she didn't want Cosmo to peep in at her. Can you imagine?"

"No, I , uh, er . . ."

"And that's not all. About a month later, she sold her house and moved to Scottsdale. I figured she collected on her late husband's insurance policy or investments and had the resources to buy a place in the magic zip code. Imagine my shock when I spied her at the Stardust Theater for that public hearing about the transfer station giving some poor woman a ration of grief for having a cute little kitten tucked into her shirt. Frankly, if Mr. Meow-mow wasn't so big, I would have brought him, too. He just loves the attention."

As if on cue, an enormous long-haired orange tabby appeared from behind the couch and meandered toward us. The woman immediately snatched him up and Lyndy and I had no choice but to pet him. Thankfully Lyndy must have read my mind because neither of us mentioned the fact that the cute little kitten belonged to my mother and didn't say a word as the woman went on.

"Cosmo must have had a pickle when Enid got elected to the Maricopa County Planning Commission for her new district. Or maybe it was the other way around. Talk about a coincidence. Two obnoxious peas in a pod. Say, you don't think she killed him, do you?"

"Um, uh, right now we're gathering information that could help our client, but everything is confidential so we cannot disclose who that is. You've been very helpful, Miss . . ."

"Oh, goodness. I never did introduce myself. Jane Moore. From Feasterville, Pennsylvania. Retired from teaching and been living here for over fifteen years."

I reached out my hand to shake hers. "Again, thanks for your time, Miss Moore."

"Yes," Lyndy said. "Thank you for speaking with us."

"You're most welcome. And between you and me, I hope Enid doesn't decide to relocate back here. The people who bought her house are lovely. I play Bunco with them on Thursdays."

As I approached the front door, I turned and faced Jane. "Would you happen to know if Enid's former neighbors on either side of her house are still there, or did they move?"

"I know that the beautician lady from down the block moved to Sun City and the Fergusons, who lived directly behind me, are now at the Presidential Arms. Deluxe two-bedroom suite. I know they'd love company but both of them suffer from mild dementia, so I doubt they could remember much about Enid."

"And the other house?"

Jane took a deep breath and closed her eyes for a second. "It was years ago. The poor man was found dead in his kitchen. Authorities said he forgot to turn off the gas all the way on his stove. But if you ask me, someone did him in. You see, he never cooked."

# Chapter 19

"Another murder," Lyndy said over and over again as we walked to my car. "A cold case. A genuine cold case. Do you think it has anything to do with Enid?"

"I hope not. I really hope not."

"But?"

"Ugh. I guess it wouldn't hurt to look into it. At least that's a paper chase. Anyway, Jane saved us a lot of time. Not to mention giving us the lowdown on Cosmo and Enid."

"Now what?"

"A swing around the block to the house behind Cosmo's where that man was found dead. I know none of the people living there were around when Enid was here, but I want to check on some sight lines."

"Sight lines? I thought that was a theater term."

"It was the only one I could think of. I want to see if that house has a bird's-eye view into Cosmo's place, because that would mean Cosmo had the same view into his."

"Meaning?"

"Cosmo might have seen something. Something Enid did."

"You can't be thinking she murdered her neighbor all those years ago."

"Lately, nothing surprises me. If Enid did that deed and Cosmo saw her, it would have explained the payoff she made at the Scottsdale library. You heard what Jane said. She thought Enid came into quite a bit of money when her husband died. Well, maybe she found a way to come into more money if she weaseled it out of that poor old man next door."

"And you think the book club ladies have vivid imaginations."

"*That*, or the fact I live with a detective who keeps reminding me that most cases have far-reaching tentacles. Come on, this should only take a second."

I pulled around the block to West La Vina Drive where Enid had lived and parked the car between her house and the one next door. "This should only take me a second," I said to Lyndy. "I'm going to walk between those two houses and scope it out."

"You mean trespass?"

"If anyone comes out, I'll tell them I thought I saw a small dog running loose."

Lyndy chuckled as I exited the car. In all honesty, I couldn't believe how brazen, not to mention conniving, I'd become. I could feel my pulse quicken as I stood fifteen or twenty yards from Cosmo's place, and I wondered if Nate and Marshall had that same sense of trepidation and excitement when they took similar chances.

Enid's block wall obscured part of the view but it didn't hide the perfect diagonal line that ran from the back of the deceased man's house to Cosmo's expansive patio, with its four-panel windows in the middle, flanked by French doors on one side and a bay window on the other.

It was a floor plan I was familiar with since my aunt Ina's house in Sun City Grand had the same setup: a huge great room that opened onto the patio along with a master bedroom suite that did the same, hence the French doors. The bay window on the opposite side framed the kitchen's eating area, allowing for privacy as it faced the rear of the house and not the street.

Given the angle, I was positive Cosmo could have witnessed all sorts of goings-on across the way from any pivotal hot spots in his house. To be sure, I meandered closer to the home of the deceased until I found myself on the far corner staring at that backyard patio. Like Cosmo's, it too had the bay window eating area and the long sliders. Not wanting to press my luck, I hurried back to the car.

"I need to find out if the man who lived over there was found dead in his kitchen," I said as soon as I opened the car door.

"Huh? What did I miss?"

"Cosmo would have had an unobstructed view of the man's kitchen, so if anything took place there and he happened to be looking that way, it would have been impossible to miss. I'm beginning to think if I want to know more about Enid's involvement with Cosmo, I might be better off finding out about her relationship with the former neighbor. And I know exactly where to begin."

"Don't keep me guessing. Where?"

"On the county assessor's website, where else? I have to find out who owned the house. Tax records don't lie. Once I get a name, it should be as easy as a walk in the park."

Yep. Those were my famous last words—a walk in the park. They might as well have been a walk on the moon because, as I found out later that day, the legal owner of the house turned out to be none other than Enid herself.

"You're not going to believe this, Lyndy," I shouted over the phone. "Not in a million years. The owner? The dead man? The neighbor? He wasn't any of those. Okay, wait, maybe he was dead, but he didn't own the house. The name on the tax records and the person who later sold the house was none other than Enid Flox herself."

"Whoa. Slow down. You're making me dizzy. Enid, you said?"

"Uh-huh. Enid. According to the tax records, she owned that house, so it stands to reason the man who was found dead was her tenant. The records indicate she sold both homes when her husband passed away, but I'm not sure if the tenant died while Enid's husband was still alive or if it happened once he passed away. Aargh. Talk about a widening web and a growing paper chase."

"And you've still got your original problem. You don't know who the man was. No name. No nothing."

"Worse than no nothing. No way to search. Without a name, I can't go into Vital Records under Death, or pull up the Sun City West obituaries from the *Independent News* or Legacy.com. Honestly, I need to clear my head and then maybe I'll be able to think straight."

"How about a half hour at the pool and then we call out for subs and have them delivered to my house. You said Marshall won't be back until late. Order a sub for him, too."

"That's the best plan I've heard since we got back from Cosmo's block. Okay, fine. See you in fifteen minutes. Um, make it twenty. I may regret this, but I'm going to give my mother a call. She might remember something about someone being found gassed to death in their house."

"Yeesh."

It was a little before five and I needed to call my mother before her "unofficial-official" dinnertime began. Since she retired and moved out West, mealtimes became more regimented than in the service. Dinner especially, with a window of opportunity between five fifteen and five thirty. Citing digestive issues along with the TV lineup, my mother never swayed. That meant I had a fifteen-minute window and I had to move fast.

"Hi, Mom. Thought I'd catch you before dinner."

"Barely. But it doesn't matter. It's chicken salad. One of Cecilia's recipes. And easy ingredients for Streetman and Essie to digest. Of course, now I have to mush Essie's chicken since she's still a kitten. I found if I softened it first with warm water it was easier to mash."

*Oh no. Cat recipes. She's going to make me listen to cat recipes. The dog was bad enough.*

"That's great. Wonderful, really. Listen, the reason I called was to find out if you remembered hearing anything about an elderly man who was found dead in his home a few years ago because he left the gas stove on?"

"Phee, that could have been anyone around here. Remember that incident with Jeanette, the neighbor across the street who's since moved? That's not uncommon when some people reach a certain age. Best bet is to forget about all those alarm getups and give up cooking entirely. We've got wonderful restaurants, take-out, and delivery. And why are you suddenly interested in some unfortunate man who forgot to turn off his stove?"

"Because his house was diagonal from Cosmo's. I checked it out with Lyndy."

"I thought you were going to look into that dreadful Enid Flox."

"I am. I mean, I did. Lyndy and I had a nice chat with one of Enid's former neighbors earlier today. A woman by the name of Jane Moore."

"Hmm, don't recognize the name. So, the petition premise worked, didn't it? Did she sign it?"

"What? No. I wasn't about to muddy the waters with that transfer station petition. And besides, it isn't even written yet!"

My mother paused long enough to let it sink in. "Oy! I've been so busy calling all my club contacts about the letter-writing blitz that I forgot about that petition. *Someone* needs to write it. Someone who can throw in enough legalese to make it sound formidable."

"Well, don't look at me. You've put enough on my plate. How about having one of Herb's cronies do it?"

"Are you kidding? We need someone who won't drag out an old typewriter. And someone who's good with words. I know, I'll ask Louise. She's always doing crossword puzzles."

It was a good thing we were on the phone because I must have rolled my eyes at least three times. "Yes. Louise. Great idea. Anyway, I—"

"Not so fast. Why did you drop Enid like a hot potato and start asking around about some unfortunate neighbor of Cosmo's who left his stove turned on? I thought you were trying to find out who killed Cosmo, not dredge up household accidents."

"If you must know, I think everything is connected. The house where that man died belonged to Enid. Her name was on tax records until she sold it. Sometime before or after her own husband died."

"Oh my gosh. And now Cosmo. We could be looking at one of those Black Widows."

"Um, I think that term is reserved for women who marry wealthy men and then kill them for the money. We don't know what kind of relationship Enid had with her former tenant or with Cosmo, for that matter. But once I find out, it might bring us closer to finding out if she was involved in their deaths."

"I thought you said it was an accident. The stove . . . the gas . . ."

"Enid's former neighbor, Jane, didn't think so. Makes me wonder if maybe it wasn't an oversight or an accident on the part of that poor man. But I need to find out who he was."

"She didn't tell you?"

"She didn't know."

"All right. I'll make some calls. I have to call Louise anyway about the petition, and you know how fast she can spread gossip around. Worse than

Myrna. I guarantee she'll be on it before I can call the other ladies."

"Thanks. Let me know what you find out."

"Do you want to say hello to Streetman and Essie? They're right next to the phone on the couch."

"Um, no sense disturbing them. Pat them on the heads or whatever you do. Enjoy your chicken salad."

"We'll all enjoy it."

I was off the phone and on my way to the pool before I had time to let that image sink in.

# Chapter 20

The swim felt good but it really didn't clear my head. That came later when Marshall got home and said the one word that should have immediately sprung to mind—*Google*.

"Try googling 'accidental deaths Sun City West,' or 'gas asphyxiation Sun City West,' he said when I told him my dilemma. He had just polished off the mixed cold cut sub I brought home and thanked me profusely for not having to "rig up" something from the freezer.

"I feel like the village idiot. Google should have been the first thing to come to mind."

He gave my shoulder a squeeze as he got up from the table and tossed his sub wrapper into the trash. "That's because you've got a zillion things floating around in your head and they're all jockeying for position. Not that mine's much better. This case has really gotten Nate and me rattled."

For the next twenty minutes he gave me the salient details about his and Nate's investigation in Verrado. "It's the magnitude of the case," he said. "Seventeen break-ins turned into twenty and the person or persons we're after seem to be pretty good planners. They flipped the surveillance cameras to the opposite side, but only in the area with the new thefts. Needless to say, we'll be monitoring the physical position of those cameras as well as what we get from the videos. Tomorrow we'll have Augusta help us out with calls to the usual high-end consignment places as well as scouring Craigslist."

"She'll eat it up. Augusta loves doing that sort of thing."

"Too bad she doesn't love dusting for fingerprints or we'd have her do that, too." Marshall must have noticed the expression on my face because a second later he laughed and said, "Only kidding." He went on to explain that he and Nate pulled some partial prints and sent them to a private lab but they weren't optimistic.

"There's a pattern somewhere," Marshall said, "because whoever's behind this seems to know exactly when and where to stage their version of a smash and grab. All we need is that one small clue that will pull everything into place."

"Aargh. Wish I could say the same. One thing leads to another and I'm meandering all over the place."

"Do what you always do. Take one thing at a time. Working logically and sequentially is what you do best."

"That's why I'm in bookkeeping and accounting."

"And now poking, prodding, and crime solving."

"I suppose that's a hint for me to start on that search, huh?"

Marshall smiled. "You can get on with the search and I'll get into a much-needed shower. Honestly, I bathed first thing in the morning but after a day in this heat it's as if I haven't been near water. And if it's this bad today, I can't imagine how many showers I'll need when that heat wave kicks in."

"Don't remind me. I probably should check the weather app for more info but I've been avoiding it."

"App or not, you'll know it when it gets here."

I wiped the kitchen table and then made myself comfortable on the couch. With iPhone in hand, I wasted no time typing in the keywords that I hoped would bring me one step closer to finding out who Enid's next-door neighbor/tenant was.

"Accidental deaths" included everything from motorcycle and golf cart accidents to falls from ladders and succumbing to heatstroke. No mention whatsoever about meeting one's maker from asphyxiation. I moved on to a tighter word search but no luck there either. The closest I got was a mention about a man who drove his car into the block wall behind a local gas station. *Gas* being the key word.

I gave up about the same time as Marshall emerged from his shower. And while he was relaxed and refreshed, I was frustrated and tired.

"Tomorrow's another day, hon," he said. "Give it a break. Maybe you'll get lucky and one of those book club ladies will come through."

"I hope so. Because this may be the one link I need to put everything in place."

As things turned out, I got my link but it didn't bring me any closer to finding out who did Cosmo in or why. In fact, it added more questions to an already growing list.

• • •

"We'll be back in the office before five," Marshall said the following morning while I brushed my teeth. "I'll catch you then for a quick hello and goodbye. Nate and I both have to do some follow-up work on our other cases, so I don't think I'll make it home before seventy thirty or so."

"Want me to pick up something we can reheat? Or salads?"

"Anything's fine. I've got to run. I'll grab coffee on my way to Verrado. Hate to rush like this." He leaned over the sink and planted a kiss on my forehead. "I'll try for your lips tonight."

"You'd better."

I heard the front door close a few minutes later while I continued my morning routine. At least I had time for a cup of coffee and a slice of wheat toast before heading to the office.

Augusta was hard at work at her desk when I breezed through the door at a little before nine. She looked up from a stack of papers and motioned to the counter. "Help yourself to the donuts. Got filled, glazed, frosted, and bear claws. Everything but those cronuts. Still can't decide if they're worth the price."

"Yum! Thanks. Are we expecting someone?"

"Nope. Unless it's a drop-in. *I'm* expecting a long day and I wanted lots of fortification. I got in at seven. Mr. Williams phoned me last night and asked if I'd scour the consignment shops and Craigslist for the stolen jewelry. Some of the victims had photos so he emailed them to me. That helped. I figured I'd start with Craigslist and then make calls to the retail places. I'm also going to try eBay, too. You never know. Hey, any news on that break-in? Your mother's friends must be one step below pushing a panic button."

I dusted off some of the white powder that my jelly donut left on my blouse. "Not as panicked as one would think, but it gets better. Well, not better, weirder. I had brunch with all of them, men included, on Saturday. While we were at the restaurant, who should walk in but Bowman and Ranston. They told Herb a similar break-in had taken place at Therm Whittaker's house. His recipe box was stolen."

"Therm Whittaker. From Cosmo's grilling team, right? Hard to forget a name like Therm."

"According to what the deputies told Herb, they thought some nutcase broke into both places for whatever reason."

"I take it you don't share their opinion."

"It's bizarre, even for Sun City West. Herb believes Therm or Clinton broke into his house for the marinade recipe and tried to cover it up by fabricating a break-in at Therm's. Meanwhile, the deputies are no closer to solving Cosmo's murder. My mother's convinced it's only a matter of time before Herb is charged with the crime. That's why I've been on overdrive trying to track down all sorts of clues and connections."

"Uh-oh. Dare I ask what you got into this weekend?"

"Not as much as I would have liked but I'll give you the lowdown."

I plopped a K-Cup into the Keurig and spouted off all sorts of stuff, including Lyndy and my makeshift investigation and the reason behind it.

"Let me get this straight," Augusta said. "One of your uncle Louis's musician friends told him he saw Enid handing over a chunk of money to Cosmo at some library in Scottsdale. Have I got it right?"

"So far, so good. There's more. Enid lived in the house behind Cosmo's before her husband died and she moved to Scottsdale. Yesterday, Lyndy and I spoke with Cosmo's neighbor and she thought Enid came into some money from her husband's death."

"But you don't."

I shrugged. "I'm in the information-gathering phase but I may have hit a dead end. Turns out the man who lived next door to Enid happened to be her tenant. He was found dead from a supposed gas leak since he allegedly left the stove on. But get this! According to what Cosmo's neighbor said, the man didn't cook! Oh, and there's more—Lyndy and I think that maybe Cosmo, who lived behind the guy on the diagonal lot, might have had a bird's-eye view into the man's place and might have seen Enid over there doing heaven-knows-what. And that 'heaven-knows-what' might be the very thing that resulted in Cosmo extorting money from her. *If* that was what she did in the library."

"Good grief, Phee. I've read murder mysteries from *New York Times* bestselling authors and none of them were as complicated at this is. Keep it simple for me, will you?"

I took another bite of my donut and reached for my coffee cup. "In order to find out what went on between Cosmo and Enid, I need to find out more about her relationship with that tenant of hers. After all, she might have been responsible for his death." I swallowed some coffee and took a step closer to Augusta's desk. "Unfortunately, I'm at a dead end. I can't find out who the man was."

Augusta crinkled her eyes. "Couldn't you ask *his* neighbor? The house next door to his. Seems to me you've been talking to everyone else."

I looked at the ceiling and then back to Augusta. "There *is* no house next to his. It's a lot and a half that extends to the corner. And forget Google. It was useless. And vital records only works if you've got a name. So, I'm at the mercy, heaven help me, of my mother's gossipy friends. Hopefully one of them will remember something about some poor man who succumbed to asphyxiation."

Augusta looked down at her stack of paper. "Craigslist is sounding better and better."

I chuckled. "At least my real work doesn't pose any mysteries. Addition and subtraction don't lie. And if they do, it's not the numbers, it's the person who put them there." I took another donut, wrapped it in a napkin and smiled. "Best darn breakfast I've had in ages."

# Chapter 21

A t a little past one, after Augusta and I chowed down on our to-go lunches from the deli, two things happened almost simultaneously. One unexpected. One not. She found a listing on Craigslist that matched one of the stolen items: a butterfly brooch with green and blue inlaid stones. The ad said to contact the buyer and meet between the 101 and West McDowell Road. Location to be disclosed once transaction is agreed upon.

"That sounds suspicious," I said.

"Nah. They all read like that. Very Raymond Chandler. I'll let Mr. Williams know and keep on perusing. The jewelry section for Phoenix alone has over a thousand pages, but I'm sorting from newest listings so I only have to go back from the time of the first robbery."

"That makes sense."

It was at that precise moment when the phone rang with my mother at the other end. No surprise there. Augusta held out the receiver and leaned back in her chair.

"Go ahead," I whispered. "Put it on speaker."

"I heard you, Phee. Is that Augusta or one of the men?"

"Nate and Marshall are in Verrado. It's Augusta."

"Fine. She can listen in. I called to give you wonderful news about that man who died from gas inhalation. Cecilia found him. You can call and thank her later."

"Who is he? I mean, *was* he. And how'd she find out?"

"She remembered hearing something about it a few years back and made some calls. The man was a former parishioner in her church's diocese. She phoned their office and asked them to send her a spreadsheet with the information."

"And they did that?"

"Names, addresses, emails and phone numbers. Yes. Not the business records like who paid and who's going straight to hell."

"Mom!"

"You know what I mean."

"I can't believe they emailed her a spreadsheet."

"They were going to just send her a list but she's friends with the church secretary, and when she explained why she needed it, the woman sent her something on Excel."

"That's the spreadsheet."

Augusta turned away and tried not to laugh.

"Anyway, Cecilia was able to sort through the names by their addresses. All alphabetical. That may be something your office should look into."

"We already know how to do that. Sorting, organizing and filtering data has been around for years. The trick is to have some data to begin with."

"Don't get snippy."

By now Augusta closed her eyes and tried to keep still.

"Sorry. Tell me, what did she find?" I asked.

"I told her that Enid lived on West La Vina so she searched there and found two listings. The first is some woman who's alive and kicking and the other is your victim. They put an asterisk next to the names of the deceased."

"Did they say when?"

"No. It only refers to a notation on the bottom of the page that says the person died."

"Never mind. What was his name?"

"Desmond Bartley. Not going to confuse that name with anyone else."

"No, I suppose not. Wow, Mom. This has been a tremendous help. It shouldn't be too difficult to find out more about him and go from there. I'll talk to you later."

"Wait! Not so fast. Herb called me just as I got off the phone with Cecilia. There's been a change regarding the Master Grillers contest."

"Change? What kind of a change?"

"Most likely those two deputies had something to do with it. They were the ones on the scene at Herb's house."

"Had to do with what? You lost me."

"Herb got an official letter from the contest committee. It began with their sincere regret that someone had stolen his recipe for the contest. Apparently, the marinade recipes had to be submitted ahead of time but the committee allowed for minor adjustments. That being said, the theft invalidated their entry."

"Oh, no. But wait. Therm's recipe was stolen, too."

"I know. I'm getting to that. Herb, and I imagine Therm and Clinton as well, were asked to enter a new marinade for consideration, but get this, they now have to re-compete with the other three teams who were in the semifinals."

"The three teams they beat out already?"

"Yes. I just said that. But that's not the problem. Herb and his crew have to come up with an entirely new barbeque recipe. And then perfect it."

"Oh, no. He must be really ticked."

"He's past that. He's now on to full-blown panic. Maybe I should give him Alte Tante Rosie's brisket recipe."

"She baked that. She didn't barbeque it. And it wasn't ribs. Plus, he needs his own original recipe. Not yours or *you* would be in that contest."

"Poor Herb. I guess he and his team are on their own. He did mention that the men were going to have a strategy session to figure something out. Once they come up with a new recipe Herb will need you to taste it."

"What? Again? I don't have time to taste test another marinade. And Marshall can't spare a second. He and Nate are at their wits' end in Verrado."

"It's not right this minute, Phee. I'll let you know in plenty of time. Meanwhile, don't forget to thank Cecilia."

*Who's thanking me for all this work?*

"No problem."

I handed the receiver back to Augusta and took a breath. "I'm glad you heard all of that because the last thing I would've felt like doing was to repeat it."

"Repeat it? I could barely keep up with it. It's like a never-ending soap opera in Sun City West."

"I know. Too bad I can't change the channel. Anyway, my mother did manage to come through. I've got a name and from there, I'll be able to find out who this Desmond Bartley was and why he was found dead from asphyxiation. Meanwhile, I've got real spreadsheets staring me in the face."

"And I've got to shoot off a text to Mr. Williams about that brooch."

I meandered back to my office and worked for two solid hours before making a beeline for the Keurig. Augusta looked up from her desk and motioned me over once I plunked my coffee into the slot.

"Found another stolen item on Craigslist. Same seller. This time it was earrings. Cute little bovines with pink eyes. Almost wanted them for myself. I texted Mr. Williams and he told me to arrange a meeting with the seller."

"All the way over by the 101 and West McDowell? How are they going to find the time when they're mired in those interviews in Verrado?"

"They're not. And the sale won't actually take place. He asked if I could set it up for tomorrow morning. A parking lot in that area. When he explained what he had in mind, I offered to do it myself. Not rocket science and besides, I'm always carrying. Just in case."

I nodded and Augusta kept talking. "I'd get a description of the seller's car and give him or her a bogus description of mine. Then, I'd simply drive to where that car is parked and get the license plate. Along with a good photo of the car. Next, I'd hightail it out of there."

"Good plan. With that info, Nate and Marshall would be able to find out who the seller is without blowing the operation. Right now, all they can get him or her for is selling stolen goods, but if they catch the culprit in the act, it's an entirely different story."

"That's what Mr. Williams said. I'm going to respond to the seller as soon as I set up my bogus email for the transaction. What do you think? Yahoo? Gmail?"

I shrugged. "Pick one."

It took Augusta less than a minute to get a Gmail address for the transaction. Then, she clicked the Reply box on the ad and leaned back in her chair. "Might as well continue to scour the list while I wait for that stinking thief to make a move."

I removed my cup from the Keurig and told her to let me know the second she got a response. "Give me a shout-out, okay?"

"It's an email. Not a missive."

"It's a break in the case. Not to be missed."

"Oh, brother."

Meanwhile, I had a few minutes of my own before getting back to my spreadsheets and I was chomping at the bit to google Desmond Bartley. I began with the most innocuous site—the Sun City West obituaries in the *Independent*.

Two lines in and it was no wonder the unfortunate demise of Mr. Bartley was classified as such—a tragic accident. The man was ancient, even by Sun City West standards. At ninety-seven years of age, whoever found him most likely made the assumption the man had cognitive issues and didn't probe any further.

I could hear my mother now, "Just because we're senior citizens doesn't mean we're on the road to senility."

*Sorry, Mom. But I think that's exactly the road in question as far as Desmond is concerned.*

I continued to read the abbreviated story of Desmond's life but stopped short when it got to the part about survivors. There was only one and the instant I read the sentence, I froze. "Mr. Bartley is survived by his great-niece, Enid Flox, from Sun City West."

"He wasn't her tenant," I shouted out to Augusta as I opened my office door. "He was her great-uncle. But why kill him when he probably only had a few years left?"

"Who? Who had a few years left?"

I caught a breath and explained what I'd found out about Desmond.

"Darn it all," I said. "The man was older than Methuselah. I was really convinced Enid murdered Desmond. Not only that, but I was certain Cosmo witnessed it. That would have explained the payoff money."

Augusta spun her chair around and looked directly at me. "And what was the motive, Miss Marple?"

"Motive. My gosh, I hadn't even considered motive. Only means and opportunity. But I'm positive there's a motive. There has to be."

"Start with the house. You said Enid owned it and then sold it once Desmond inhaled those gas fumes and entered the pearly gates. And she unloaded her house, too, and moved to Scottsdale once she became a widow. If you ask me, the answer's in the real estate."

"You may be on to something, Augusta."

# CHAPTER 22

I stared at the spreadsheet in front of me and then minimized it in order to visit databases for property ownership. Most carried a modest cost and I was willing to chalk up the money to find out exactly how and when Enid acquired the house where Desmond was found dead.

Thankfully, it was a quick search but it gave me the willies. The house was purchased in 1998 by Desmond Bartley and sold to Enid Flox two decades later for one dollar.

"What do you make of that?" I asked Augusta. It was now twenty to five and we expected Nate and Marshall to breeze in any second. I paced back and forth a few feet from her desk.

"Hmm, maybe they worked a deal where she owned the house and he'd live there for free. She'd pay the taxes and other related expenses. Like one of those reverse mortgages. Most likely he planned to will it to her anyway. You know, keep it in the family."

"I suppose. It's still kind of odd. And I can't seem to get that unsettling remark of Jane's out of my head. She pretty much insinuated Desmond died suspiciously even though it was ruled accidental."

"Yeah, it does make you wonder, doesn't it?"

"Up until my aunt Ina mentioned what my uncle Louis overheard about Enid, I worked in my usual orderly and well-thought-out manner with this unofficial investigation into Cosmo's death. Then, all of sudden, I'm playing one of those video games and zapping asteroids as they approach. This is *so* not like me. In fact, Marshall said he admired the way I tackled things logically and sequentially. But I'm not. I'm chasing after a cold case. A cold case! And why? Because I'm doing exactly what Bowman and Ranston do—latch on to one idea and sink my teeth into it to the exclusion of everything else. Well, not anymore." I raised a fist in the air. "I'm not going to concoct a theory and force everything to fit."

"Good for you. Are you done? I've heard inspirational speeches that were shorter. But nice touch with the fist. It rivals Scarlett O'Hara but I think she was holding a potato."

"Thanks a heap. I know what I need to do—draft a murder book with a detailed suspect list and look for connections. Find out more about Cosmo and who else had motives to do him in. If Enid and that cold case stand out, then it's because the evidence is more compelling."

"I take it that will be your evening entertainment?"

"Uh-huh. Marshall will be exhausted once he finishes up in the office.

He'll eat and conk out on the couch. Then he'll make his way to the bedroom and fall asleep as soon as his head lands on the pillow. Meanwhile, I'll be at the kitchen table trying to make sense of this mess."

"I'll be watching a Dirty Harry marathon if you want to know. DVR'd it last month. Tonight will be *Magnum Force*."

"Good to know. I'm going to finish up in my office. Call out when the guys get back."

"You'll hear them. Trust me."

Sure enough, at a few minutes before five, I heard Nate's voice. "Hi, Augusta. Is that a box of donuts on the counter? Please tell me you and Phee didn't wipe it out."

"I can't speak for Augusta," I said as I walked over to where he and Marshall stood, "but I only ate two. How was your day? Did you make any progress?"

Marshall gave me a quick hug and sighed. "If you define progress as interviewing a plethora of landscapers and home repair servicers, then we made stellar progress."

"Only three of the landscaper servicers worked for homeowners who had break-ins. We're looking further into that. And none of the HVAC or painting services that we interviewed had been hired by those homeowners. Frankly, the best lead we have so far is the one Augusta found," Nate said. Then he turned to her. "Sure you're okay with tomorrow's plan?"

Augusta stretched out her arms and rolled her shoulders. "Piece of cake. The thief got back to me and we're meeting at seven a.m. in the Starbucks parking lot across from the Circle K on West McDowell. Male voice. I'll drive close enough to the white Chevy Equinox he described, snap a photo or two, and keep moving."

"Remember," Nate said, "whatever you do, don't get out of your car."

"Honestly, Mr. Williams, I'm not about to leave an air-conditioned car in this heat."

"Fine. I'll touch base with you in the morning."

"If you must know," Augusta said, "you and Mr. Gregory weren't the only ones to make any progress today. Phee made real progress. She found out who the old man in the house next to Enid Flox's house was. Turns out the guy was Enid's nonagenarian great-uncle. And there's more. Lots more."

"Okay," Nate said, "spare us the suspense. Which one of you ladies wants to dish it out?"

I flashed "the eye" at Augusta before I spoke. "It turns out Enid's great-uncle, a man by the name of Desmond Bartley, sold her his house for a dollar in 2018. He was probably going to leave it to her in his will anyway, but it *is* rather weird, don't you think?"

Nate shook his head. "Not all that unusual really. Sometimes when family members reach a certain age, they deed over their property so it doesn't become an issue once they pass away. Especially if the will might be contested."

"I still have a funny feeling Enid was in a hurry for money and needed to sell her house and her great-uncle's in order to purchase her current place in Scottsdale. And if so, I'm back to that nagging theory that she was the one who left the gas on. Which brings me to my next theory. The one where Cosmo witnessed the heinous act and used it to get money out of Enid."

Marshall, who was now standing next to me, gave my shoulder a squeeze. "You'll need more than those theories, hon."

"I'm way ahead of you. Tonight, after I pick up Chick-fil-A salads on the way home, my official murder notebook begins. I can't go off on tangents. I need to focus. Besides, last thing I need are those book club ladies and my mother breathing down my neck. I can hear them now— *'Do you want Herb to land in the Fourth Street Jail?' 'How can we sleep if there's a murderer loose?'* or worse yet, *' We have a plan. We have a new plan.'* If that's not enough to keep me glued to this investigation of mine, nothing will be."

"Just don't overdo it. Take a breather. Remember, that's what Bowman and Ranston get paid to do."

Augusta and I let out audible groans at the same time.

"Speaking of which," I said, "are they any closer to solving Cosmo's murder?"

Nate shook his head. "Last I spoke with them, they were unable to contact next of kin because there weren't any. Closest they got was the ex-wife in California."

"No wonder the news anchors released the information so quickly. Usually it takes forever. Um, what does that mean in terms of his will? His house? He was having major renovations done."

"Interesting situation." Nate crossed his arms and rolled his neck. "Bowman and Ranston were able to chat with Cosmo's attorney regarding the will."

"Oh my gosh. I know where this is going. I should have realized it immediately. Murderers tend to be people who have a vested interest in the estate. Who was it? Who's getting his money? Maybe those deputies will wrap this case up after all and spare everyone the anguish. So who? Who?"

"Slow down, Phee, you're making us dizzy." Nate reached behind and grabbed the nearest donut. "He left his entire estate to the Thunderbird School of Global Management, and before you say another word, the answer is no. The school is hardly considered a suspect in his demise. They receive all sorts of monies from endowments, estates, and trusts. Cosmo's is probably a drop in the bucket for them."

"Drat."

Augusta extended her fingers and gave her bouffant hair a lift. "Look on the bright side. You can work on that murder notebook of yours all night. Much better than doing laundry or cleaning."

I turned to Nate. "I don't suppose Clinton, Therm, or any of the planning commission members are affiliated with the Thunderbird School of Global Management."

He laughed. "Believe it or not, Ranston actually checked that out. And the answer is no."

"Another reason to be on the bright side, Phee," Augusta said, "You're thinking just like Ranston."

I shot her a look just as Marshall leaned over to kiss me on the check. "You're amazing, and thanks for picking up salads."

"If this is going to get mushy, I'm out of here." Augusta stood, powered off her computer and straightened a few things on her desk. Then, to Nate, "Talk to you later, Mr. Williams."

"I'd better be going too," I said. "Don't stay here all night."

Augusta and I walked out together and she locked the door behind her. "Don't want anyone sneaking in while those two are at their desks. Even if their guns are at the ready."

I cringed at the thought and wished her luck tomorrow. "You could break that whole case, you know."

"Or I could just be getting it started."

Neither of us knew how prophetic her remark would turn out to be until the following morning. Marshall and Nate were already in Verrado when I showed up to work at a little before nine, ready to regale Augusta with the detailed murder map I had tucked under my arm. It spanned two adjoining pages in my marbled composition notebook and featured notations that would have made a biblical scholar proud. Unfortunately, I never got the chance to show it to her. Not right that minute, anyway.

Augusta had the receiver pressed against her ear and covered the mouthpiece. "Damn license plate was stolen from another car."

# CHAPTER 23

"**W** hat happened?" I asked when she got off the phone.

"The white Equinox was parked to the left of the Starbucks drive-through so I got in the line and ordered a java mocha latte. While I waited for my order, I took a handful of photos of the car and the license. Perfect. Couldn't have gone any smoother. I emailed them to Mr. Williams as soon as I left Starbucks and pulled into the Circle K lot. Then I drove back to the office, and that's when I got his message. He has connections with the Arizona Department of Transportation and someone ran the plate for him. Turns out it was stolen off of a Mazda in Goodyear."

"Goodyear. That's not far from Verrado. Maybe the thief or thieves is working out of there. So now what?"

"Mr. Williams will try to make the buy again. Only this time with those deputies. I've been back and forth with calls to Ranston. Bowman took the day off for some dental work. Didn't need to hear the details."

"I don't understand. I thought the HOA didn't want to involve the sheriff's office."

"They don't, but the operation won't take place in Verrado and should be pretty low-key. Mr. Williams said, and I quote, 'We can't afford to dilly around with stolen license plates when we've got a flesh-and-blood suspect right under our noses. Might as well have the MCSO deputies nab him.'"

"Who's going to make the buy? I mean, *transaction*?"

"That's what we were talking about when you walked in. One look at Bowman and Ranston and the seller will bolt out of there like his pants are on fire. And I say *he* because the person driving the car was a man. No one else in the car. Got a good photo of him through the window."

"What did Nate say? Is he going to meet with the guy? Or is Marshall?"

"Here's where it gets interesting. According to Mr. Williams, Bowman and Ranston are up to their noses with Cosmo Pruett's murder, and since they haven't officially been asked to investigate the Verrado thefts, they said they'll help us out but they, in turn, will need some assistance with their little old homicide case once things get sorted out in Verrado."

"What kind of help? Please don't tell me it's interviews. Nate and Marshall will cringe."

"Nope. They're looking into Cosmo's social life. Not just his *dating* social life, but all that other stuff that goes on in Sun City West. The clubs, the contests, you name it."

"I think I understand. To be honest, I'm taking the same approach.

Well, similar. I'm dying to show you my murder map but it's now ten after nine and I need to get to work. Maybe at break time."

"Sounds good to me. Meanwhile, I've got to pull up Craigslist again and offer to buy those earrings if they haven't already been sold. This time I'm using a real description of Mr. Williams's car. He wants to do it ASAP so I've got to get a move on. If all goes well, he'll get it worked out with the deputies, and once an arrest is made for stolen goods, maybe they'll offer that scoundrel a deal for info about that ongoing crime ring in Verrado."

"I'll keep my fingers crossed."

"Oh, one more thing. Herb hasn't been vindicated yet. Far from it. From what Mr. Williams said, Ranston is covering all his bases. That's why the big push to delve into Cosmo's personal life. They don't expect to find anything or anyone noteworthy. That means they'll have a stronger case against Herb. Got that threat of his written down verbatim."

"Seriously? It wasn't a real threat. Herb was furious and spouting off."

"Not according to Ranston."

"Oh, brother. That's a weak motive if ever I heard one."

"Face it, Phee. It beats profiting from Cosmo's death because the only known recipient is a college."

"The only known recipient *of his will*. Not the prize money from that contest. And what about revenge? That's always high on the murder charts."

"I'll be happy to play Nancy Drew with you during lunch. Sounds like break time won't be long enough."

I laughed and traipsed into my office, where I set aside all thoughts about Cosmo's death and focused on invoices and billing. It was a work-induced Nirvana until ten thirty, when my mother called to inform me the letter-writing blitz was a huge success.

"You did that in one day? One day?" I was incredulous.

"It wasn't that difficult. Cecilia rounded up a bunch of her church ladies and they got down to business right away in the church's social hall. Apparently a few of them made phone calls and brought in at least forty other women. Can you imagine? Myrna had good luck, too, with the bocce club. Only they had to do their letter writing in that little alcove by the table tennis courts."

"Sounds pretty—"

"I'm not finished. Lucinda dropped by the clay and ceramic clubs and had everyone write letters. She also sent out club emails with a sample fill-in-the-blanks letter. Too bad we didn't think of it sooner. Tomorrow we start with the petitions. Louise found an old petition online about saving the dolphins so she tweaked it and it sounded pretty good when she read it to me. She and I will drop off petitions at all the club rooms first thing in the morning and pick them up at night. We'll do this for the next few days before the heat wave renders us senseless. Before I forget, how did you make out with that name I gave you? Desmond something-or-other."

"Bartley. Desmond Bartley. And it was very interesting. Turns out he was Enid's great-uncle and he sold her his house next door to hers for a dollar before he died."

"Harrumph. Didn't want any greedy relatives to come out of the woodwork and swoop in to contest the will if he wanted it to go to her."

"That's exactly what Nate said."

"But?"

"I have this gut feeling Enid killed him and I can't seem to shake it. The case is so cold no one will look into it. The man was in his late nineties, after all. The thing is . . . I checked out the sight line between Desmond's kitchen where his lifeless body was found and the large sliding glass windows at Cosmo's house. It's a direct view. What if he saw Enid in the act and—"

"Spit it out. Blackmailed her. You think he blackmailed her and she finally had enough and bashed him behind the head with a river rock."

"Well, frankly, yes. I do. But I realize it's speculation on my part and not indicative of a theory based on solid evidence. Therefore, I decided to take another approach. Study the original suspects and their links to Cosmo. Then I can always revisit Enid."

"Just don't revisit so long that the next visit we take will be to the Fourth Avenue Jail to see Herb and most likely Paul."

*The Fourth Avenue Jail. Only a matter of time for me to hear those words come from her mouth.*

"And if you're revisiting," she went on, "make sure you revisit the scene of the crime. They always do that on TV. That's always the first place where they look on *NCIS*."

"That's because it's where the body is."

"At first, yes. But they keep going back again and again. On last night's episode, which was a repeat, they went back three times."

"It's a TV show. Oh, never mind. I've got to get back to work. Um, nice job with the letters and petition."

"I'll keep you posted."

*Like clockwork.*

I hated to admit it, but my mother was certainly the better detective in this would-be investigation. At least she knew to return to the scene of the crime, even if it took the *NCIS* screenwriters to get her there. I had no choice. If I was to get anywhere, I'd have to start at the beginning.

My mother's call had eaten into my midmorning break so I took a quick stretch in the outer office, grabbed another cup of coffee and asked Augusta when Nate and the deputies planned their meet-up with the seller.

"Tomorrow. Early. Ranston's going to plan the thing tonight. You'd think it would be a simple deal, but nope. He's going to meet with Mr. Williams and Mr. Gregory once they leave Verrado. Mr. Gregory said to tell you to grab a bite for dinner because he doesn't know when he'll be home. Said he'd call or text."

"That's fantastic."

"Huh? Did you hear what I said? About dinner?"

"Not a problem. I need to drive to Sun City West after work to scope out the area where Cosmo's body was found. Tonight's my best bet. It stays light until after eight. Plus, in a few days it will be too hot."

"You're going to be walking along the railroad tracks?"

"You make it sound like I'll be right on top of them."

"Well?"

"It's only been ten or eleven days. Maybe the area is still cordoned off. If not, I have a general idea of where to look. But finding the spot where the body was found isn't as important as figuring out how he got there. My mother said Herb and Paul snooped around and Cosmo's car is still in the parking lot. That means someone had to have driven him to the railroad crossing."

"I'm sure those deputies have asked the supermarket for their surveillance video of that night. Especially since Cosmo called the sheriff's office about the fish in the engine."

"Yeesh. Don't remind me. Anyway, Marshall and I talked about that video. The car was slightly out of range so the supermarket wasn't much help. Worse yet, the social hall doesn't have video surveillance. But it does have something better—the rec center's night maintenance guy. I met him a few times in the past when I had to walk Streetman after dark. Don't ask. The dog park lighting was awful so I walked him around the social hall. If it's the same maintenance man, I may be in luck."

"Wouldn't the deputies have spoken with him already?"

I laughed. "I don't think they know there's an outdoor maintenance man at night."

I beat Marshall to the punch and sent him a text explaining I had some very safe snooping around to do and not to worry. He texted back, *I always worry. Be careful.* This time the text included some interesting emojis. A heart, a frog and some grapes. Either he sent me a code or he pushed the wrong images.

I texted back a heart and a pizza. No mistakes there.

# CHAPTER 24

I pulled into Starbucks for an iced mocha latte and a slice of their lemon cake. No way was I going to wait until Marshall got home in order to eat. Besides, pizza was just as good at nine p.m. as it was at six.

As I sipped on the latte I glanced at the clock—six twenty. Another half hour until I'd get to Sun City West. I had stayed in the office a tad longer to finalize some of my billing, which unfortunately had taken a backseat to my mother's calls. No matter. The railroad tracks weren't going anywhere and I'd always run into the night maintenance guy after seven.

The area where Cosmo took his last breath was a few yards down from the hospital on the Sun City West side of the tracks. However, he wasn't on the hospital side. He was found near the grand entrance sign that welcomed visitors. Had they spied the body, they might have opted to visit another retirement community.

The closest I could get to the spot in question was the far side of the hospital's parking lot. It was a no-man's-land and I had my choice of parking spaces. I took the one nearest the road and crossed to the opposite side when there was a lull in traffic. Not the best move, but it was daylight and no cars were in sight.

Once I reached the grand welcome sign, I realized the crime scene was no longer cordoned off. That meant two things: the forensic team had completed its investigation and I now had to play "guess where they found him" since the area was now unmarked.

River rocks were abundant and Cosmo's killer had his or her pick of the size, shape, and texture for their murder weapon. A dusty towpath separated the river rocks from the tracks and I followed it south for a few yards. Absolutely no shade anywhere. Not even a small cactus. Tiny beads of sweat stung my eyes but I used the backside of my hand to wipe them and kept walking.

A number of railroad workers used the towpath to access junction boxes and the tracks themselves if they were in need of repair, so it wasn't unusual for me to see what appeared to be indents in the sandy dirt from wheelbarrows. Only wheelbarrows leave one rut or track mark line, not two equidistant ones.

I first spied the two lines by the entrance sign and didn't think much of it until those indents continued for a good twenty yards until they neared the tracks. I took off my sunglasses to get a better look and that's when I noticed lighter indents. Again, in lines of two and equidistant from each other.

It had to be indents left over from a hose or possibly something one of the switch operators used on the tracks. But whatever it was, it didn't set off any red flags for the forensic crew.

The tough part was that I didn't know what I was looking for. Not like finding the killer's blue thread from a loose button in the study of an old mansion. Only in cozy mysteries . . . Still, something about those idents plagued me. They began and ended in the area where Cosmo had been killed but that didn't mean they had anything to do with his death.

The medical examiner's office was certain cause of death was from blunt force trauma to the head. But the exact time of death had wiggle room. In my mind, Cosmo could have been clobbered elsewhere and then dumped on the tracks. But wouldn't the killer have used a wheelbarrow?

Then again, two killers could have dragged the body, making it appear as if they were helping an intoxicated buddy of theirs. I studied the area for footprints but it was a waste of time, and the same beads of sweat had now become rivulets that poured down my face. I wasn't going to make any headway by pursuing this jaunt any further so I headed back to my car.

By now traffic had picked up and that meant there was no way I could cross RH Johnson Boulevard and access the hospital parking lot. I had to walk alongside the road until I reached the traffic light before making my move.

Forget the rivulets that emanated from my forehead. A steady surge of sticky sweat draped the back of my neck and made its way down my back. Whoever said Arizona's dry heat prevents sweating should be drawn and quartered. I got to my car in time for my back to adhere to the driver's seat.

Thankfully there was another Starbucks across from RH Johnson and Meeker Boulevards and I couldn't pull in fast enough. This time for the Venti lemonade. As I took my last gulp of the cold liquid, I considered my next move. Most of my conversations with the night maintenance man consisted of me apologizing for Streetman's erratic behavior—snapping, growling, and biting the tires on his Sun City West golf/utility cart. At least the dog wouldn't be with me.

It was eight ten and I had pulled into the main recreation center complex on RH Johnson Boulevard. Bowling was in full force and I wondered if it was a league night. No matter. I found a decent parking spot a few rows up near the welcome courtyard. As I was about to get out of the car, I got a text from Marshall.

*Hope you've eaten. Mtg. is still going on and on.* It was followed by a heart emoji and one of a smiley face with lots of Zzz's all over it.

I texted back *Starbucks* and added more hearts and a happy smiley. Then I took off to find the maintenance guy.

On nights when I'd bring Streetman to the rec complex, we ran into the man by the "great lawn," an area reserved for outdoor seating behind the swimming pool. Since there were no signs posted that prohibited dogs, I felt comfortable allowing Streetman to roll on the grass and do what dogs do, careful to pick up after him.

No one was in sight on the sidewalk that ran uphill from the bowling alley to the social hall. Even at dusk it was too unpleasant for a walk. But I wasn't strolling. I was sleuthing. A nice, pleasant word that sounded better than snooping or prying. Taking the little path that ran adjacent to the courtyard area and the social hall, I made my way downhill to the grassy lawn in hopes of finding the maintenance man.

There was no doubt he was on the job because clear plastic trash bags filled to the rim were placed by the side of the walkway waiting for him to load them into his golf/utility cart. He once explained to me that he emptied the bins and replaced the trash bags first before lining them up for a quick toss-in and disposal.

I looked around but no one was in sight. It was now dusk and the solar pole lights came on automatically. Given the dust in the air and the low-level lighting, the great lawn looked more like something from a Bronte novel rather than a playground for active seniors. The miniature golf to my right was deserted as well. Heat has a way of doing things like that.

Past the great lawn was one of the bocce areas. I headed in that direction hoping I'd come across the maintenance man. Instead, I came across a man and a woman arguing in the alcove that connected the zymurgy club room and the outdoor sports. They stopped the minute they saw me but I had already heard the gist of their conversation. When the woman said, "a minimum of two carrots," I thought they were talking about salads and figured the guy didn't make the right purchase at the store. But it was when she said, "I'll accept slightly under two carrots if they're surrounded by baguettes," I knew she wasn't talking loaves of bread. She meant carats, spelled with one *r* and an *a* instead of an *o*.

Interrupting their spat was the last thing I meant to do but it was inevitable. I was already at the entrance to the alcove and couldn't very well back off without having it appear really awkward. Bizarre as it sounded, I wished I had Streetman with me, if only to have an excuse for infringing on their privacy.

"Um," I muttered. "You haven't by any chance seen the night maintenance man, have you?"

The man pointed to the exit of the alcove that faced the dog park area. "He drove past here in that club car of his a few minutes ago. Looked like he was going uphill by the fitness center."

*Terrific. Uphill in the heat.*

"Thanks." I walked past them and glanced at their faces. The man appeared to be in his late sixties but the woman was younger by at least a decade. Blonde, but definitely not natural, slender, and well-dressed in white capris and a stunning color-block top. Apparently her partner, and most likely future fiancé, didn't share the same flair for dressing.

He was shorter by a few inches and his loose-fitting beige cargo pants coupled with a well-worn red golf shirt gave him the appearance of a garden gnome. Maybe it was his white goatee and mustache but no matter, I had a hard time picturing them as a couple.

Turning to the left, I trudged up the hill toward the fitness center. I was already exhausted from my prior jaunt at the railroad tracks and this latest trek didn't do my body any favors. At the crest of the hill, I spotted the familiar Sun City West golf/utility cart with its orange detailing and the words *Club Car* emblazoned on the side. The driver had gotten out and tossed a bag of trash onto the extended cart before taking off again.

Rather than chase after him and exhaust myself further, I backtracked through the alcove again. I figured the guy would have to loop around to snag the bags he had already lined up. The man and woman were still face-to-face, only their disagreement seemed to have heated up.

I caught the man's words, "The money won't be a problem" and "you need to be patient," but I missed the full gist of the woman's response. The second she spied me, she stopped talking. Funny, but people usually do that mid-sentence. In her case it was mid-word. I heard, "Poi—" and my mind immediately went to *poison*. Of course, it could have been *point, poise*, or even *poinsettia*, but somehow I thought I had gotten it right. I eyeballed her, offered a quick nod, which may not have been the best idea, and kept moving.

When I finally got back to the pathway between the courtyard and the social hall, the maintenance man had just finished tossing the last of the bags into his cart.

"Hi!" I called out as I hurried toward him. "I need to speak with you."

The guy, who had now taken a seat behind the steering wheel, turned and motioned me over. "It's too hot to stand. You're welcome to take the passenger's seat if you want."

"I'm fine. I'm only going to be a minute."

He crinkled his nose and titled his head. "Hey, I almost didn't recognize you without your partner. Did he give you the slip? It's still light out. We can cruise around and look for him."

"Thanks, but he's home with my mother. It's her dog. Streetman. He tends to be on the neurotic side."

The man laughed. "Tends? This golf cart still has bite marks on the bumper. But don't worry. He's not the first dog to have done that. Anyway, what can I help you with?"

"A murder."

"Beg your pardon?"

"Oh, sorry. Not committing one. Looking into one. I'm Phee Kimball with Williams Investigations in Glendale. I'm not a detective but I do help out from time to time in Sun City West since I'm familiar with the community."

*Not exactly a bold and outright lie. More like an extended introduction.*

"I'm not sure how I can help you but I'm willing to give it a shot."

"Thanks. Remember the night of that public hearing from the Maricopa Planning Commission?"

"Man, do I! If ever I thanked my lucky stars to have an outdoor job, that was the night. That stinking smell lingered for a full forty-eight hours. Had to cancel lots of club activities in the area. Say, is this about that guy on that planning commission who was found dead by the railroad?"

"Uh-huh. Cosmo Pruett."

"Awful thing. News said it was a homicide."

"According to the medical examiner's report, it was. But the victim may not have been killed where his body was found."

"You think he was killed here? I didn't see anything. Or hear anything, for that matter. Place was pretty quiet. Like I said, they had to cancel all those club activities around the courtyard."

I nodded. "Shortly after the meeting was canceled, Cosmo went back to his car, which is still parked over there between the social hall and the supermarket. He phoned the posse because someone put a dead fish in his engine."

"Yeah. I heard about that. I was at the other end of the complex by the fitness center and pool. Didn't learn about it until I got to work the next day. The maintenance crew couldn't stop laughing about it. Of course, the man's death is no laughing matter, but this was before all that."

"Sometime after the dead fish incident and the next morning, Cosmo wound up dead. I have to think that since his car is still where he left it, and no one in their right mind would drive a car that stunk from dead fish, he must have called someone to get a lift home. Did you notice anyone parked near his car when you swung back from the fitness center and pool?"

The maintenance guy rubbed the nape of his neck. "Hard to say. I usually don't pay too much attention to who parks where as long as they keep off the sidewalk. Got some nutcase who insists on driving his golf cart on the sidewalk but he goes so fast I can never get a license to turn him in."

"So I take it the answer is no."

"Not exactly. There was one car parked next to his. Looked like the driver put something in the hatchback and then took off. Probably groceries. Some folks prefer to park away from the crowds. Sorry I couldn't

112

be more help."

"Did you happen to notice what kind of car it was?"

"Those SUVs all look the same, but I did notice a bumper sticker. It said, 'Beauticians do it with style.' Not much help, eh?"

"No, that's fine. Every bit of information is a help. Um, er, did the sheriff's deputies speak with you about that night?"

The man shook his head. "Not yet. But I'll tell them the same thing I told you. Didn't witness a gosh darn thing."

# CHAPTER 25

I thanked him and started for my car when I realized he might be able to provide more information about that SUV, including its color. It was a long shot, but maybe he saw the license plate and remembered it, especially if it was one of Arizona's vanity plates. Then, with any luck, I could find the driver and ask if he or she saw anything.

Pivoting so fast I almost lost my balance, I caught him just as he was about to take off in his club car. "Uh, I've got one more question if you don't mind. Were you able to get a good look at the car? Or the license?"

He gave a nod. "Not the license but it was one of those silver SUVs. Could've been a Ford, or a KIA. Maybe a Chevy. They all look alike. The lighting is lousy in that area so it's hard to say."

"Thanks anyway. I appreciate it."

"And thank you, too."

"Me? For what?"

"For keeping that dog with your mother."

He drove downhill toward the bowling alley and I walked back to my car. That's when I realized I'd forgotten one more thing. I never looked at Cosmo's car. Not that I expected it to yield any pertinent information, but like Nate always told me, "Sometimes what appears to be the most insignificant clue turns out to be the very thing that solves the case."

*Okay, insignificant clue, here I come.*

Since I was now closer to my car than Cosmo's, I drove to where his was parked and pulled up alongside it. The car was a new silver metallic Buick Envision and thankfully, the fetid fish aroma was gone. At least from where I stood. I had no idea what the interior smelled like.

I used the flashlight feature on my phone to peer inside but nothing stood out. Either Cosmo was a real neat freak or the car had just come from the showroom. The interior was in keeping with most SUV interiors only this one had a dizzying dashboard with more features than most commercial planes. The console seemed larger and the seats roomier. I made a mental note to let the book club ladies know in case any of them were in the market for a new car purchase.

If Ranston and Bowman had searched the vehicle for clues to Cosmo's death, surely they would have mentioned it to Nate and Marshall. Especially since Williams Investigations had been approached to assist with the case once the situation in Verrado was resolved.

Given the pristine interior, sans any lingering fish odors, it didn't appear as if any sort of struggle took place in the car. No torn seats, no scratches, and a rearview mirror that wasn't off-kilter. Had there been a struggle, I doubted the assailant would have had time to readjust the mirror. Nope, nothing noteworthy as far as I was concerned, and the only prize I managed to go home with was a heat exhaustion headache.

It was past nine when I pulled into our garage. Marshall had made it home first and I kept my fingers crossed he'd ordered a pizza. Starbucks munchies could only take me so far. As I turned the key in the utility room door, I heard his voice.

"You missed the pizza delivery guy by three or four minutes. It's still hot. Mushroom and olive. Didn't think we needed pepperoni and sausage so late at night. Geez, I'm sounding like those book club ladies."

"Bite your tongue. I'm starving."

"Napkins and paper plates are already on the table. I'll grab us some Cokes unless you want an iced tea."

"Coke's fine."

We were at our food in seconds and it was only after we'd consumed the first few bites of our pizza that we were able to converse.

"I was about ready to chew my arm off," I said. "Thanks for ordering the pizza."

"I passed the point of wanting to chew my arm off and go for Ranston's head instead. Less planning went into D-Day. I swear if the man said 'Let's go over this again' one more time, Nate would have tossed him from the nearest window."

I laughed. "I take it the sting operation is finalized."

"Oh, it's finalized all right. You'd think Ranston was directing a Broadway production. Try not to laugh again, but he actually had Nate run lines with him in a role-play to prepare for the encounter with the seller."

I nearly choked on my pizza. "Yikes. I'm sure Nate must have enjoyed that."

"Let's just say acting isn't his forte. Anyway, how'd your night of sleuthing go?"

"Like a balloon after someone sticks a pin in it."

"That bad?"

I nodded and took another bite of the pizza. The tangy green olives hit my taste buds like a bullet and I quickly washed it down with the Coke. "I got nowhere. Except maybe for the indent lines by railroad tracks. And don't worry, I wasn't that close to the tracks."

"What indent lines? I'm not sure I understand."

I gave Marshall the lowdown on the parallel indent lines I saw near where Cosmo's body was discovered but he didn't find it unusual. He propped up an elbow and leaned his head on it. "If the forensic crew let it go, it's probably not worth pursuing. Must have been indents from a long pipe or hose that the maintenance crew used."

"Yeah. Still, I wished I would've uncovered something that had been overlooked before."

"It's a process, not a race. Our best leads come from the people involved with the victim. Eventually someone caves."

"Yeah, but that's usually when they're presented with forensic evidence they can't escape from. Right now, all we have is the medical examiner's report, and that was as nebulous as could be when it came to the murder weapon. A river rock. Might as well have been a grain of sand."

Marshall wiped the sides of his lips with a napkin and took a quick sip of his Coke. "The river rock makes the most sense under the circumstances but the medical examiner didn't specify. The report merely suggested something large and possibly round. Heavy, too, I'd presume."

"So it could have been anything, huh?"

Marshall shrugged. "Whatever it was, it holds the key to motive. A river rock suggests a spur-of-the-moment act while, let's say a rolling pin or a bat, would indicate something a bit more thought-out."

I looked at the table and realized we had devoured the entire pizza. "You're right. I need to put the forensics on hold and work on my original plan the way I intended. I've got a detailed murder map, you know. I did it when you and Nate stayed late to play catch-up."

"Usually eating so much makes me logy, but I've got a second wind. What do you say you show it to me once we clear off the table?"

"Done!"

For the next half hour, I spewed about all my suspects, including Clinton and his gold-digging girlfriend, as well as Therm, Enid, Abigail, and the planning commission's second in command, Neville. I even showed Marshall the clumsy artwork I'd sketched to go along with the names. It was like a new version of Clue but without the board and the cute game pieces.

"I seriously doubt it could have been one of those anti–transfer station folks from Sun City West," I said. "I mean, yeah, they were all adamant against the idea, but to go as far as to commit murder against the chairperson of the planning commission is a bit far-fetched, don't you think?"

"Last on my list for sure. Got to admit, you've got the suspect list covered, but if you really mean business, do an incident list as well."

"An incident list? What do you mean?"

"Jot down the weird things that occurred after Cosmo's body was found. You know, things that seem to be pulling the case in one direction or another."

"Like the fish Paul found by his front door? And the deck of pinochle cards Herb found?"

"Uh-huh. And what about those pinochle cards that were stashed in the jacket pockets of four of those planning commission members? The ones that made a double pinochle."

"I hate to say it, but everything points to Herb. Maybe even Paul."

"Exactly. Making it way too obvious. Now think who could have done it. Oh, and leave plenty of room on that list because perpetrators don't stop with one or two attempts to throw investigators off course."

"I feel like I'm on a merry-go-round."

"Join the club."

We turned in a few minutes later since both of us had reached that point of total collapse. Little wonder that when the phone rang the next morning before our alarm went off, we bumped into each other's arms, necks, and heads as we scrambled to answer it.

Marshall was the winner, but given his reaction when he lifted the receiver, he didn't quite see it that way. "Uh, I think it's your mother, hon. You may want to take this."

I reached over and took the phone. "Mom? Is everything all right?"

"Not according to the paper. The *Independent* was in my driveway when I took Streetman out. The headline says, 'Recipe Theft Puts Master Grillers Contest on Hold.'"

"Um, you kind of knew that was going to happen. Didn't Herb mention something about having to re-compete against the other semifinalists prior to his team and Cosmo's being selected as finalists?"

"Yes, yes, the new marinade sauce. But I didn't think they'd put the contest on hold. Neither did anyone else. According to the paper, new arrangements with the Food Network are in the works. Whatever *that* means."

"It means the contest will be rescheduled." *I hope or I'll never hear the end of this.* "Listen, Marshall and I need to get ready for work. I'll touch base with you later, okay?"

"Call me when you've narrowed in on the killer. And don't wait too long to revisit the scene of the crime. The killer always returns to cover up evidence."

"In crime novels and on TV. Honestly, Mom."

I wasn't about to tell her I'd already revisited the scene where Cosmo's body was discovered because I'd never make it to the office on time. Besides, I was convinced it was the scene of a body dump and not a murder. Too bad I couldn't piece together what happened between the time Cosmo discovered the dead fish in his engine and the person who parked next to him closed their SUV's hatchback and took off. Maybe Marshall was right. Maybe if I concentrated on the suspects and the incidents, I'd get closer to narrowing down which one of them fit into the timeline.

I crossed my fingers I wouldn't be alone in my endeavor. The deal between the deputies and Williams Investigations was a quid pro quo for sure. If the arrest from the sale of those stolen items on Craigslist could yield a confession regarding the series of break-ins and thefts in Verrado, then Nate and Marshall would have to honor their end of the commitment and help tackle Cosmo's murder.

As I let the cool water trickle down my face in the shower, I hoped Ranston wouldn't flub up on his lines.

# CHAPTER 26

"Any news from Nate or Marshall?" I asked Augusta when I returned to the office from a quick donut run at ten.

"You've been gone less than fifteen minutes and no. No calls." She peered into the box and selected a double chocolate cake donut. "But you did get a call from your mother, who told me she wasn't about to monkey with that cell phone of yours."

"Aargh. I better find out what she wants."

Augusta took a bite of her donut and held up her hand like a stop sign. "I'll save you the trouble. After receiving that official letter from the contest committee on Monday, Herb got a phone call at a little past nine from the chairperson of the contest." She took another bite and went on. "They're having another qualifying contest this Saturday at Palm Ridge. Only the five semifinalist teams and their invited guests."

"Oh, crap. I'm one of the guests, aren't I?"

Augusta finished the donut with one bite. "It's not like someone's wedding, or worse yet, one of those awful retirement parties where everyone tells the person how much they're going to enjoy their new life. Besides, you don't have to bring a present."

"No, I'm pretty sure my mother will bring two fur-covered ones with her. Did she say what time?"

"Six thirty in Summit Room A on their outdoor patio."

"Terrific." I rolled my eyes. "Hmm, there's one good thing. It will give me a chance to see who Therm and Clinton invited. That new beautician who did my highlights is convinced Clinton may have done the deed in order to reap more money if they win. Seems he has a girlfriend he's trying to impress."

"Harrumph. Nothing worse than middle-aged or senior men trying to impress women."

"Bernice, the stylist, thinks the woman is one of those gold-digging hussies. Her words, not mine."

"Taste testing and hussy hunting. Sounds like a fun evening for you, Phee."

"Very funny. But I doubt we'll be able to sample the food. I imagine the teams only marinate enough ribs for the judges to try. We'll only be the spectators."

"Then you and Marshall better eat first, huh?"

"Marshall . . . Can't wait to give him the happy news. I don't think that's how he intended to spend a Saturday evening."

Augusta grabbed a napkin and put another donut on her desk. This time a French cruller. "Intentions, hell. He's married now. Goes along with the territory."

I moseyed back to my office and concentrated on payments due. I always pushed the deadline ahead in my mind so that I wouldn't be late. Lunchtime caught me completely off guard and it was only when Augusta announced, "Are you up for gyros again? They deliver," that I sat bolt upright.

"Yes! Two chicken ones."

Twenty-five minutes later we were both savoring the pungent blend of tomatoes, onions, and tzatziki sauce. We sat in the break room with the door wide open in case anyone was to walk in. Fortunately, none of Nate or Marshall's other cases were time-sensitive so Augusta was able to reschedule them for the times when the men weren't in Verrado.

"Think they'll nail the creep with the stolen earrings and brooch?" I asked.

"And license plate. Don't forget the license plate. Some poor unsuspecting person now has to deal with ADOT to get a new plate. And they'll probably have to pay for it, too."

"It should be a simple arrest, shouldn't it?"

Augusta all but choked on her gyro. "Ranston and Bowman are in charge. The word *simple* isn't in their vocabulary. My take is that they'll haul the culprit in for questioning and he or she will wish they never heard of Craigslist. Yep, much easier in the old days when P.I.'s dealt with fences and pawnbrokers."

As soon as I wiped the last of the tzatziki sauce from the sides of my mouth, I went back to my office to continue working. Seconds later Augusta shouted, "Mr. Williams is on the line and Mr. Gregory's going to call your cell phone."

Before I could answer, the familiar ringtone went off and I answered the call.

"Good news and bad news, hon. We nailed the guy dead to rights and he gave it all up in exchange for a lesser charge of dealing with stolen property. Geez, who wouldn't with Bowman threatening him with malfeasance and subterfuge? Even if they don't fit the crime. I don't even think the thief knew what they meant."

"Then it's all over and you can wrap up the Verrado case."

"Uh, no. Here's the bad news. Our dealer in stolen goods was working with his brother-in-law and a merry little band of robbers. Three more heists are planned for tonight and—"

"Uh-oh. You and Nate plan to catch them."

"Actually, Bowman and Ranston plan to catch them, along with some local backup and help from Nate and me."

"I think I see where this is going."

"It's going to take us all night. Well, not *all* night, but late enough. Our thief said his buddies planned to get the first break-in underway around dusk. One thing for sure—these men aren't slouches. They did their homework. They learned when their victims planned to be out of the house by keeping track of their weekly schedules. Talk about planning accordingly."

"Uh, were these random victims?"

"You've heard the term *casing the joint*, right?"

"Uh-huh."

"These guys cased the cars first. Looked for high-end newer models that spelled money. Then they did the usual internet snooping to find out which families would be more likely to possess fancy jewelry given their lifestyle."

"Did they have a connection to the development?"

"And then some. Listen, we can chat about it over breakfast tomorrow."

"Breakfast?"

"When I said bad news, I meant it. The *roundup*, for lack of a better term, will take us well into the night. And once that's done, the paperwork back at the MCSO office will be monumental. I don't even want to think about it. Unless of course the whole thing fizzles out like a bum firecracker."

"It won't. I have faith in you and Nate."

"Not Bowman and Ranston?" Marshall laughed. "Never mind. Nate and I need to finalize the operation with them this afternoon. If I thought the morning meeting was grinding, this one will be downright oppressive. Thank goodness the restaurants in Goodyear make deliveries here."

"If you can, keep me posted."

"I'll do my best. Try to have a nice evening. Maybe a swim or something, okay?"

"Be careful."

"Don't worry."

Ending the call with the usual words of affection, I pushed the red End Call icon with the upside-down phone. My stomach was as topsy-turvy as the icon and I knew it wasn't from my gyro.

"Looks like they're on a chase," Augusta said when I stepped into the office. Nate had given her the same rundown as Marshall did with our call. "Wish I was up there to watch it unfold."

"Unfold or unravel? Ranston has a unique way of blowing things out of proportion and Bowman isn't too far behind. Hope they don't overdo it."

"You mean like a SWAT team?"

"Uh-huh. I'll grant you, they're dealing with seasoned thieves, but not with domestic terrorists."

"Relax. Mr. Williams and Mr. Gregory should even out the equation."

I did a mental eye roll, smiled, and went back to my office. Augusta was a source of never-ending clichés and her influence had already infiltrated the way I expressed myself. At least it was better than a daily encounter with the book club ladies. And that came soon enough at the end of the week.

Like the seasoned detectives they were, Nate and Marshall, along with Ranston and Bowman, corralled the entire Verrado bandits in a night-long escapade. Caught with pockets loaded with jewelry, credit cards, and over four hundred dollars in cash, the men couldn't explain what they were doing in the foyer of a three-bedroom golf-course-view ranch home.

Two other accomplices had their plans foiled before they could get their hands on any booty in another house a few blocks away. Thankfully, the owners of the third house on the hit list would never find out. The thieves were placed under arrest before that break-in was to take place.

I learned all of this when Marshall staggered into our house at a little past two. I was half awake, half dozy, sprawled on the couch with an old black-and-white movie playing on Turner Classics. The minute I heard his voice, I muted the sound and rushed over to him.

"Boy, is it good to see you. I thought you'd be in bed by now," he said as he gave me a giant hug.

"There was no way I was going to get any sleep until you got back."

"You were giving it a pretty good imitation when I walked in the room."

"Very funny. Are you hungry? Can I fix you anything?"

"All I want is to crawl into bed and put this night out of my mind. Honestly, if Ranston said the word *criminality* one more time, I think Nate might have slugged him."

"During the arrest or during the paperwork?"

"Both. Aargh. Let's get some sleep, tomorrow's another day."

Thursday was another day all right, and those deputies didn't waste any time faxing over the information they had on Cosmo Pruett's murder once they tied up the Verrado caper. Regarding Cosmo, there was nothing our office didn't already know, but having the official blessing made it easier for me.

Like it or not, I had committed myself to finding the real culprit because the last thing I needed was to help my mother sneak Streetman and Essie into the Fourth Avenue Jail to visit Herb.

# CHAPTER 27

"**D**id you tell Marshall about the rigmarole this Saturday?" Augusta asked when Marshall and I got into the office the next day. He headed straight for his desk and I made a beeline for the Keurig.

"No. The poor guy's still dealing with last night's aftermath. No need to throw more stuff at him right away. Besides, it's two days away." Two days that flew by with little to no progress on the murder case . . .

Bowman and Ranston were still convinced Herb was responsible for doing Cosmo in as well as faking his own break-in. Not to mention the one that took place at Therm's. Apparently, the deputies dropped the idea of a local nutcase and went with what they already knew—Herb had an indisputable motive. But motive was one thing and evidence was another.

With no discernible fingerprints near Therm's stolen recipe box or any witnesses to support their theory, they were powerless to make an arrest. But they weren't powerless to make nuisances of themselves at the semifinalist grilling competition on Saturday. They got word of it from the rec center since the sponsors were concerned there might be trouble given the reason for holding a repeat competition to begin with.

And while Bowman and Ranston were notified by the recreation centers of Sun City West, I was the one who broke the news to Marshall that very same morning right after I'd told Augusta there was no hurry. I had second thoughts when I sat at my desk and decided to get it over with. Like pulling a Band-Aid from a day-old cut. I took a deep breath, rapped on his office door and made the announcement before he could utter a word.

"The barbeque competition resolved its setback," I said.

"Huh?" Marshall looked up from his computer screen.

"Herb's grilling contest. His team, as well as Therm and Clinton, have to re-compete against the other three semifinalists due to the theft of those marinade recipes."

"Yeah, you mentioned that before. Tough break for Herb. Hope his next marinade holds up as well."

"Um, you can see for yourself on Saturday."

Pushing himself back from the desk, Marshall stretched out his arms and grimaced. "Please don't tell me we got roped into another taste test at his house."

"No."

"Whew. You had me worried for a minute."

I gulped and stepped closer to his desk. "We actually have a wonderful opportunity as far as the investigation into Cosmo's murder is concerned. The five teams in question will be competing once again. This time at six thirty on Saturday. The outdoor patio at Palm Ridge. Invited guests only."

"And you're thinking one of those guests may be our murderer?"

"It's a possibility. And it shouldn't be too hard to scope them out. We only need to focus on who Therm and Clinton invited. The other teams don't matter. They weren't in the final competition to begin with."

"Are you sure you don't have a P.I. license tucked away with your other degrees?"

"Nope. Just a solid foundation in yenta-ing."

By the end of the day, Bowman and Ranston had also called our office with the same message, only their delivery was short and succinct: "Suspect surveillance Saturday night."

Needless to say, Nate and Marshall had to endure yet another fatiguing planning session, date and time to be arranged, at the posse office in preparation for Saturday's affair.

My mother was elated when I informed her that not only were Marshall and I going to be in attendance but that Nate would be joining us as well. It was a little before five and I wanted to get the call over with before heading home.

"Hallelujah," she all but shouted in my ear. "Herb and his crew need all the support they can get. I'll tell him so he can add Nate's name to the list of guests he has to provide to the organizers."

"Uh, that won't be necessary. Nate's going as part of the investigation. Into, well, you know."

"I suppose those irritable deputies will be there too."

"Well, yes, as a matter of fact."

"Harrumph. I know what that means. You don't have to spell it out. They think the murderer will be there. It has to be one of Therm's or Clinton's guests. I'm right, aren't I? This is going to turn into a regular nail-biter and I'm not referring to the judges' decision. I've got to call Myrna."

"Call Myrna all you'd like but do not tell her to bring that arsenal of self-defense sprays with her. She's liable to get us all arrested. Paul's moose urine was enough. And speaking of Paul, I suppose he's been invited, too, huh?"

"He *and* the book club ladies. *And* your uncle Louis. Everyone will be there."

*All we need is Lady Gaga and the show will be complete.*

"Did Herb give you any idea of what to expect?"

"More like what not to expect. No samplings for the audience. Of course, we all knew that ahead of time. I'm planning on having the ladies over for some cold salads before we trek over there. Your aunt and uncle have early dinner reservations somewhere. You know, you and Marshall are more than—"

"Nope. I mean, no thank you but we'll grab dinner here and head over."

"Maybe afterward we can all go to the Homey Hut for dessert."

"Um, uh . . ."

"Oh, and getting back to the competition. From what Herb told me, the teams are expected to arrive with the ribs two hours before the guests are allowed inside so they can begin their grilling. I imagine he'll be parboiling and marinating those things for hours beforehand. Wouldn't tell me the new recipe but it's something he and the men cooked up."

"They haven't tasted it before?"

"Who knows. Anyway, propane grills will be set up outside on the patio but guests will be inside. They'll have the seating arranged so that the guests can watch as the judges taste the ribs and make their decision."

"You never mentioned who the judges were."

"Wait a sec. I wrote it down. I knew someone would ask. Hold on."

I let my eyes drift from the ceiling to the walls while I waited.

"Okay, I'm back, Phee. Obviously, the Food Network wasn't about to send the actual judges to a qualifying event."

*I'm surprised they're sending any to this event in the first place.*

"So who are they?"

"I'm getting to it. They selected master chefs from three renowned restaurants in the valley. Here goes: The Peoria Grill on Union Hills. You can't get out of there without plunking down at least seventy dollars for a meal. Everything is à la carte. Your aunt told me."

"Enough with the Peoria Grill. Who else?"

"Hmm, the Brazilian Steakhouse on Shea Boulevard in Scottsdale and the Burgundy on Central Avenue in Phoenix. Come to think of it, the Burgundy is one of Louis's favorites, but if you ask me, I can get three decent meals at the Texas Roadhouse for what he and your aunt pay for one."

"Thanks. I was curious, that's all."

"I wish they would have samplings once those chefs are done with the tasting."

"It wouldn't be samplings. It would be full-blown meals given the audience."

"I wasn't thinking of the audience. I was thinking of my Streetman. He enjoys a quality barbeque with high-end beef."

*As much as he enjoys the tidbits and droppings from the park that I make him spit out.*

"Maybe you can take him to McDonald's the next time you're out and about with him. Which reminds me, you're not going to bring him on Saturday, are you?"

"You sound worse than that shortsighted facilities committee from the rec center. Their secretary sent me a certified letter. Certified. Can you imagine? Low and behold, Enid Flox registered a complaint with them following the unfortunate incident at the Stardust Theater. Streetman has been banned from the rec center buildings indefinitely but I doubt they can make it stick."

"No sense in tempting fate. I'm sure there will be other venues you can sneak him into."

"And don't forget Essie. I can't leave her out."

"Just leave her home. Leave both of them home. We'll see you on Saturday."

"If something comes up, I'll call."

Thankfully nothing came up and before we knew it, Marshall and I were off to the Palm Ridge Recreation Center on Saturday. We finished off some leftover chicken and potato salad before getting into the car so our stomachs wouldn't announce our arrival.

When we walked inside the cavernous Summit Room A, the book club ladies frantically beckoned us to hurry over and grab a seat.

"It's not like a theater production where the curtain's about to go up," Marshall whispered.

"No, it'll be more dramatic. Trust me. I don't know *how* but it will be."

He shrugged and we walked toward Lucinda, who pointed to two chairs at the end of the row. "Quick. Sit in the cushy chairs before you get stuck with the folding ones."

The moment she said that, I heard a familiar voice. "I'm not about to plant my butt in a damn folding chair." It was Deputy Ranston and I tried not to cringe as he continued. "It took me close to five months for it to heal from that stab wound."

Marshall and I looked at each other and tried not to giggle. The stab wound was actually caused by a pair of scissors when Ranston sat in the wrong chair at the wrong time while investigating another case. "Here," Marshall said, "you can have my seat. I'm more comfortable milling around."

"And I need to find my mother," I quickly added. "So your partner can take my seat."

"Bowman's milling around, too," Ranston grumbled. "I plan to sit and take notes."

*Yep, every teacher's dream.*

"If you're looking for your mother, Phee," Shirley shouted so as to be heard above the cacophony of voices, "she went to the ladies' room with your aunt and Myrna."

*Oh, heaven help me. They better not be coming up with "a plan."*

"Um, have you seen my uncle Louis?"

"Over there," Shirley said and pointed, "talking with one of the judges. At least I think he's one of the judges. Who else dresses so formally in Sun City West?"

I turned my head and sure enough there was Uncle Louis waving his arms and laughing as he and a hefty man with dark eyebrows conversed about who-knows-what. I imagined my uncle knew him. Food connoisseur and bon vivant that he was, Louis Melinsky had connections all over the valley. Mostly chefs from high-end restaurants and casinos, as well as fellow musicians and gamblers.

"Where's Herb and his pinochle crew?" I asked.

Shirley motioned to the patio doors. "They're all outside hovering around the grill off to the left. The competition's out there, too. Therm and Clinton as well as a handful of other people from the semifinals. Only contestants are allowed outside." As if to validate her statement, Shirley walked toward the patio doors.

"Lordy! Where'd that woman come from?"

"What woman?" I swore my head spun around quicker than that girl from *The Exorcist*.

"The bleach blonde who's all over Herb. She's got an arm draped around him. He's lucky if that grilling fork doesn't land on the floor."

I approached the patio and peered outside. Shirley wasn't kidding. Any closer to Herb and she'd be a permanent fixture. Then she turned her head and I gasped.

"What's the matter, Phee? What's that strumpet up to?"

"I'm not sure, but I don't think she's as interested in Herb as she is getting her hands on his marinade. I've seen her before, and if I'm not mistaken, Herb's about to fall for the oldest game in the world."

Shirley pushed past Cecilia and Louise and plowed through the patio doors. The pungent aroma of barbequed ribs hit me the minute the door swung open. "Unleash that man, you vamp!" she yelled. "Before I do it for you! And get away from that bowl of marinade!"

# CHAPTER 28

Ranston, who appeared to have made himself comfortable in one of the few upholstered chairs, all but knocked it over as he raced toward Shirley. "No catfighting on the premises!" he bellowed. "No catfighting."

Then, out of nowhere, Bowman thundered toward the patio, barely colliding with his partner. As the two of them pushed their way through a door meant for one person, my mother's book club, along with Paul, who must have arrived shortly after Marshall and I did, converged on the scene. It was a chaotic frenzy that was fueled all the more by Bowman and Ranston.

Luckily, I was spared being trampled by the crowd, having moved off to the side of the patio doors when Shirley charged through them. Someone gave me a slight shove and I bumped into the person standing right behind me.

I flinched as I turned to see who it was. "Nate!"

"At your service, kiddo, although I doubt I can do much. It's a regular brouhaha on the patio. Wait. Hold on. Looks like your husband may have it under control."

We stepped forward, and sure enough Marshall somehow managed to get Herb and the blonde a few yards back from the crowd while Bowman and Ranston shouted for everyone "to remain calm or risk arrest."

Next thing I knew, one of the event organizers, a lanky gentleman who appeared to be in his forties, spoke into a handheld mic and made it clear that if the invited guests did not return immediately to their seats in Summit Room A, they would be escorted out and placed on probation at the rec center.

"What if they don't live in Sun City West?" I asked to no one in particular.

"They'll thank their lucky stars," someone shouted back.

While Marshall and the deputies ushered the defeated audience off of the patio, Shirley approached the blonde, who had now removed herself from Herb's shoulders yet remained in close proximity. Close enough, I imagined, to get a good whiff of his aftershave.

With her arms crossed against her chest, Shirley glared at the woman. "You best not be trying anything sneaky."

"Me? I was only interested in the yummy ingredients Mr. Garrett used for his marinade. The ribs smelled luscious when I stepped outdoors for some air."

Shirley wasn't having any of it. "Plenty of good air-conditioning in the event room. And besides, no guests are allowed on the patio."

The woman turned to Herb and widened her eyes. That's when I spoke up.

"Air my foot. Whatever it is you're up to, it won't work. I saw you with your gentleman friend the other night by the great lawn. I overheard you as well. Voices carry. And, if I'm not mistaken, isn't that him to the left of us? Short man. White goatee and mustache. Wouldn't you know it? Looks like he's one of the semifinalists."

"That's Clinton Badger," Herb said. Then he faced the blonde. "Did that pissant send you over here to mess with our marinade?"

The blonde covered her lips and shook her head before answering. "Absolutely not. I was curious about the marinade, that's all."

Shirley and I exchanged glances just as the organizer spoke. "Only contestants on the patio. If you are not a contestant, you must go into Summit Room A immediately."

"Good luck," I said to Herb. I grabbed Shirley by the wrist and we hightailed it off the patio and into the room. As I held the patio door open for her, I caught a glimpse of the blonde giving Clinton a thumbs-down sign with her hand.

"I wouldn't put it past her to sabotage Herb's marinade," I whispered to Shirley. "If their team makes it this far and they wind up against Therm and Clinton in the final round, we'll have to get a security detail for them."

"Lordy. I didn't want to say anything but that was my thought all along. I mean, a woman that good-looking throwing herself all over Herb? I don't mean to sound superficial and judgmental but some of these vixens will do anything for money."

As I took my seat, I suddenly remembered the first syllable of the word she uttered by the great lawn—"poi." Maybe it really was *poison*, and if so, Herb and his cronies would have more to concern themselves over than having the winning ribs.

As the guests got settled for the second time in less than fifteen minutes, the event organizer who had spoken before marched in front of the first row and exhaled. This time there was no need for a mic. "Thank you, ladies and gentlemen, for joining Sun City West and the Food Network for our semifinalist competition in the Master Grillers contest. As you are aware, two unfortunate incidents involving intellectual theft of property resulted in our having to schedule another semifinalist competition."

"Intellectual theft?" someone shouted. "It's a barbeque recipe, not biological warfare."

The organizer clasped his hands and took a breath. "According to Wikipedia, and I quote, 'Intellectual property includes intangible creations of the human intellect.'"

To which the person responded, "And a hodgepodge of family concoctions."

I tried to see who the agitator was, but when I turned around, he had already finished speaking. The organizer continued without acknowledging the last remark. "Allow me to introduce our judges: executive chefs from three esteemed establishments in the Greater Phoenix area."

With that, he introduced the two men and one woman from the three restaurants my mother had mentioned. The portly chef with whom my uncle Louis spoke was the one from the Burgundy. I listened to the introductions but the words drifted over me. I was more concerned about the blonde, whose intentions left me on edge.

She was now seated mid-center in one of the rows opposite ours. As I scanned the audience, I found it remarkable that for a gathering of less than forty people, most of whom were invited by Herb and his pinochle crew, it came across as a stadium filled with raucous, unpredictable fans. Uncanny how loud voices can accomplish that.

The organizer explained that the five teams on the patio would finish grilling the ribs and once they were done, they were to deliver them to the long rectangular table off to the right of the room before taking their seats in a specially designated area.

The three judges, who were to wait in the lounge area outside Summit Room A, would be brought in for a blind taste test. Herb had told my mother each team had an identifying number and that's what was to be used.

The next ten minutes were sheer agony. At least for me. My aunt Ina got into a long dissertation about medieval cooking, suggesting that instead of the usual fare the book club ladies bring to their pot luck dinners, they try something different like fortified gruel, which turned out to be gruel reinforced with meat, and cinnamon brewet, another type of meat dish, only with spices that are usually found in pastries.

That was enough to get Paul started on a dissertation of his own. This time about fish recipes that should have been tossed back into the water along with the fish. I stood on the pretense of needing to stretch and panned the area for Nate, Marshall, and the deputies.

Ranston was back in the comfy chair taking notes while Bowman stood off to the side of the judges' table looking like a dog waiting for food scraps. I spied Nate and Marshall chatting on the opposite side of the room and joined them before anyone could ask where I was going.

"That blonde," I said, making sure no one was close enough to hear me, "was with Clinton on Tuesday. The night I went to the rec center complex to talk with the maintenance man. I think they're a couple. And

I'd bet money her only interest in Herb's marinade was to sabotage it. Too bad we can't search her to see what she's got in her pockets or her bag."

Nate rubbed the nape of his neck. "Not without a search warrant, kiddo. And if it makes you feel any better, you're not the only one."

"Then those deputies realize what's going on?" I was ecstatic.

Nate looked at Marshall, who gave my shoulder a squeeze. "Not the deputies. Me. I watched that woman's body language and it was like a well-rehearsed play. I said something to Bowman but he didn't buy it."

"He's got to get his head out of the sand. Doesn't he see what's going on? Clinton and Therm are dead set on winning. I'm positive they eliminated their other team member to get a bigger piece of the pie. They're working it from two angles. It stands to reason foiling the competition would be next. Only thing is, I don't know how far they'll go."

"Hey," Marshall said, "maybe they'll get knocked out of this round and that will be that."

Nate continued to rub his neck. It was more a habit of his than a reaction to a kink or twist. "No sense speculating. Might as well see what the judges have to say."

"I'm on my way back to the peanut gallery," I said. "Keep an eye on the blonde."

"Hurry up, Phee." My mother's voice was urgent. "That's the last of the ribs being brought to the table. They're about to start tasting them. Herb and the men are back in their seats already."

The three judges stood expressionless behind a long table with a white cloth and fancy skirting. They each had five small plates in front of them with two sample ribs. The organizer informed the audience that the tasting was underway and that everyone should refrain from making comments. He also explained the procedure. After each taste test, the judge would clear his or her palate with lemon sorbet that was also provided. Again, he reiterated, "no unnecessary chatter."

*Who was he kidding?*

"See if any of them raise their ears," Paul said. "It's a sign the ribs are too sour."

Then, like clockwork, the other comments followed. Too numerous to keep track of who said what.

"Watch to see if one of them licks his or her lips."

"If they go for the second rib, it's a shoo-in."

"Watch to see if anyone guzzles that sorbet stuff. A bad sign for sure."

"Think they'll lick their fingers?"

"This isn't Kentucky Fried Chicken."

I must have done at least five mental eye rolls and one silent scream. The judges remained expressionless throughout the entire tasting. Not a single sign of pleasure or displeasure whatsoever.

"How much longer is this going to last?" Louise whispered. "I can tell if something tastes good in two or three seconds." *This from the person whose idea of gourmet cooking is spam and eggs.*

"No one spat anything out," my mother whispered back. "Must be a close contest."

I shifted in my seat to glance at the spot where the contestants were seated. Herb and his cronies were huddled together and for the first time since I'd known them, none of them were talking. Clinton and Therm were seated to the left of Herb's crew but with an empty chair between them. I tried not to read too much into it.

Behind them were at least seven or eight other men from the original semifinalists, creating a sea of gray in the audience. I tried not to look obvious as I shifted and re-shifted in my chair.

Then, out of nowhere, my mother let out a gasp and I looked all around to see what had gotten her so alarmed. "What? What's the matter?" I asked, but my words were drowned out by Cecilia who shouted, "Is it a mouse, Harriet?"

And that's when a series of shrieks took over the room.

# CHAPTER 29

M y aunt had used the mouse ploy before, but under very different circumstances. There would be nothing to gain from feigning a rodent sighting in Summit Room A. I leaned closer to my mother and asked again, "What? What on earth's the matter? I don't see anything."

My mother clasped her hands and grimaced. "I can't believe it. With all this fuss about Herb's barbequed ribs and Cosmo Pruett's murder, not to mention Essie joining our household, I completely forgot about the Christmas in July Doggie Contest. At least I remembered to enter Streetman a few months ago."

My jaw dropped and I stood. Then I announced, "There's no mouse. False alarm. Everything's fine." I sat and leaned closer to my mother. "You almost caused a riot. Over what? Another dog contest?"

"It's not another contest. Streetman could be on next year's Sun City West calendar. I don't know how I could have forgotten about it. Christmas in July is going on right now. Goodness, there's the gingerbread special cookies at Betty's Café, nutmeg and spice latte specials at Putters Paradise, and the trinkets-trinkets-trinkets sale at the resale shop by the posse office."

*Yep, a retailer's dream come true . . .*

"It's okay, Harriet," Shirley said. "We've got the tree outfit with all those cute ornaments. And it's not another shindig. All we have to do is take the dog's photo and send it to the calendar committee. What's today? Saturday? We'll make the deadline on time."

I tried to get the image of the tree costume out of my mind but it was impossible. When I first saw Streetman in that outfit, he pulled at those ornaments as if they were porcupine needles. I shuddered and focused my attention once again on what was happening in the room.

Thankfully the judges were unfazed by the goings-on in the audience and continued to taste the ribs. I watched as they dutifully wiped their lips and spooned sorbet into their mouths. As if on cue, they stepped away from the table and exited to the patio.

"The judges are conferring and will render their decision momentarily," the organizer announced before exiting to the patio as well.

"If Herb and the men are axed," Paul said, "I'll make sure Clinton and Therm pay the price. Don't you think it was a tad coincidental that Therm had a break-in at his place, too? A *staged* one if you ask me. Yep, Herb better be in the running or those two creeps better finalize their wills."

Oops. Wrong words. Wrong time. Wrong place. Bowman, who was

only a few feet from the judges' table, was in earshot of our group and must have heard every word Paul said. In seconds, the deputy trounced over to where Paul was seated and motioned for him.

"Uh-oh," Myrna said. "Herb better skooch over because Paul will be joining him in lockup."

Shirley put a finger over her lips. "Hush, all of you. We're only going to make this worse."

Bowman had his back to us, but worst of all, his huge torso obscured Paul from our sight. The men stood against the rear wall and it was impossible to gauge what was going on.

"Think Bowman will arrest him for making inflammatory remarks?" Lucinda asked.

My aunt adjusted the crimson ribbon that held one enormous braid to the top of her head in lieu of the usual two braids that hung down her neck. "Don't be ridiculous. If they arrested everyone for making inflammatory remarks, they'd have to lock up the residents in all of the Sun Cities. Inflammatory remarks are acceptable for people of a certain age. They know none of us filter our thoughts anymore. We're lucky we can spew them out."

No sooner did my aunt say "spew them out" when Paul thundered back to his seat muttering something about "fishing in the wrong pond" and "idle threats." Cecilia asked him if everything was okay and he nodded. "Bowman's covering his you-know-what, that's all. Oh, and he gave me an unofficial restraining order to stay away from Therm and Clinton. Geez, can you imagine?"

A few groans followed but they ceased the moment the organizer returned to the room. He and the judges stood in front of us and no one made a sound.

"Thank you, everyone," he said. "I'm sure our contestants appreciate your time and your patience. It was unfortunate that our original decision could not be honored due to the aforementioned theft. And given those circumstances, there is always the chance that those who were in the finalist position would no longer hold that honor. The contestants knew that upon entering the competition but nevertheless—"

"Lordy, just spit it out," Shirley shouted. "Some of us have sciatica problems."

The organizer turned to the judges and nodded. "Very well. It is my pleasure, well, my *duty*, to announce that the two finalist teams are Mr. Clinton Badger and Mr. Therm Whittaker, as well as . . ."

It seemed to take him an eternity to spit out the name of the other finalists, and as I sat perfectly still eyeballing my mother and her friends, the words *damage control* sprung to mind. I bit my lower lip and held my breath as I heard the words, "Mr. Herb Garrett, Mr. Wayne . . ." but I couldn't hear the rest because everyone around me erupted in screams, shouts, and whistles.

Herb and the men gave each other fist bumps while Therm and Clinton huddled off to the side. No sign of exhilaration. Nothing. It was as if the outcome was expected. Something was off but I wasn't sure what. Seconds later, the blonde tossed her bag over her shoulder and started for Therm and Clinton.

I'm not sure exactly what came over me. A moment of sheer lunacy perhaps. Or a last-ditch effort to get some answers. It didn't matter. I recognized her bag as one of the Vera Bradley models my mother had. One with the snap closure. In that instant, I knew I had to act fast. Too bad I didn't have the flair for the dramatic my aunt did. But I gave it my best.

"Ew!" I squealed as I zeroed in on the woman. "That's a cockroach on your shoulder. Quick! Brush it off!"

She flung her bag to the floor, at which point I bent down under the guise of retrieving it but gave the magnetic closures a pull, and when I lifted the bag, the contents spilled out.

I slapped the side of my cheek and gasped. Meryl Streep would have been proud. "Oh, no! I can't believe that happened."

Meanwhile the blonde screamed, "Get it off me! Get it off me!"

By this time everyone rushed over to her aid and in the melee I was able to see what had spilled out from her bag: eyewear, a packet of tissues, lipstick, cell phone that thankfully was in one piece, a small zippered purse, and a glass spice container of Silver Spring coarse-cut prepared dried horseradish. Not exactly a go-to item usually found in a lady's bag.

Horseradish—a bitter herb if ever there was one. Memories of my cousin Kirk and me choking it down during Passover or spitting it out when no one was looking hit me in a split second. "Who carries horseradish with them?" I shouted. Loud enough for everyone to hear. I quickly stashed the other items back in her bag and placed it on one of the seats. "Were you planning on adding that noxious condiment to Herb's marinade?"

The blonde continued to brush her shoulders looking every which way around her. "Forget the damn horseradish. I think a roach crawled down my blouse. Oh my gosh. I can feel it crawling around."

Fearing she was about to tear her top off, I made a move that should have earned me an Academy Award. "Look! There it is! On the floor in front of you!" I proceeded to elbow my way closer to where she stood and with one solid stomp I all but crushed my own ankle. Then to offer some authenticity to the situation, I bent down and said, "Did you want to see it?"

"Ugh! No! Are you crazy?"

I shook my head. "Not crazy enough to carry powdered horseradish with me. Did you want to explain *that* or should I call those two deputies over?"

"No. No need to do that. I can explain."

*"I can explain." The three most overused words of the century.*

Now eye to eye with her, I stood my ground and motioned for her to speak.

She swallowed and sniffled. Interesting combination. "I suppose it's no secret Clinton and I are acquainted." *Is that the word for it these days?* "I was worried that the new recipe he and Therm came up with would be lacking in flavor sensations and there's nothing quite like a kick of horseradish to get things moving. I was going to put a dash in their dish, not Herb's."

"You expect me to believe that?"

"It's the truth. I'm their unofficial third party in this competition. That's how I was able to get on the patio in the first place. Clinton told the organizer that I took Cosmo's place."

Just then, Clinton shouted at the woman, "Hurry up, Marianne. We haven't got all day. Visit another time."

I looked past her shoulder to see Clinton stomping his foot, but Therm was nowhere in sight. I knew I was sunk. No way to prove anything. No one can be arrested for intentions if there are no actions to substantiate them.

"I guess it's off to the finals once again," she said. This time with a smile on her face as she strutted over to where Clinton stood.

"What was that about?" my mother asked. "None of us could figure out what you were up to."

"Trying to catch a conniving little weasel by the name of Marianne but my plan went south."

"Weasel or murderess?"

I shrugged. "At this point I couldn't even pin jaywalking on her. But Shirley was right. The woman was a femme fatale going after Herb like that. I managed to see what she had in her bag and it was horseradish. Horseradish. She said she brought it to liven up Clinton and Therm's marinade but I'm convinced it was to ruin Herb's."

"It doesn't matter. Herb and his men are still in the running and—"

Just then Wayne shouted, "We're off for a brewski at Curley's! Don't be stick-in-the-muds, join us! Got a lot of celebrating to do!"

My mother bellowed back, "So do we! At the Homey Hut. Chocolate silk pie special on Saturdays." Then to me, "How about it, Phee?"

I shook my head. "Marshall and I are exhausted. Maybe another time."

"If you and Marshall don't join us, poor Louis will be the only man there. Unless Nate decides to come."

"I doubt that. Besides, Louis went with the guys the last time. He can do the same thing this time. He's a big boy."

Sure enough, I spied Louis chatting it up with the pinochle crew while Nate, Marshall, and the deputies exited to the patio. I figured they had to be planning their next move because no one would willingly go outside on a hot July evening.

I congratulated Herb, although I doubted he heard me. He was busy whooping it up as he and his crew left the building. My next move involved saying good night to the ladies. Easier said than done. The comments flew at me like crazy.

"Are you sure you don't want to go to the Homey Hut?"

"You don't have to worry about putting on weight. You look fine."

"Just because the chocolate silk pie is on special doesn't mean you have to order it."

And then, the all-time winner of the evening: "Was that screaming woman Cosmo's killer?"

I started to answer when I was hit by a barrage of more inane questions.

"Is that what's going on?"

"Are the deputies going to nail her?"

"How did you figure it out?"

I waved my hands in the air in a frantic gesture to slow things down. "I didn't figure out anything. No one is getting arrested. Enjoy your pies."

My mother grabbed me by the wrist. "You don't have to be so grumpy, Phee. It doesn't suit you. You look as miserable as Therm did when he left the place."

"What? What did you see?"

My mother brushed the streakier side of her reddish blonde hair off to the side of her face. "One minute he was speaking to Clinton and the next he got up in a huff and left the place. You'd think for a winning spot the man would have been elated."

"What else did you notice? Anything?"

"*I* didn't notice anything, but when Cecilia returned from the ladies' room she overheard him say something about allergies and his esophagus. Maybe he had indigestion."

"Maybe." Or . . . oh my gosh. What if the horseradish was really meant for Clinton's team? And Therm in particular.

# CHAPTER 30

I rushed to the patio and spat out my words as fast as I could. "You've got to check on Therm Whittaker. Right now. I think Clinton's girlfriend might have slipped some horseradish into their marinade and I think Therm might be allergic. Oh my gosh, she's knocking them off one by one so she and Clinton can split the winnings."

Before the deputies had a chance to question me, I told them exactly what I discovered in Marianne's bag and what Cecilia had overheard. "Can't you make a wellness check?" I asked.

Ranston scratched his nose and looked at Bowman. "What do you think? We're done here."

"I'll call in and get the address." Then to Nate and Marshall, "We'll give a holler if we turn up anything. Meanwhile, we'll have our office send over the footage from the Stardust Theater. See if we missed anything. Got word the planning commission is going to announce its decision on that transfer station pretty soon. We need to identify our key players if it gets ugly."

With that, the deputies said good night, or something I presumed was "good night," and left the patio.

"Geez, I hope Therm's all right. I have a queasy feeling about this. Um, from what they said about the Stardust Theater, I take it they've relaxed their stance on Herb and now think some nutcase went overboard and murdered Cosmo over the transfer station deal. Am I right?"

Nate chuckled. "More or less. They're all over the place. With nothing definitive, they're jumping from hoop to hoop."

"Sounds like my mother's friends. One minute someone's talking about a book and next thing you know they're discussing colonoscopies. They switch topics faster than TV channels."

Nate stood. "No sense sticking around here. I've got a cold sub at home and an even colder beer. Unless all hell breaks loose, try to enjoy what's left of the weekend. Monday's shaping up to be a load of fun. Bowman told us they got search warrants for Cosmo's house and his car. It certainly took long enough."

"Is that because it wasn't the scene of the crime?" I asked.

Nate shook his head. "Someone lost the paperwork. Anyway, we'll be joining them first thing on Monday. Doubt it will turn up much but you never know."

"I hope Therm will be okay," I said, "even if he and Clinton were up to no good."

Marshall and I said good night to Nate and walked to the car.

"It'll take me the entire ride home to decompress." Marshall reached across the console and gave my shoulder a quick rub. "All I want to do is fill a bowl with ice cream and watch something mindless on TV."

"You didn't get enough *mindless* tonight?"

"More like agitation. Hey, maybe the search warrants will help us turn up something. All we've got is a list of suspects and some not-so-solid theories."

"At least things are looking brighter for Herb," I said.

"Herb maybe, but not so much for Paul. Geez, I wish that guy would keep his mouth shut."

"You don't think Bowman and Ranston took him seriously over that remark about drawing up a will?"

"Who knows. Paul may be on their radar but he doesn't have a motive."

"Thank goodness for that."

I followed Marshall's suggestion and piled three giant scoops of chocolate chip ice cream into a bowl before settling down to watch whatever the Hallmark Channel had on its lineup. We were halfway finished with our decadent snack when his phone's ringtone gave us a jolt.

He took the call immediately and mouthed, "It's Bowman. This can't be good."

I watched his expression and it never wavered—consternation coupled with surprise. When the call ended, I had already surmised the outcome.

"Therm was poisoned, wasn't he?"

"An allergic reaction. A bad one. Therm was smart enough to call the EMTs and they were on scene when the deputies arrived. Bowman and Ranston are at the hospital now. They just took a statement from Therm, who's going to be okay."

"What? What statement? What did he say?"

Marshall gave his ear a quick scratch. "Said horseradish was in the marinade but in a small quantity and when he tasted it earlier in the day he was fine. When he tasted it again at the competition, he noted it was stronger and thought Clinton spiced it up at the last minute. Didn't want to make a big deal of it because ultimately, it turned out to be a winning marinade that kept him and his partner in the finals."

"But what about his esophagus? Didn't it close up?"

"Uh-huh. That was the reaction."

"Yeah. The one Marianne was after."

"Unfortunately, we can't prove a thing. Bowman and Ranston were on their way to pay Clinton a visit."

"A lot of good that will do. He'll probably cover for her. Face it, she either orchestrated that on her own or did it with Clinton's blessing. I suppose Clinton didn't want to kick-start the marinade himself in case Therm was watching. In any case, the only thing Therm should be watching is his own hide."

"By the way, I forgot to mention it, but as soon as Bowman and Ranston brought us in on this investigation, we contacted Rolo to see what he could pull up on Cosmo's banking accounts and business ventures. He should have something for us this week."

"That's right. That haywire business deal with someone on the planning board. Wow. I'd forgotten all about it once Gloria Wong told my mother about Cosmo's romance with Abigail McFadden that fizzled out. Good grief! Is there anyone who isn't a suspect?"

Marshall spooned some melty ice cream and slurped it. "Better off with too many suspects than too few."

"Was that a quote from someone famous?"

He laughed. "Yeah, your husband."

With our stomachs filled with ice cream, we conked out and didn't wake up until the next morning. It was a blissful Sunday at home beginning with a leisurely swim and culminating with our own barbeque— hamburgers and franks. Even my mother refrained from pestering us. Only one email with a photo of Streetman in his Christmas tree costume with Essie sitting on top of him trying to tear Shirley's handmade doodads apart. No doubt about it, that neurotic chiweenie and his kitten made quite the pair.

I sensed my mother would feel better if she knew definitively that no one was going to come out of the woodwork to claim Essie. But like most strays, the kitten's origin may have been a mystery that never got solved.

• • •

When Monday got underway and Marshall headed off to meet Nate and the deputies at Cosmo's house, I resigned myself to work on the quarterly taxes and use every available bit of break time to dig up whatever I could on Abigail McFadden.

True, rumor had it *she* was the one who dropped Cosmo, but lately, I couldn't trust anything I heard.

"Whatever you want to do for lunch will be fine with me, Augusta," I said the second I got into the office. "Please don't tell me you brown-bagged it today."

"No, I didn't. And good morning to you, too, Phee."

"Oops. Sorry. It's just that I need to use every available free second to find out more about Abigail McFadden. She's the last link in my suspect lineup for Cosmo."

Augusta moved her tortoiseshell readers to the tip of her nose. "The ex-girlfriend, right?"

"Uh-huh."

"See, I listen to what you say. Why the sudden interest?"

"I need to rule her out of the equation so when I pin the murder on Clinton's conniving little minx, I won't be wrong."

"Hmm, isn't that what you complain Bowman and Ranston do?"

"This is different. I give every suspect an equal opportunity. Only in Marianne's case, I'm giving her a slight edge over the competition."

"Marianne? Is that her name?"

"Yep. I overheard Clinton call out to her at Saturday's competition. Oh my gosh, I should have mentioned that as soon as I walked in. Herb's in the running. Unfortunately, so are Clinton and Therm."

I then took the next three or four minutes to fill Augusta in on what had transpired Saturday night.

She readjusted her glasses. "Good to stay on top of things. All I got from Mr. Williams this morning was a message he and your husband were going to be snooping around Cosmo's house with the deputies."

"Yeah. Seems there was a snafu with the original search warrant."

Augusta rolled her eyes and smiled. "Why doesn't that surprise me?"

"Anyway, I'm going to plunk in a quick cup of coffee and I'll be holed up at my desk until lunch."

"The usual ham and Swiss sub from the deli?"

"Perfect."

The task of completing the Arizona quarterly tax withholding form was about as perfunctory as it gets. Still, it kept me occupied along with a review of our business income and expenses. I was so engaged that I didn't hear Augusta ask if I wanted to share the giant apple fritter she got from a new donut shop that opened a few doors down.

"No, thanks," I called out. "I've got a Coke and that should hold me until lunch."

"Guess we don't need a calendar to tell us it's summer. When your Coke intake exceeds your coffee habit, it's time to crank up the AC."

I laughed and went back to my spreadsheets before turning my attention to Abigail. I'd worked for a solid two hours and needed a break. Or, in this case, a good round of snooping. Facebook was my go-to place and I breathed a sigh of relief when Abigail's profile came up.

The backdrop was a typical Arizona sunset and the insert photo showed her holding a large long-haired white cat. I immediately thought of Enid and wondered how those two got on considering Enid's remark about toxic cat dander. The smaller photos off to the left depicted picnic scenes, cat poses, and what appeared to be a family or friend celebration. Very ho-hum and no help whatsoever.

I scanned the list of friends wondering if I'd find Cosmo but she either deleted him or he was never there to begin with. Under the "About" section, it listed District 4 of the Maricopa County Planning Commission but little else. I went back to friends to see if anything else would pop out at me but nothing did. No recognizable names or faces. I was about to move to another site when something caught my eye.

It was a photo of a beaming Abigail in front of a Chinese take-out place. Both of her hands held up plastic bags laden with food. But it wasn't the cuisine that interested me. It was the store next to it—Angel Hair. That was Bernice's place.

Most likely it was a coincidence but I wondered if the two women were acquainted and if so, how did any of that fit in with Cosmo, Clinton, and Marianne. Too bad it wasn't soon enough for me to schedule another haircut.

I tried Twitter and LinkedIn next but no sign of Abigail. She was, however, on Instagram, but only with photos of her cat. My mother, thankfully, hadn't discovered Instagram yet so the civilized world was spared endless pictures of Streetman and Essie. I stopped my yenta-ing and went back to my spreadsheets. And while my search wasn't exactly a washout, it wasn't a roaring success either.

"Well, did you find out anything?" Augusta asked when I stepped out front for a quick stretch.

"Yeah. Abigail McFadden likes Chinese food."

# CHAPTER 31

At a little past one when Augusta and I finished lunch and wiped the potato chip and bread crumbs from the break room table, Nate and Marshall returned from their sojourn at Cosmo's house.

"Don't worry about us," Nate announced. "We grabbed a bite at Mr. Taco's."

Augusta gave him a sideways glance. "I wasn't worried, Mr. Williams. I figured if you got hungry enough the grape jelly and peanut butter in the break room would sustain you."

Nate shuddered and walked to the mini-fridge for a Coke.

"Well?" I asked, looking directly at Marshall. "Did you find anything of importance?"

He shook his head. "The place is under renovation and oddly enough, the construction company is still working on the master bathroom remodel and an entertainment wall. Cosmo paid the first half of the cost up front and the second is due upon completion. Guess the Thunderbird School of Global Management will have to deal with that situation. We were able to go through his desk and some scant files but nothing that would point to why he was murdered."

"What about his computer?"

"Sent to the forensic lab. It's password-protected so Bowman and Ranston didn't want to mess with it."

I laughed. "They should have at least tried Cosmo's name or birthdate. Scary, but that's what my mother and all of the book club ladies use."

"I'll try to pretend I didn't hear that," Nate said. "Anyway, the car's been towed to the lab as well. The exterior was dusted for prints when Cosmo's body first turned up but only partial prints were found. Impossible to extract a decent print and match it. The technicians need to get inside the vehicle to see if any viable prints can be pulled. If Cosmo was forcibly removed from his car, the evidence may still be there."

I stepped closer to Augusta's desk. "But no one saw anything."

Marshall leaned against one of the file cabinets and stretched. "It was a long window of opportunity, hon. Between the time of the dead fish incident and estimated time of death, Cosmo could have gone into the supermarket, could have left with someone and later returned . . . that's what viable prints may be able to tell us."

"Or Phee's gossip line," Augusta added. "She usually gets better results that way."

Nate threw his hands in the air. "At this point, we'll settle for a soothsayer. Anyway, our next step is to review that Stardust Theater footage that the deputies sent over and pray there's something worthwhile on that computer."

The men started for Nate's office when I remembered something and gave Marshall a tap on his arm. "Wait a sec. Did the deputies mention how their conversation with Clinton went on Saturday?"

"It was the party line, all right. You nailed it. Clinton told them he was concerned that their marinade was too mild and told Marianne he thought it needed a boost. He claimed he asked her to pick up some dried horseradish since he and Therm only brought the existing marinade and the ribs to Palm Ridge."

"A likely story."

"Likely or not, there wasn't much the deputies could do about it. The question remains, 'Who had the greater motive?' If it wasn't Cosmo's teammates, it brings us back to the transfer station opponents. Let's hope we see something on the video that Bowman and Ranston missed."

"Shouldn't be too hard," Augusta whispered under her breath as Nate opened the door to his office.

I tried not to laugh as I returned to my own office, but deep down I was worried. If those lab techs couldn't pull anything from Cosmo's computer, we were dead-ended. Too bad it would take another two days for things to turn around.

• • •

It began with a phone call from my mother on Tuesday night.

"I really hate to ask you this at the last minute," she said, "but I'm joining the book club ladies tomorrow for lunch at Arcadia Farms Café in Scottsdale. Louise and Ina have been raving about it. From there, we'll most likely pay a visit to the Poisoned Pen Bookstore."

"Let me guess. You need me to let the dog out."

"Herb was going to do it but he called a few minutes ago with some flimsy excuse about going trout fishing with Paul and Kenny at Lake Pleasant. Said it was a last-minute thing. Honestly. So, can you stop by on your lunch hour? There's some potato kugel in the refrigerator that I took out of the freezer. You can even have lunch with Streetman and Essie."

*Or I can jump into Niagara Falls.*

I tried not to sound whiny. "Fine. I'll do it. But it will be a quick in and out for the dog. I've got a lot of work to do at the office."

"Come through the garage. Use the code on the outside lock. You know it. Then unlock the utility room door. It's like a vapor-lock for the cat.

Can't use the front door, even with the security door because she can slip out."

"Uh-huh."

"Once you get inside, turn off the alarm. It's the same code. Make sure you put Essie in the bedroom first and close the door. She follows the dog everywhere and I don't want her to escape. She'll come right over to you. Not like Streetman. You may have to coax him with dog yummies that are on the counter in a small plastic container."

"I think I can handle this."

"What about handling Cosmo's murder investigation? Have you, your husband, or your boss made any headway? And what about those deputies? What have they been doing?"

"I'm not privy to Bowman and Ranston's schedules but Nate and Marshall have been reviewing footage from that night at the Stardust Theater while they wait for some forensic reports to come in."

"Tell them to hurry things along. The Master Grillers contest is a week from Saturday and Herb needs to concentrate on his grilling. He can't have a murder hanging over his head. Besides, Myrna, Paul, and I need to prepare as well. It's not every day someone gets to MC an event from the Food Network."

"Um, what exactly *is* your role?"

"First, we introduce ourselves and give some background about the competition. I only hope Paul can keep his mouth shut about Cosmo. Then, we give a rundown on the gourmet food trucks that will be selling barbequed specialties. We'll also interview some of the square dancers who will be performing. After that, we'll move on to the competition, where—"

"I get it. I get it." *Why do I ask these things?* "Have a good time tomorrow. If Aunt Ina says the food's good, it must be. She and Uncle Louis are so discriminating."

"Discriminating? Try picky and kvetchy when it comes to food. And thanks, Phee. Streetman will be overjoyed to see you."

"As long as he doesn't pee on the floor, I'll be overjoyed as well. Have a good time tomorrow."

I imagined Herb, Paul, and Kenny would have a fun day as well, although the thought of putting stinky bait on a line to catch a slippery fish had absolutely no appeal for me whatsoever. Augusta felt differently when I told her the next morning and even offered up her best selections for bait, including nightcrawlers, salmon eggs, and something called Berkley Powerbait Dough. I didn't want to ask.

"Can't think of a better way to relax," she said. "Unless it's an hour at the gun range."

"Or a leisurely cup of coffee at a cozy café."

145

She crinkled her nose. "Nope. That always ends with too many trips to a restroom."

I trotted off to my office and buried myself in my work, pausing only once for a quick break around ten, about the same time Nate and Marshall headed out to meet with Bowman and Ranston. When lunchtime came, I took off for Sun City West and told Augusta I'd be bringing back lunch from whatever take-out place she wanted.

"Chick-fil-A. Sandwich and mac and cheese. Evens out the meal."

Traffic was light and it didn't take me that long to get to my mother's house. True to her word, Essie came right over demanding to be picked up and cuddled. Streetman dove under the coffee table and eyeballed me as if I was the enemy. Not wanting to waste time coaxing him, I put the cat in the bedroom and grabbed two treats from the container. The dog immediately moved to where I stood but, having gone through this before, I knew my move. I opened the patio door to the now fenced-in yard and walked three or four paces before holding out my hand to him.

Streetman gobbled the treat, lifted his leg on the nearest bush and then lifted it again on the gravel. I reopened the patio door, made sure he saw me, and tossed the remaining treat into the room. The dog charged toward it, at which point I closed the patio door, locked it, and patted myself on the back for outmaneuvering my mother's chiweenie. Then, I opened the bedroom door and watched while Essie strolled to where the dog stood.

Relieved all had gone as planned, I walked to the utility room door that led into the garage and was about to lock up and leave when I felt my phone vibrate. I stopped to take the call figuring it might be Marshall or Augusta.

"Phee, it's me, your mother. I called the office first but Augusta said you already left for my house."

"Don't tell me you called to check up on me? Because everything's fine. The dog peed twice and got a treat. Essie's nuzzling him right now."

"Good. Listen, I called because we're seated at Arcadia Farms. It's lovely. You and Marshall have to try it."

"You called to rave about the café?"

"No, I called because that horrible Enid Flox is seated right behind us with some other woman."

"And?"

"And you may be right about her. We can hear everything they're saying. I'm not at the table right now because I don't want her to hear me."

"Fine. Fine. What did you overhear?"

"Not her. The woman next to her. She said, 'You finally went through with it.' And then Enid said, 'What choice did I have?' And then the first woman said, 'It must have been horrible for you to be on the same planning commission.' And then Enid said, 'It was serendipitous really. That's when I knew what had to be done.' Phee, are you listening? Did you hear what I said?"

"Yes, yes, I heard. It was kind of vague, though." I glanced over my shoulder and Essie was still nuzzling Streetman.

"Not that vague. The woman asked Enid if she planned on slumming it again in Sun City and Enid said she'll have to because she needs her roots done and she gets discount prices from the beautician. Can you imagine? That snob actually used the words *slumming it*. I had all I could do to restrain myself."

"Showing restraint is a good thing. Besides, Enid didn't come right out and say she killed Cosmo."

"Heavens. It's not as if she's about to wave a banner but we can read between the lines."

"Unfortunately, reading between the lines is a blank space as far as law enforcement goes. Do you recognize the woman she's with? Have you seen her before?"

"I wasn't about to turn around and stare. None of us were. But I did take my compact out and adjust the mirror to get a somewhat decent look at her face. No stranger to Botox if you ask me. And her skin is pulled so tight it looks as if it might crack. That happens when people are too thin. An extra pound or two does wonders covering up wrinkles."

"Okay, fine. If anything else jumps out at you, make a note of it. We'll talk later."

"Myrna says her phone can record conversations but she doesn't know how to do it."

"That's probably for the best. Don't be too obvious or you may wind up in trouble."

"Don't worry. We'll keep our ears glued to their conversation. Even if that means stuffing a chunk of bread in your aunt's mouth."

"Just make sure it's buttered."

# CHAPTER 32

"How'd you make out with the little nipper?" Augusta asked when I got back to the office. I handed her the Chick-fil-A meal and she immediately forked out some mac and cheese. "I think your mother's concerned. She called here."

"Both of them are fine. My mother got ahold of me on my cell. You'll never guess in a million years who was seated behind her at that restaurant so I'll tell you. Enid Flox. You know, transfer station Enid Flox. Former neighbor of Cosmo's Enid Flox. Possible murderess Enid Flox who was paying off Cosmo. That's who. I suppose that's not too surprising she dined at Arcadia Farms considering she lives in Scottsdale."

"Scottsdale, huh? I doubt she'll be voting in any transfer stations there."

"My mother and her friends overheard Enid chatting it up with another woman. Something about going through with it and not having a choice. My mother's convinced they were talking about Cosmo's murder."

"Or getting a root canal."

"I told my mother to keep listening and to be discreet."

Augusta, who had just gulped some iced tea, all but spat it out. "Those book club ladies? Discreet? I'll say this much. You've got a good sense of humor, Phee. Hey, before I forget, I scanned through the *Glendale Star* over lunch and they mentioned the Sun City West transfer station proposal. It doesn't look good for your mom's community. Hold on, I'll pull it back up on my screen and read what it says."

I moved closer to her desk and peered over her shoulder. "Oh, no. I can read the headline from here."

"Letters and Petitions Won't Deter Sun City West Transfer Station."

"Can you print off a copy of the article so I don't have to lean over your shoulder? I'm too lazy to pull it up on my computer."

"Hold on." Augusta pushed the Print Screen button and hummed.

I grabbed the sheet of paper from the printer and bit my lower lip. "It's not really definitive. It says 'sources close to the planning commission.' That could be anyone. It's not a done deal yet. And it doesn't say when they're going to render their decision. Although Bowman and Ranston thought it was pretty soon. Oh, geez, once the book club ladies see this, they'll go ballistic. Not to mention Aunt Ina."

"It's a Glendale newspaper," Augusta said. "Not Surprise or the Sun Cities."

"Trust me, if it's in the Glendale paper, it's in all of ours, too. Oh, no, once my aunt sees this she'll be hammering my poor cousin Kirk to fly out here. And I promised him there was no need to worry."

"What do you plan on doing? I recognize that look on your face. You're up to something."

"Not something. Someone. Do you have Rolo's phone number handy? He's not still into that burner phone deal, is he?"

On the last case Williams Investigations had, our cyber-sleuth, Rolo, was so convinced the phones were being tapped that he insisted on prepaid ones. I seriously doubted what I was about to ask him would give rise to that sort of concern.

"Here you go. Knock yourself out." Augusta jotted the number on a Post-it and I marched into my office, clutching it in the palm of my hand. Seconds later, Rolo took my call.

"Whoa. Second call from you guys today. Must be important," he said.

"Uh, hey, Rolo, I, um, wasn't aware there *was* a first call. I've been in and out of the office. I'm calling to see if you can look into some banking accounts from a few members of the Maricopa Planning Commission. Looking for deposits from a waste disposal management company. They may be going under a bogus name."

"I know. I told your boss I'd have it by tomorrow morning the latest. Easy-peasy. You guys need to get your signals straight."

"Uh, yeah. We should. Well, thanks and have a good afternoon."

"Will do. Started a new apple cider, honey, and vinegar diet for two weeks. Thinking about getting my own apple press if it works."

I gulped. "Sounds promising." *And horrible.* "Good luck with it."

I was at Augusta's desk in less than ten seconds. "Can you believe it? Nate and Marshall beat me to it. They called Rolo about looking into monetary transfers into the bank accounts belonging to some of those planning commission members. Could be they were getting bribed by the waste management company to push through that transfer station deal."

"Still wouldn't explain the guy's murder."

"No, but it may explain what was really going on between him and Enid."

"What do you mean?"

"I thought he might have seen her turning on the gas in her late great-uncle's house and was blackmailing her. But now I'm beginning to wonder if maybe he found out she was taking a bribe and he needed to get in on the action. So, she had to pay him off. You know, to make sure he got his share of the bribe."

"It's possible. But that would have to be one hell of a bribe, depending upon how much she paid him."

"Those companies have beaucoup bucks. Still, it's only one of a zillion theories floating around in my head. Anyway, I've got to get some real work done. Catch you in a bit."

I returned to my office and let my mind quiet down with the straightforward and exacting processes that only bookkeeping can provide. I'll take data entry, financial reconciliation, and account-balance-maintenance over speculation, wild-goose chases, and ungrounded theories any day of the week.

A short while later, Marshall sent me a text. Seemed they hit pay dirt with something on Cosmo's computer so he, Nate, and the deputies were going to review it and go from there. I knew what that meant—a long night. I texted back that we'd catch up later and that I was going to take a swim once I got out of work.

What I didn't count on was a phone call from Shirley at exactly five minutes before five.

"Thank the good Lord you're still in the office, Phee. I've been with your mother all day so this is the first chance I had to call you."

"Is something wrong?" The muscles in my neck tightened up. "Did Enid turn around and get into a spat with my mother?"

"No, no. Enid and that pencil-thin friend of hers with enough jewelry to sink a ship left before we did."

I let out a sigh. "That's a relief. What's going on?"

"I entered the photo I took of Streetman to the contest committee on time. He's officially one of the contestants."

"That sounds like good news."

"That part is, yes. Oh, Lordy! I sent the wrong photo and it's too late to change it."

"But you said it was a photo of the dog. Not something else."

"Oh, it's that dog all right, but the cat's in it, too. Essie is on top of Streetman's back chewing and pulling on the hand-sewn ornaments. Streetman's head is partially turned toward her and her little kitten teeth are showing."

A sudden cough took over my throat and I couldn't stop. Then the cough turned into an awful chortle sound that compelled Augusta to make hand gestures as she mouthed, "What's going on?"

"Phee? Are you all right?" Shirley asked. "I can't tell if you're agitated or if you're laughing."

"Laughing if you must know. That's hysterical. Look at the bright side. Maybe the calendar committee has a good sense of humor."

"But what should I tell your mother?"

"Nothing. As far as she's concerned, a photo of her beloved chiweenie was entered into the Christmas in July calendar contest."

"I hate being so, so . . . duplicitous."

"You're not. You're just being a good friend. By the way, were you or the other ladies able to hear more of Enid's conversation? I'm sure my mother will tell me, but since we're on the phone I thought I'd ask."

"Your aunt and Myrna are loud eaters so it was difficult. Seemed the only thing we were able to hear revolved around Enid's appointment at the beauty parlor. Either she's a friend of the hairdresser or a relative because she said no one can argue against the price."

"So nothing more about Cosmo?"

"Not that we were able to hear. I hope I haven't kept you. You know how your mother is about that dog."

"Only too well. But I'm afraid Streetman's going to take a backseat if an article Augusta and I read in the *Glendale Star* shows up in our local papers. It pretty much insinuated that the transfer station will be a done deal. If you come across the article, maybe you can break the news gently to the book club ladies." *So I don't have to.*

"The *Glendale Star?* I'll pull it up on my computer right now. Have a nice evening, honey."

"You, too, Shirley."

Augusta stood, hands on hips, with her head shaking. "A bad photo of the dog and no more scuttlebutt on Enid?"

"You're getting pretty good at deciphering parts of conversations."

Augusta smiled as she flicked off the lights. "I've had lots of practice."

# CHAPTER 33

I texted Lyndy about meeting me at the pool in an hour and she responded with an overly jubilant emoji. As I prepared a quick tuna salad and took out some frozen banana bread to defrost, I wondered how Nate and Marshall could operate with a constantly changing landscape. One minute it's one clue and the next it's something else entirely.

The suspect list was mind-boggling and every time I zeroed in on someone, I found myself bumping into a wall. Not enough solid evidence. Or *any* real evidence, for that matter. It was no wonder I vented like a frustrated adolescent whose parent just confiscated the car keys.

"No one is any closer to solving Cosmo's murder," I lamented when Lyndy and I took a break from the four or five laps we completed. Oddly enough, the pool had only one other person in it—an older man snoring away on a chaise lounge. I figured maybe the dinner hour kept everyone at home or perhaps the swimmers had gotten their fill earlier in the day, but it didn't matter. Having the Vistancia pool to ourselves in the middle of a heat wave was a miracle.

I shook the water from my hair and leaned against the wall in the deep end, where Lyndy had already settled in. "I got nowhere with Abigail," I continued, "no motive. No nothing. Now, Enid could have two possible motives but nothing I can prove. Then there's Therm and Clinton. And don't let me forget Marianne, Clinton's paramour."

"Paramour? What romance novel did you pluck that word from?"

"Hey, it's better than trollop, hussy, floozy, or vamp. Those are the words my mother and her friends plucked."

Lyndy giggled. "Figures. Keep going. Sorry to interrupt."

"Those three have the strongest motive to knock off Cosmo. Money's quite the motivator. But again, no evidence." I went on to tell her about my mother's encounter with Enid earlier in the day as well as the latest bombshell from the *Glendale Star.* "Right now Rolo Barnes is looking into a possible bribery scheme involving members of the planning commission regarding the transfer station. Maybe Cosmo knew something. Or maybe he was the one raking it in and someone stopped him in his tracks. Literally, not figuratively. And now those deputies may have their sights set on Paul because, heaven knows, that man cannot keep his mouth shut."

"You're doing pretty well yourself," Lyndy said. I splashed her and we both laughed.

"Seriously, the only other person who springs to mind is Neville Lindblossom, the vice chair of the planning committee, but who would knock someone off to take over as the chair of a county committee? It's not as if any money was riding on it."

"Oh, what the heck, Phee. As long as you're snooping into everyone, add Neville to the list. Hey, I'll do one better. *I'll* add him to the list. I don't have much going on so I can check out social media for you. And the busybody gossip line. I'll see if my cranky aunt's heard anything."

"You're the best!"

Lyndy smiled. "I'll remember that. Hey, do you happen to know what time that Master Grillers competition is? I'm supposed to take my aunt. All I know is that it's a week from this Saturday and it better not be in the heat of the day. Only an idiot would schedule that."

"Don't worry. It's pretty much a late-day and early-evening affair, according to my mother. The entertainment will be in the social hall with tables set up so once people purchase stuff from the food trucks they can go inside to eat. The competition won't start until seven or eight, but I'll find out for sure."

We took a few laps, grabbed our towels and went home. The light was blinking on the landline when I got in the door and the caller ID indicated it was Marshall.

"I'll be home soon. Don't go to any trouble with dinner. Cosmo's computer was quite the treasure trove but not exactly what we had in mind. Nate's still scratching his head."

I checked the time of the message and realized I had just missed him. Drat! That meant I had to wait at least a half hour or more until I knew exactly what kind of treasures the lab techs were able to extract from Cosmo's computer. I tossed my towel into the wash and raced to take a quick shower.

"I'm home!" Marshall announced as I finished towel drying my hair. "I swear I've seen more of Bowman and Ranston in the past few days than the months before."

I walked into the kitchen and gave him a hug. "It only feels that way because they're so intense."

"Intense. Is that a euphemism for something else?"

"Pick whatever words you want."

He opened the fridge and took out an iced tea. "I'll be floating by midnight but honestly, it's like I can't get enough liquid in me. I knew Arizona was hot, but this is, well . . ."

"Like Satan's living room?"

"More or less."

"I've made tuna salad and banana bread. Tell me what was on Cosmo's computer while we eat."

"If I *could* tell you, I'd be working for the CIA, not partnering in Williams Investigations. Good thing we've got Rolo on board. The first file was something out of a prepubescent's dating handbook."

"What??"

"Oh, you heard me. Cosmo had a file list of women he dated, or possibly cheated on while he was still married. He ranked them from one to five stars with side comments."

"Ew. Any names of interest?"

"Only Abigail's. Boy, did she make the right choice to dump him. Not that it mattered in the long run, but still . . ."

"What else did you find?"

"Here's where it gets interesting." He reached in his pocket and handed me a flash drive. "Scan for viruses first, then have a field day. We're sending it to Rolo, too. It's a spreadsheet with what appear to be bank routing numbers—double nine sequence for bank and account. We didn't have time to study the totals but Cosmo may have had some sort of pyramid scheme going on. Let me tell you, Bowman and Ranston were really glad to drop this one in our laps."

"I thought Rolo was already looking into Cosmo's accounts."

"He is, but this gives him a shortcut."

I nodded. "As soon as I'm done here, I'm booting up the computer."

Three swallows of tuna salad, two bites of banana bread, and I raced to the computer. "I'll run the virus scan and hope it doesn't take too long. Don't clean up yet. I may want more banana bread."

Forty-five minutes later, Marshall and I studied Cosmo's spreadsheet like kids on a scavenger hunt. "You were right," I said. "Look how the amounts add up. I've seen this before. It's a multilevel marketing operation, only that kind of operation deals with tangible goods so it's not really illegal. I can tell you this much, the banking codes aren't any that I recognize. Not Wells Fargo, JP Morgan Chase, Bank of America or Citi. I know those routing numbers by heart. Give me a sec. I'll check Capital One, HSBC and PNC."

Marshall leaned back while I grabbed my iPhone and did a few quick searches. "Nope, none of those big guys."

"I hate to say it, hon, but this has Rolo written all over it. At least we know one thing. Whatever Cosmo was up to may turn out to be the very thing that got him killed."

"I'm not so sure. I mean, yeah, he was probably up to something nefarious, but I still think his murder was closer to home. Kind of personal. Right now, Enid, Clinton, and Marianne are the top runners as far as I'm concerned. I only wish there was some way to draw them out."

"I'm sure you'll think of something, only please don't let it be one of your mother's wacky plans that she and the book club come up with. Meanwhile, let Rolo take a gander at Cosmo's files. Maybe that's as far as we'll have to go."

I honestly wanted to share Marshall's optimism but I knew better. Especially when it involved my mother's community. Words like *impetuous*, *reckless*, and *impulsive* immediately sprang to mind. But in a million years, I never would have imagined just how far they'd go. But that was the least of my worries at the time.

• • •

The article that appeared in the *Glendale Star* also appeared in every news outlet from Peoria to Buckeye, including all of the Sun Cities. Even the ones as far away as Sun City Festival and Sun City Anthem. It gave the word *syndication* a whole new meaning and it gave me a royal headache the next morning when my aunt called the office.

Augusta had just finished a conversation with a new client when the phone rang again. This time from my aunt. I was a few feet away from the phone, having made myself a cup of coffee.

"For you, Phee," Augusta said and winked. "Your aunt Ina."

"Tell her I'll be right there. I'll pick up in my office."

"Lucky you," she mouthed as I marched to my office and closed the door behind me.

"Hi, Aunt Ina. What's up?"

"A disaster, that's what's up. Your uncle Louis is in the shower so he doesn't know about it yet."

"About what?"

"The transfer station. What else? It's in today's *Independent.* I'm surprised your mother hasn't seen it. She usually gets that paper on Wednesday. Sometimes earlier."

"Um, yeah. I read an article about it in the *Glendale Star*, but you know how these things go. It's only after the final vote when anyone can be really sure."

"We can't wait for the final vote. That's like waiting for the final nail in the coffin. Hold on a minute, your uncle is shouting." Then to Louis. "What? What do you want?" Then, "I'm talking to Phee. What? No. No one's planning a funeral. I used an expression. That's all. I left some lox and pickled herring on the table for your breakfast." Then back to me. "Your uncle has ears like a bat. Too bad he only hears one word at a time."

*That's better than the book club ladies and Herb's crew.*

"I'm not sure what else can be done at this time. You've all sent letters, had lots of clubs and organizations send letters, and you've even had petitions against the transfer station signed and delivered."

"The article says the vote will take place a week from this coming Monday. That's only ten days away and everyone's so wound up about that murder, not to mention the Master Grillers contest, that I'm afraid we'll be smelling refuse all the way into our senility."

"Try to calm down, Aunt Ina. I'm sure we'll think of something to convince that planning commission to vote no."

"Think fast, Phee, or your uncle will never be able to enjoy the full pleasure of his smoked herrings again. Garbage odors travel, you know."

I was sure she meant the transfer station, but frankly, the aroma of smoked herring travels too . . .

# CHAPTER 34

"I better give my cousin Kirk a heads-up," I said to Augusta. "And I'm doing it now so I can beat my aunt to the phone. She'll wail, carry on, and plant a guilt trip on him. It's a family thing."

"Glad I grew up on a dairy farm. No time for family issues when the cows had to be milked."

I nodded and made a beeline for my office. Seconds later, I had Kirk on the phone.

"If your mother calls about the transfer station, ignore it. There was an article in the local papers insinuating it was a done deal. But who knows about these things? The vote is in a week or so and the community is still putting pressure on the planning commission to nix the idea."

"I'll do what I always do—let it go to voicemail and deal with it later."

I laughed. "Boy, do we think alike. Anyway, I promised her I'd do whatever I could to help sway the vote. Of course, I have no idea *how*, but I'm hoping for an epiphany."

"If any of those commission members are on the take, you'll need more than an epiphany. That kind of thing happened a year or so ago in the community next to ours. Always something going on in the Boston area. It wasn't a transfer station, though. It was a housing development with zero lot lines. Drew a tremendous amount of attention from the press."

"Did it go through?"

"Nope. Died on the spot when it was discovered the vice chair of the committee was the contractor's brother-in-law. Nepotism, favors, and all that."

"Oh my gosh. Neville!"

"Who?"

"Uh, sorry. Neville Lindblossom. He's the vice chair of the committee. He's been under my radar until recently. I *did* tell you about the murder of the committee's chair, didn't I?"

"If the name is Cosmo, you did. Along with your mother and mine."

"Good, because I've got so much going on I keep forgetting who I told *what* to."

"I think it's because we're creeping out of middle age."

"Speak for yourself."

"Judy's seriously thinking of using that note app on her phone to remind her of what she told her friends. She said she didn't want to turn into one of those people who tell you the same story over and over again."

"Tell your wife not to worry. Most of us have already forgotten. Thanks, Kirk, for mentioning the vice chair. I need to get on it."

"Hey, anything I can do to keep my mother off my back, I will."

"Give Judy my love."

If Kirk hadn't brought up Cosmo's second in line, I would have let things be. Thankfully Lyndy offered to have a look-see and I knew she'd share anything pertinent with me. Still, I made a note to touch base with her.

The day rolled by at its usual pace. Nate and Marshall were in and out of the office as they juggled new client meetings with their ongoing investigations. Meanwhile, I centered on my work, feeling a genuine sense of fulfillment when the numbers added up. Unfortunately, nothing else did and Thursday rolled into Friday.

• • •

Too tired to take something out of the freezer, let alone prepare an actual meal, Marshall and I chose to have dinner at the Lakeside Grill in Vistancia. It was located in a popular shopping center close to home and featured a variety of comfort and bar foods—something we both loved. The heat wave forced us indoors rather than dining on their patio, but we were able to snag a table by the large picture window so we could people watch as we ate.

Ordering was a no-brainer. It was Friday night and their endless Atlantic cod fish fry was not to be missed. With sides of coleslaw and French fries, we were in heaven. So absorbed in our eating that at first I didn't notice who walked in.

It took me a minute but the voice from the table behind ours was one I'd heard before. I turned my head slightly so as not to be obvious and then quickly turned back.

"That's Marianne," I whispered to Marshall, barely audible. "Clinton's girlfriend. I caught the side of her face. That's her all right."

"I'm looking at the two girlfriends across from her but she's facing outward. I can't see her face."

"It's her all right." I made sure to keep my voice low and mouth a few words. The restaurant wasn't what I'd call noisy, but it wasn't quiet either. It was your typical sports bar/family spot. "I doubt she'll say anything incriminating but hey, you never know."

"Guess that means we'll be chewing our food quietly, huh?"

I gave him a playful kick under the table and continued to munch on the fried fish. We caught bits and pieces of their conversation but nothing that made me put down my fork to listen. Mostly small talk about the best workout gyms and bathing suits that covered flabby thighs. I popped a vinegar-coated fry into my mouth and proceeded to wash it down with an O'Doul's when Marianne announced, "That's right, girls. I'm coming into some money. Not a dead relative, although someone *did* die. But it wasn't as if he left me any money." Then she giggled. "More like a better chance at the roulette wheel."

My eyes widened and I put a finger to my lips. Marshall leaned closer and we both held still, but just like that, Marianne stopped talking and one of the other girls took over. "I absolutely *love* roulette. We've got to do a road trip to Vegas. It's so damn boring here in the summer."

Then the other girl spoke. "It'll have to wait until that barbeque contest is over. Won't it, Marianne? That's what you were referring to, wasn't it?"

"Clinton promised me some fun moolah along with a shiny you-know-what for my left ring finger."

By now I was twitchy. I tapped my foot under the table and squirmed in my seat. I took a few deep breaths as well as another sip of the O'Doul's.

"But what if he doesn't win?" the first girlfriend asked.

"Oh, *he* will. They've got it covered."

At that point I grabbed Marshall by the wrist and mouthed, "She's going to mess with Herb's marinade *and* get rid of Therm."

Marshall made one of those calming gestures with his hands that frantic parents do when they're afraid their kids are going to have a meltdown in public. "Listen some more and we'll talk in the car."

Too bad for us that the topic of Marianne coming into money was quickly shoved aside when one of her girlfriends mentioned concert tickets for Talking Stick Casino. From there, the subject morphed into music lineups and gambling before the girls stood and left.

I was relieved Marianne didn't notice me, but then again, how could she? I was bent over my plate like my great Alte Tante Rosie spooning matzo ball soup into her mouth.

"You can come up for air now," Marshall announced. "They're gone."

"We need to alert Bowman and Ranston that Marianne may pull a regrettable stunt at the competition a week from tomorrow."

"Texting them now. Those two need time when it comes to digesting things like this. Nate and I have gotten used to it."

"It's like a horse race, isn't it? With Enid and Marianne neck and neck."

Marshall put his arm around my shoulder as we exited the restaurant. "Usually a third or even a fourth horse pulls up from behind. Don't get too focused on your top contenders. A new name may emerge for all we know."

"I'll laugh if it turns out to be Neville. Lyndy couldn't wait to pull up the dirt on him. I think she's getting hooked on armchair sleuthing."

"Smart gal. It's the safest kind."

• • •

I had the following day off and for once I didn't have to start off my Saturday at Bagels 'n More with the book club ladies. My mother, along with Shirley and Lucinda, was volunteering at a local food bank so I was spared. That meant I could get in some swimming, give the house a good cleaning, and pick up a few groceries before turning to my murder map for another round of guesswork. What I didn't count on was a six fifty-five reveille from Ranston. All he needed was the bugle to complete the call.

"Mrs. Kimball . . . Gregory . . . whatever, this is Deputy Ranston."

"Kimball-Gregory. Phee. Hold on, I take it you want to talk to Marshall."

"I can tell you. He's only going to tell you anyway. We made an arrest in the Pruett murder. Got her dead to rights on a tip-off."

"Oh my gosh—Marianne. Did she murder Therm, too? Is that what happened? She must have done it right after Marshall texted you and Deputy Bowman."

"What are you talking about? We don't know about any other murders or Marianne."

The pinprick hairs that stood at attention on the back of my neck gradually subsided. "Then it was Enid, right? Enid Flox."

"For your information, Miss Abigail McFadden, a Sun City West resident, was arrested on suspicion of murder. That name should be familiar. She's the other District 4 planning commission member. Hmm, looks like the commission's going to be short a few votes."

"Abigail? What? How?"

"Who's on the phone, hon?" Marshall called out. "I'm just about done shaving. I'll be right there."

"They've made an arrest," I shouted. Then, back to Ranston, "You said tip-off. What did you mean?"

"Our office got an anonymous call late yesterday afternoon claiming we'd find evidence of Cosmo's blood on one of Abigail's golf clubs. Even told us where the golf club was. Got a search warrant and the rest is history. Lab confirmed the results pronto." He went on about the golf club as I tried to process his two key words—*Abigail* and *arrest*.

"Um, where's Abigail now?"

"Still at the posse office. Can't transport her to the Fourth Avenue Jail until later today."

"Can she have visitors?"

"I'll make an exception for your office."

"Okay. Thanks."

Marshall walked toward his dresser and took out a shirt. "Who did they arrest?"

"Abigail McFadden, but I'm positive she's been set up. We've got to speak with her. Ranston said it's okay."

"What evidence did they have?"

"Ugh. Here's the worst part—tangible evidence. Cosmo's blood on one of her golf clubs. Not easily explainable."

"Was he specific?"

"Oh, yeah. A Callaway Hyper X Driver. Those are the ones with the really flat side surface, aren't they?"

"Uh-huh. Did Ranston say anything more about who tipped him off?"

"No, but it's *way* too convenient. Too tidy."

"My thought as well. Hang on, my phone's vibrating. It's got to be Nate."

In that instant, my swim plans, my housecleaning, and my grocery shopping evaporated along with taking another gander at my murder map. "I'm going with you," I said. "Well, in a manner of speaking. I'll take my own car to the posse office."

"Breakfast at McDonald's on the way?"

"Yep. Let's get going before they run out of Egg McMuffins and black coffee."

"Then some serious arrests will have to be made."

# CHAPTER 35

Abigail looked as if she'd lost everything in a tornado. Her rosy complexion, which I noted when I first saw her at the public hearing, was now gray. In addition, her hair hung listlessly to her chin and it looked as if she had slept in her clothes. She was seated in a small room at the posse office with only a table, four chairs, and a tinted window that couldn't have been more than a foot square.

"Do I know you?" she asked when Marshall and I entered the room. "You look familiar."

"We're Phee and Marshall Gregory, from Williams Investigations. We were at the public hearing in the Stardust Theater. You don't have to tell us anything, but rest assured, we're not law enforcement. I'm the company's bookkeeper/accountant and my husband is a detective."

"I can't afford to hire a private detective," she said. "I'll have to wipe out my savings to get a decent criminal attorney."

"We're not looking to be hired," Marshall said. "We're here because we've been assisting with the investigation into Cosmo's murder and frankly, your arrest was a bit unexpected."

"Unexpected?" she sobbed. "It was outrageous. I don't think I've stopped shaking. When those deputies showed up with a search warrant, they knew exactly where to look and what to look for—my garage, my golf cart, and my golf clubs. Goodness. I haven't played golf since last March. I pulled a tendon in my leg and by the time it healed, the weather had turned wretched. I'm not one of those golfers who relish getting up at four to tee off at five thirty. Summer golfing is out for me."

"Mind if we sit?" I asked. I had already approached the table and started to pull out a chair.

"Please do."

Marshall propped his elbows on the table and rested his head on his fists. "And yet, the evidence was striking."

"I know." Abigail started to sob again. "I can't explain it. All I can tell you is that I clean my clubs thoroughly when I return from the golf course. Clean *and* polish. I'm kind of a fanatic when it comes to that sort of thing."

"Who else might have had access to your house?" Marshall asked. "A cleaning service? A neighbor or relative with a spare key?"

Abigail shook her head. "No one. Absolutely no one. And there were no signs of any break-ins whatsoever."

I tried to envision how someone could have set her up and suddenly I

162

remembered my uncle Louis's house in Sun City Grand before he and my aunt were married. Aunt Ina always pitched a fit because Louis insisted on leaving his garage door open an inch or two in order to let air in during the summer.

"Abigail," I asked, "do you close your garage door all the way or do you leave an inch or two for air?"

"Only in the summer. Like now. Oh, no. You don't suppose—But how? I mean, it's only an inch or so."

Marshall clasped his hands and stretched. "An inch or so is all it takes. With the door up from the ground, the lock mechanism doesn't activate. That means anyone with enough strength can manually force the door up and close it down, leaving the same inch or so as to be unnoticed."

"But how were they able to get Cosmo's blood from the real murder weapon onto my golf club? And when?"

"The *when*'s the easy part. Most likely the night of the murder while the evidence was still malleable. Then they waited for the right time to accuse you. As for getting the blood on the club, that's fairly easy, too. All they would have needed was a Q-tip or a small brush like the kind women carry around in their makeup kits. Add a tinge of Cosmo's blood and a few grains of sand from the ground and—"

"I know," Abigail whispered. "My Callaway club then became the weapon that killed my ex-boyfriend. Listen, you need to believe me, I had no reason to do such a thing. None whatsoever. We were already through so why bother to kill him? It's not like I was after money or he was blackmailing me. Can I really be tried for murder over some trumped-up evidence?"

I gulped. "I'm afraid so. But motive's a strong factor. Did Cosmo ever mention someone who had it in for him?"

Abigail shook her head. "No. He wasn't particularly fond of Enid, but given her personality, I don't know too many people who would be. Myself included. She even threatened to have me removed from the planning commission for fraternizing with Cosmo. Can you imagine? We were consenting adults. And besides, there was nothing in the regulations that would have prevented it. Heck, I'm surprised she didn't notice Neville sniffing around. He asked me out once but I politely declined."

"Yikes."

"Cosmo never expressed any concerns that Enid might do something to him. As far as everyone else went, I honestly can't say." She patted her hair for a minute and rubbed the dampness from her cheeks. "Cosmo was involved with all sorts of business dealings. I know that much. But he didn't act as if any of that posed a threat. Oh my gosh. I'm really doomed, aren't I?"

I hate giving people false hope, but when I looked at her tearstained cheeks and disheveled appearance, I genuinely felt sorry for her. Unfortunately, the wrong words came out of my mouth. "It wouldn't hurt to hire an attorney." Then I quickly added, "Just in case."

Thankfully Marshall was able to remedy the situation. If only for a minute.

"I'm sure the deputies will review the circumstances under which the evidence was found in your garage and determine its legitimacy."

"So you think I've been set up?"

Marshall and I exchanged glances before he answered. "The evidence came a bit too easy. Still, it's tangible and that won't change."

Abigail folded her hands and looked down. "Someone set me up to be the scapegoat."

"Then we'll need to find out *who* and *why*. If you think of anything, please have your attorney call us."

"Why are you doing this for me? I can't pay you."

"No," he answered. "We're paid by the county, and if the real murderer is out there, he or she needs to be caught." We closed the door behind us as we left the room and reentered the outer office.

"So, what did you think?" Ranston pushed himself back from the small desk where he was glued to the computer.

"It's a damn setup," Marshall said. "Even you guys know that."

"No kidding."

My jaw dropped the second Ranston said those words. "Then why did you arrest her?"

"To ferret out the real killer. Which reminds me," he said to Marshall, "Bowman and I need to meet with you and Nate to come up with a game plan for next Saturday. Later today? Got a feeling whoever saw to it Cosmo fell off the perch may try it again. Transfer station my rump. They're interested in that big money payoff for grilling some stupid ribs."

"Can you believe that?" I shook Marshall's arm all the way to our cars.

"Typical Bowman and Ranston. Go figure. Once news of Abigail's arrest gets out there, she'll be out on bail. Less than twenty-four hours would be my guess. They can't drop the charges because they're sitting on solid evidence but thankfully they know it was planted."

"Poor Abigail."

"No. Poor us. Nate and I will now have to sit through some mind-numbing meeting listening to Bowman and Ranston go over their plan, one excruciating step after the next. Hope the rest of your day is better."

"I only have one piece of unfinished business—Neville. I'll give Lyndy a buzz and see what she's found."

"Sounds good."

"Cold sandwiches and chips okay for dinner? I can't bear the thought of even turning on the microwave in this heat."

"Or firing up the grill. Cold sandwiches sound fine. Don't knock yourself out."

"No, Boar's Head, Oscar Mayer, and Hillshire Farm have already done that."

I called Lyndy as soon as I got home and we decided to meet in an hour and a half at the closest Starbucks for a Frappuccino. We also agreed to follow it up with a quick dip in the pool. That gave me enough time to get a load of laundry in and straighten up the house. We had enough food in the fridge and pantry so I had no problem putting off the grocery shopping.

"Did you unearth anything mind-boggling about Neville?" I asked Lyndy before she even had a chance to pull her chair from the table and set her drink down.

"He's an actuary with a firm in Fountain Hills near Scottsdale. An actuary. Good golly, Phee, that's even more boring than what you do. No offense meant."

I laughed. "It's probably a toss-up. Calculating insurance risks and premiums or balancing ledgers. Did you find out anything else?"

"He's on LinkedIn but what I saw was even more boring. Nothing on Facebook or any of the more exciting social media sites. Still, I was able to do some prying. He's single and lives in a condo in Scottsdale. A rather pricey condo, according to Zillow, and in a prime real estate location. And get this—he has an art collection that was featured in a local news article a few years back. And I'm not talking Elvis renderings on black-velvet canvas."

"I suppose if someone's single and didn't have to shell out money for their children's college expenses, that might explain it. But artwork, huh? I'm beginning to wonder if Neville was part of the alleged business deal of Cosmo's that went belly up. At least according to Gloria Wong, the latest voice in my mother's gossip link."

"If Cosmo and Neville both lost money on a shared business deal, it wouldn't make sense for Neville to kill his partner. Especially if they were both embroiled in a shady transfer station deal."

I took a giant sip of my caramel frap and set the glass in front of me. "I don't suppose we'll ever find out before next Saturday and I can't very well ask Rolo because he's already looking into offshore banking accounts for us."

"Whoa. Hold on. Why Saturday? Why do you need to know before next Saturday?"

"Aargh. Neville was my last link in this so-called investigation of mine, and I jumped right into it before telling you what's going on."

"You mean you've discovered something?"

"Yeah, but nothing I didn't already know about Bowman and Ranston."

"Huh?"

Lyndy was mesmerized as I proceeded to tell her about Abigail's arrest and how she was being used in a ploy so that the deputies could ferret out the real killer at Saturday's Master Grillers competition. Had the Food Network known, they might have swapped places with *America's Most Wanted*.

"Crystal-clear evidence on her golf club? Gosh, I'm not even in this business and I can shout the word *setup* from fifty paces. That poor woman. Tell me, what do those deputies expect to happen on Saturday? Other than the grilling contest and your mother's crew stuffing their faces along with my aunt?"

"They think whoever killed Cosmo most likely did it for a greater share of the winnings or to rig the competition altogether."

"Ew. That's not sounding good. If it's the first thing, then that would mean Therm or Clinton, right?"

"Or Marianne, Clinton's money-hungry girlfriend. If she's behind this, I wouldn't put it past her to ensure Clinton is the only one in the competition. I can picture it now—a slow-acting poison delivered seamlessly to Therm. Slow enough for him to hold on until the winning team is announced."

"That's so, so . . . ."

"Agatha Christie?"

"I was going to say diabolical."

"Want to hear what's worse?"

Lyndy grimaced.

"The second reason." I took a long swallow from my now half-empty drink. "That would mean we're back to Herb and his crew. However it shakes out, it's not going to be good."

# CHAPTER 36

"*Not going to be good.*" The classic understatement. I'm not usually prophetic, but in that instance, I could have hung a psychic shingle over my door with a neat little horoscope or even a crystal ball. Same deal with Marshall. He had been right about Abigail all along. She was released on her own recognizance later that same day but directed not to leave her residence until further notice.

The week that preceded Saturday's grand event was like a rubber band about to snap at any moment. Frantic calls from my mother about the transfer station, a looming murderer since no one believed it was Abigail, and Essie, who had now decided she only wanted to eat the dog's food. Had it only been my mother's calls, I might have skated through the week unscathed, but no, the calls also came from my aunt Ina and the rest of the book club ladies. By Thursday afternoon I was ready to chew my fingernails down to the nubs.

My aunt seemed to call every morning around nine or ten to inform Augusta and me that my uncle would be enjoying his last kippers and baked potato breakfast, or his final fillet of herring breakfast, before succumbing to the noxious fumes certain to emanate from the transfer station.

Then, there was Shirley. Panicked that Cosmo's real killer wasn't done. And Cecilia, who informed me she'd be sneaking holy water from the church into the social hall on Saturday. *Just in case.* Lucinda and Louise called me, too, if only to ask if I had heard anything more about the case.

My favorite call came from Myrna. She offered to drop off an arsenal of her best self-defense items, including wasp and hornet spray, bear spray, one large and two mini-Screamers, and some sort of sticky spray that sounded more like those confetti-in-a-can things that kids bring to parties or when they're out trick-or-treating. I graciously declined.

However, the most unnerving call of all came from Herb on the Friday morning before the grill-off.

"Hey, cutie," he said when Augusta transferred the call to my office, "I'm phoning you because I didn't want to upset your mother."

*Great. You can upset me.*

"Uh, hi, Herb. What's going on?"

"Remember when Kenny got that bearded dragon a while back?"

"Please don't tell me he plans to bring it to the competition. It's bad enough my mother shows up to events with Streetman in that tote bag, and now the cat in that hooded shirt of hers."

"No, nothing like that. He found a pet shop in Sun City that sells crickets for half the price of the one in Surprise."

I was totally lost but let him continue.

"I went down there yesterday. It's in a strip mall behind the CVS pharmacy. EJ's Reptiles."

"Uh-huh. I know where that is."

"Then you know there's a beauty parlor right next door to it. Kenny and I were leaving with a bag of crickets when who should come out of the beauty parlor but that Enid woman from the planning commission. Same one who mouthed off about your mother's cat."

It was like getting walloped in the head.

"You still listening?" he asked.

"Uh-huh."

"Good, because this takes the cake. A skinny redhead followed her out the door. They didn't notice Kenny and me in the alcove by our door. Anyway, the redhead says to Enid, 'Are you going to that Food Network barbeque tomorrow?' and Enid says, 'Might as well. If the vote goes as planned I might be persona non grata in Sun City West.'"

"Oh, no." I couldn't believe my ears. "You're telling me it's a done deal? Poor Louis and his kippers."

"What?"

"Never mind. Was that what you called to tell me?"

"Sorry, cutie, but that was only the first inning."

"There's more?"

"Oh, yeah. Next thing I know, the redhead says, 'I hope the SOB chokes on one of his marinated ribs.' Then Enid says, 'Only one way to make sure. Meet me there. You should be finished by then.'"

As if I wasn't frantic enough that Marianne was about to pull a food-related stunt, now the Borgia sisters, for lack of a better description, might indeed be planning a stunt of their own. And while I wasn't sure what the relationship was between them, I was pretty certain the redhead was Bernice. *Wonderful. And just when I find a decent beautician.*

"Herb, you need to let Bowman and Ranston know what you and Kenny overheard."

"Are you kidding? Those two will think I made it up to get the heat off my own back."

"Aargh. I hate to say it, but you may be right. Look, I'll let Nate and Marshall know."

"Tell your crew to be extra vigilant tomorrow."

When I got off the phone, I stepped to the outer office and strode to Augusta's desk.

"Looks like it might be a tied score tomorrow."

She looked up from some paperwork. "The contest?"

"No, the attempts at food tampering."

• • •

That evening, Marshall and I went over the Master Grillers program in detail. We downloaded the schedule of events from the Sun City West website, and conferred with Nate at least a half dozen times between six and nine at night. As for the deputies, it was anyone's guess.

I had a fitful night's sleep and woke with a pounding headache that didn't quit until I finished my second cup of coffee.

"You don't have to go into work today," Marshall said, "if you feel that lousy. It's only a half day."

"No, I need to keep my mind busy. Like I said earlier, I have a really bad feeling about tonight."

"Take a number and join the rest of us."

"Hold on, here she is now," I heard Augusta say the second I got in the door. Marshall gave me a wink and went directly to his office. We'd taken his car because we planned to make an early escape and take in a swim before making an appearance at the Master Grillers event around four.

Thankfully, the sheriff's office, in conjunction with the posse, had arranged for deputies and volunteers to look over the setup in order to ensure there'd be no funny business. However, knowing about Marianne, and now Enid, Marshall and Nate arranged to do some snooping around as well.

"Who?" I mouthed to Augusta, but I already had a sinking feeling I knew.

"Your mother."

I glared at her and took the call. "What's up, Mom?"

"I'll only keep you a minute. Whatever you do, don't wear sandals to the barbeque."

"Huh? Is this a trick question? There's no dress code and besides, I plan to wear mules. Very comfortable."

"Good. The paths all around the rec center were recently sculpted with sand. Don't know which idiot came up with that idea but the sand, aside from being slippery and dangerous for seniors, gets into sandals. The administration plans on redoing it with concrete but not until the fall. I wanted to give you a heads-up."

"Thanks for the tip-off."

"The book club ladies are meeting in the welcome courtyard at four. That's when the food trucks will open for business. Not your run-of-the-mill trucks either. Gourmet food trucks. I have the list."

Before I could say a word, she went on, "Mediterranean Magic, the

Lobster Shack, Roasted, Toasted, and Seared, Fire Flamed Pizza, Beignets and Bagels—"

"Cut it out. All I had for breakfast was some toast."

"You'll make up for it later. We figured we'd eat first and then go into the social hall to watch the square dancers. Did I mention the ukulele clubs from Sun City and Sun City West will also be performing?"

"I'm sure you did." *And I'm sure I tried to block it from my mind.*

"Cecilia plans to get there early so she can commandeer two of the large patio tables that overlook the pool and the great lawn. The actual competition doesn't start until seven but Myrna, Paul, and I have to be at the KSCW radio booth at five forty-five. The booth is off to the side in the social hall so we can give the listening audience a blow-by-blow description. The grand prize is nothing to sneeze at. They'll have a guest appearance on the Food Network and split a hundred-thousand-dollar prize. If Herb's team wins, they'll each wind up with twenty grand."

*And more relatives they never knew they had will come knocking on their doors.*

"Sounds like all of you have gotten over your fear that Cosmo's killer will make an appearance."

"What? None of us have gotten over our fear. We simply know how to approach a situation with calmness and decorum while we trust in our law enforcement professionals."

"Since when?"

"Since your boss and your husband got on the case. I imagine they have an entire tactical plan in place. It probably even has some nifty little code name as well. Like Anaconda or Blink."

More like Punt.

"Okay. Sounds good. See you then."

"Is she bringing the pet parade with her?" Augusta asked as soon as I got off the phone.

"I honestly didn't want to know."

When Marshall and I left the office at midday, we grabbed subs at Which Wich, a neat little franchise that we first discovered in Tucson, and made a beeline for the pool the minute we got home. He mentioned something about needing the water to cool down his core temperature but even if that was the case, it wouldn't have done a thing for our blood pressures as the evening unfolded.

We arrived at the RH Johnson Recreation Center at a little before four and immediately spotted Nate conferring with Ranston near the archway to the welcome courtyard. I knew tables and chairs would be spread out all over the courtyard, as well as the social hall, but I didn't expect to see misters hanging from every ceiling, alcove, and rafter. Unlike home patio misters, these were high-speed vapor misters that sent cooling air in every direction. The heat wave was still in full force, but now a tad more bearable.

"The plan is to keep a tight perimeter around the contestants and the judges," Ranston said as soon as Marshall and I approached. "They've got a table set up to the left of the patio for the judges. Bigwig grilling chefs. Didn't know it was a thing."

"Who?" I asked.

Ranston pulled out his phone and studied it. "John Markus from *BBQ Pitmasters*, Melissa Cookston from Memphis BBQ, and Bobby Flay from—"

I held my palm up. "No need to explain. He's a celebrity chef with restaurants in Vegas and New York City."

Ranston looked directly at me. Then at Nate and Marshall. "Like I said, 'tight perimeter.'"

# CHAPTER 37

"Why don't you head over to the welcome courtyard," Marshall said, "and visit with your mom and the book club ladies?"

"Visit?"

"A nice euphemism for 'make sure they're not up to something wacky.' Meanwhile, Nate and I will be monitoring the perimeter." He tried to keep a straight face when he said the word *perimeter* but he had to cover his mouth to keep from laughing.

"Have fun. I'll catch up with you later."

I moseyed over to the welcome courtyard and sure enough, my mother was right. The sandy pathway was slick and annoying. Sandals would have made it deadly. The parking lot in front of the complex was lined up with enough food trucks to feed a battalion. And from the look of things, that's exactly what they were about to do. The crowds had already begun to line up at the trucks of their choice, and as I passed Crepes and Croissants, I spotted my uncle Louis and waved. A few feet away, Cindy Dolton was chomping on a huge burrito but too engrossed to see me.

The Booked 4 Murder book club was in its full glory with all of the ladies at the table except my aunt and Louise.

"Over here, Phee," my mother called out. "Your aunt and uncle, as well as Louise, are making the first round for us."

I pictured a never-ending smorgasbord and I wasn't far from wrong. What I hadn't envisioned, and I could have kicked myself for not doing so, was the parade of news vans that stretched from the bowling alley all the way to the far end of the social hall. Maybe Ranston didn't have a clue who Bobby Flay was, but KPHO, FOX10, ABC15, and 12NEWS sure did.

"When we're done eating, we're heading directly to the social hall. We don't want to miss the square dancers and the ukulele clubs," Cecilia said. "Thank goodness the Rhythm Tappers stayed out of this one. I hate performing in front of people."

"What time do you start MC-ing?" I asked my mother.

"At six sharp, although Myrna, Paul, and I are supposed to be at the radio station's table fifteen minutes prior. I thought I mentioned that yesterday."

"Um, you probably did but it must have gone to the back of my mind." *Along with the recent anecdotes about Streetman and Essie.* I squinted to get a better look at my mother's top and was relieved there was no cat inside a compartment. When no one was looking, I bent down to see if she had placed that all-too-familiar tote under the table, but with the dense seating, it was impossible to tell.

A few minutes later, my aunt and uncle returned to the table laden with trays of food. Louise was a few feet behind them, only she had managed to get a young worker to carry her enormous platter of mixed shish kabobs. The aroma of roasted pork, beef, and shrimp put my taste buds on high alert and I had forgotten all about the sandwich I devoured from Which Wich.

I sat between Shirley and Lucinda and listened intently to a conversation that may or may not have involved a Telemundo episode when, like a boomerang, Cecilia brought up the transfer station vote. "It may not be a done deal after all."

Suddenly, all conversation ceased and all eyes were on her as she continued. "That is to say, I don't really know for sure, but I saw Paul earlier this morning at the gas station. He was filling up his golf cart and said something about having a plan that would all but ensure the commission votes down the proposal."

I gulped. "What plan? What kind of harebrained, ill-conceived plan?"

"He didn't say, only that it was sure to get the attention of the news media this evening and embarrass the planning commission to the point where they would nix the plan."

I leaned forward and looked at my mother. "Did you hear that? He's probably going to say something regrettable when he's on the air. You and Myrna need to cut him off before it's too late." Then I added, "You do that all the time without thinking. This time give it some thought."

Shirley put her hand on my wrist. "It'll be all right, honey. Your mother and Myrna can handle Paul."

*In what universe?*

At quarter to five, the group, having consumed enough food to last the remainder of the weekend, left the table en route to the social hall. The crowd in front of the building had almost tripled since I first arrived and the food truck lines showed no signs of slowing down. I ambled along with everyone else when I suddenly took notice of some sort of travel bag that my mother wheeled behind her. It was deep indigo with a logo of a cat and dog on the side.

Its wheels made small indents in the sand but the surface was smooth enough so as not to jostle the contents. I strode toward her at breakneck speed.

"You've got Streetman and Essie in there. Don't you?"

"Honestly, Phee. Calm down. We're in the middle of a heat wave. I couldn't take a chance the air would go out on them."

"You have a fairly new system with biannual maintenance."

"Things happen."

I bent down and took a look. Sure enough, the little fur balls were seated side by side and looked no worse for wear. In addition, a water bottle, like the kind shown in crates for lab animals, hung from the side of the carrier.

"I've seen it all," I said to her.

"Good. Now you can watch the square dancers and listen to the ukulele songs."

I caught a glimpse of Nate in the far left of the social hall and figured he, along with Marshall and whomever the deputies added, were on guard duty. Seating was at a premium and there was no way the book club ladies, let alone my aunt and uncle, would find adjacent chairs.

"We've got to split up," Lucinda said. "Let's try to get chairs close to the patio doors where the competition will take place. They've got a big area cleared out. Must be for the square dancers."

Without waiting for a response, she elbowed her way through the crowd followed by everyone else, including my mother, who seamlessly dragged the pet carrier behind her. My aunt, at one point, grabbed me by the elbow and whispered, "Does she have to take them everywhere?" to which I replied, "I'm afraid so."

I didn't expect to find Herb or his crew in the audience. Most likely they were either taking advantage of the food trucks or, as he explained to me when we last spoke, guarding over their ribs and marinade in their assigned social hall kitchen. Since so many activities take place in the social hall, including cooking classes, two full-service kitchens were added to accommodate the community need—the east kitchen and the west kitchen, separated by restrooms.

As I looked about, I saw the book club ladies grabbing the available seats by the patio and followed suit. A few minutes later, someone from the rec center approached the front of the room and announced the arrival of the Sun City West Square Dance Club. Following an exuberant round of applause, a dozen dancers took us through handholds, allemande left, promenades and what could best be described as circling around.

When the square dancing ended, the rec center announcer returned to introduce the Sun City and Sun City West Ukulele Clubs. A dozen or so women and two men lined up, all dressed in Hawaiian garb—muumuus for the women and floral island shirts for the men. With their ukuleles in hand, one of the women stepped forward and mentioned a few words about the club and beginner classes before motioning for the first number to begin. It was "Tiny Bubbles," apparently a ukulele favorite according to the announcement.

Nervous about the possibility of Streetman yapping or Essie yowling, I spent more time keeping an eye on my mother. That's probably why I didn't notice Bernice on stage with the rest of the ukulele performers until they were well into their second number—"Somewhere Over the Rainbow."

Maybe Herb got it wrong and she and Enid wouldn't pose a threat to Clinton after all. Her comment, "You should be finished by then," might have referred to the ukulele performance and not the salon schedule. I watched intently as the graceful men and women continued with "What a Wonderful World" and "Aloha 'Oe."

Then, a cacophony of loud shrieks permeated the room. The noise came from outside and for a split second I thought perhaps Bobby Flay had made an entrance to a crowd of adoring food fanatics. The ukulele chorus continued but they were quickly drowned out by more shrieks, a few screams, and the unmistakable sound of dogs barking.

To make matters worse, Streetman joined the canine choir as well, only it was more of a low growl. I stood, motioned for the ladies to remain seated, and raced out the front doors. I estimated that it must have taken me a full minute to fully comprehend what I saw in the parking lot. It was a bright green golf cart with enormous posters on either side that read, "The Transfer Station Vote is Fishy," and "Toss Back the Garbage Catch of the Day."

But that wasn't the worst of it. Dangling from behind the golf cart were half a dozen dead fish, their mouths secured to manila rope that had been attached to the rear of the cart. And as if that spectacle wasn't enough, a few neighboring dogs had either jumped their fences or broken free from their owners to chase after the fish float as the driver maneuvered through the parking lot beeping his horn.

Narrowly missing the sea of senior citizens, the driver continued the foray into the far reaches of the recreation center complex. Nothing was safe. The food truck vendors closed their windows and told the patrons to be patient while more canines found their way to what they hoped was a fish dinner.

By now, I was certain the social hall emptied out. A throng of spectators descended on the parking lot like an invading army and everyone shouted at once. Including my mother, whose voice all but rattled the nearby windows on the houses adjacent to the parking lot.

"It's Paul! Cecilia was right. This is his plan. Smelly dead fish to embarrass the planning commission."

I elbowed my way toward her and regretted it the moment she latched on to my wrist. "You've got to find a way to stop him. Look! He's circling around and doubling back. Now he's headed straight toward the zymurgy club booth with at least five big dogs behind his golf cart. They'll knock over the wine and beer glasses."

"I'm not about to chase after a golf cart dragging slippery, smelling fish. One wrong step and I'll be on the ground."

"Well, I can't do it, Phee. I'm getting too old for that sort of stuff. You're physically fit with all that swimming you do. Oh, no, those dogs are definitely going to knock over the wineglasses."

Myrna, who stood a few feet from us, shook her head. "Nope. Don't think so. They're more interested in the fish. Look how they're following the scent on the ground."

If the truth be known, I didn't want to look at anything. And certainly not at unruly dogs going after dead fish behind Paul Schmidt's golf cart. Lamentably, the news media *did* want to look. Not only that, but they were intent on filming as well. Heaven forbid their viewers miss an opportunity to watch Paul's fish parade ad nauseam. Reporters complete with camera crews took off on foot in an effort to out-scoop the next guy.

"One good thing, Harriet," Myrna went on. "We won't have to worry about Paul saying anything inappropriate over the air. Why talk when you can show-and-tell instead?"

The ruckus in the parking lot rose to a crescendo, augmented by Streetman's groans and Essie's mews. Worse yet, it wasn't limited to my mother's pets or Paul with his golf cart and canine companions. The sheriff's office, along with the local posse, had arrived on scene complete with their red and blue flashers.

If I was Bobby Flay, I would have hopped the next ride out of here and removed myself from any further Food Network competitions.

# CHAPTER 38

I watched, numbly, as the sheriff's cars joined the melee and chased Paul and his stinky golf cart around the RH Johnson Parking Lot. Then, something occurred to me and I prayed to the gods I was wrong. If not, Paul may have unwittingly created a diversion that would allow Marianne to get away with murder if she was serious about getting Therm out of the picture. Or, at the very least, food tampering, if she wanted to be sure Herb's team didn't stand a chance.

Without wasting a second, I charged back into the social hall and headed straight to the first kitchen on my right—the east kitchen. Either Herb and his crew would be in there, in which case I could briefly describe what was going on, or Clinton and Therm would be in there and I'd have to tell them with absolute clarity that Therm better not do any taste testing.

Unfortunately, I found myself face-to-face with Marianne the second I opened the door. Realizing my mistake, I muttered something unrecognizable and raced to the west kitchen, where I found Clinton and Therm engaged in a heated discussion over whether or not to add more onion powder to the marinade. That meant Marianne was in Herb's kitchen doing heaven-knows-what while Herb and his crew were fixated on the circus Paul created in the parking lot.

Convinced that Marianne tampered with their refrigerated marinade, I flew out of the building in an attempt to find one of them. Thankfully, it wasn't all that difficult. Herb and the pinochle guys stood on the low concrete wall to the left of the social hall watching the catastrophe along with the rest of the community.

I was out of breath by the time I reached him. "Your kitchen," I stammered. "Marianne's in there. Clinton's girlfriend. She's probably tampered with your marinade by now."

I expected Herb to explode but instead, he gave me a silly grin. "It's a decoy. We figured they'd be up to something. The real marinade is in a cooler in Bill's car along with the ribs. We parboiled the ribs like we were supposed to and put them in the marinade. It's fine. Got plenty of dry ice. We'll get it to the grill on time."

"Whatever you do, don't take your eyes off of it."

"Thanks, cutie. Hey, look! Things are slowing down over there. Paul's out of his golf cart and a few of the dogs are back on their leashes. Quite the show, huh?"

*Yeah, if vaudeville is your thing.*

"Um, sure. I'd better get back inside. By the way, you haven't seen the judges, have you?"

"They're sequestered in one of the admin offices by the welcome courtyard with your uncle Louis. Boy, that guy has food connections up the ying-yang, huh? Is something going on?"

*You mean other than Paul's fishy attempt to sway a vote and Marianne's attempt to cheat her way to the moolah?*

"Just wondering. Anyway, good luck. And watch your back."

As I turned to go inside the social hall, I saw Paul responding to reporters' questions. More microphones than I could count were inches from his lips. His little fish stunt had become the news catch of the day and maybe, just maybe, it would net him the result the community hoped for. And a possible fine from the rec center for creating a disturbance.

I checked the time on my cell phone and it was now five forty. Five more minutes and my mother would be at the KSCW broadcasting booth along with Myrna and Paul, *if* Paul could break away from his five minutes of fame.

Even though I chose not to wear sandals, an annoying layer of sand had gotten under the heel of my foot. Low-level mule heels are comfy as all can be but they're only one step above flip-flops and sandals when it came to attracting rocks and sand.

I bent down to shake the shoe when I noticed a number of wheelchair groves on the pathway. I imagined the residents would be overjoyed when that concrete pathway project was completed in the fall. And then it happened—one of those aha moments that only appear in TV commercials or romance novels. Like a flash in front of my eyes, I saw the folded companion wheelchair leaning against the wall in the Angel Hair salon, complete with flecks of sand in the wheel treads.

The grooves on the rec center's path were similar to the ones I observed at the train tracks. I originally thought those might have been caused by a long pipe or hose from the railroad crew. They had the same equidistant spacing and narrow tread marks.

*Good Gracious! I know who Cosmo's killer is but I don't know if she plans to perform a second act.*

I was certain who did the deed but stymied as to my next move. I couldn't very well point a finger at ukulele player and hairstylist extraordinaire Bernice and make an accusation out of the blue. I'd been down that path before and to say it wasn't pretty would be the understatement of the century.

With the competition only an hour or so away, I knew Bernice wasn't going anywhere and that would give me time to think. I'd lost sight of Nate, Marshall, and the deputies but at the moment, it didn't seem to matter. I might have had an epiphany but I didn't have solid proof Bernice was the killer.

Earlier in the day, my mother explained that she, Myrna, and Paul had a *loose* script to follow that detailed the criteria for judging, along with a chronicle of the long and glorious history of barbequing meats, and a few prepaid advertisements from local vendors. Without a doubt, they'd screw it up, but that was the least of my concerns. By the time I wandered back into the social hall, it had begun to fill up again. I spotted a few of the book club ladies milling about, as well as Lyndy and her aunt on the other side of the room.

Although Herb didn't seem too concerned about interference from Marianne, I feared Enid, with the help of Bernice, would do to Clinton what Bernice did to Cosmo.

"What's with you, Phee? You look as if you lost your best friend." It was Augusta of all people, and for an instant, I was stunned. "Must really be bad," she said. "Cat's got your tongue."

"Augusta! I didn't expect to see you here."

"And miss seeing John Markus in the flesh? They don't call him the Pitmaster for nothing. Hey, nice act going on with Paul, even though it was a waste of some perfectly good fish. Surprised those dogs didn't knock over the golf cart."

*Give it time. Anything is possible.*

I motioned for Augusta to move closer to where I stood, and when I was certain no one was near us, I said, "I'm positive Bernice, the lady who did my hair, is the killer but there's no way to flush her out and I can't prove a thing."

I went on to explain how coincidental it was that the wheelchair in her salon had sand in its treads and how I was certain a forensic lab would match that sand to the sand found by the railroad tracks.

"If only I could get Bowman and Ranston to get a search warrant for Bernice's salon and brush some of that sand into an envelope for examination. I can't believe it took me this long to realize Bernice had a motive, too. She was furious with Cosmo. Said he sabotaged her marriage to Clinton."

"Speaking of which, what about him and his gold-digging paramour?"

"Okay, okay, they have motives, too, and Marianne's probably figuring out how to knock off Therm as we speak, and—Oh, good grief, Augusta—I'm all over the place with this. There's no way I can convince those deputies to get a search warrant."

Augusta looked around and smiled. "You don't need to. Only one *you* have to convince is Bernice."

Just then, a loud, grating voice permeated the room and I shuddered.

My mother had taken over the airwaves.

"Welcome, everyone, to the Master Grillers Barbeque Competition sponsored by the Food Network. I'm Harriet Plunkett from KSCW and with me are Myrna Mittleson from our *Booked 4 Murder Cozy Mystery Hour*, and Paul Schmidt from the *Fishing with Paul* show."

"Hey, don't forget our combined Murder Mystery and Fishing Show on Thursdays," Paul added.

"We've been trying to forget for the past three months," Myrna said, at which point my mother and Paul shushed her.

"Two teams will be competing for the honor of appearing on the Food Network," my mother continued, "as well as a substantial monetary prize."

Then Paul and Myrna read off the names of the two teams.

"In just a few minutes," my mother said, "we will introduce the teams and the judges. The teams will head to their stations on the patio and grill their ribs, during which time we will regale the audience with the robust history of grilling and searing meat."

Paul immediately snatched the microphone from her. "Or, we can talk about grilling fish. Got a great recipe here for grilling mackerel. Remember, you have to fillet them first and remove the rib bones. A little lemon, a little olive oil and medium heat should do the trick. And for those of you who want to eat the fish but don't want to look at it, I suggest stuffed tomatoes with mackerel. Easy as can be. Smash the fish. Add tomato sauce, cooked rice, onion, pepper, basil and then—"

"We're not talking about fish, Paul," Myrna said. "This is a barbequed rib competition. Beef ribs. Not fish bones."

I'd become so used to the squabbling among Paul, my mother, and Myrna that it drifted off somewhere in my mind along with plaguing thoughts about Bernice and Marianne. Up until that moment, I hadn't given Streetman or Essie any thought. It was only when Shirley rushed over to the KSCW table pulling the dog and cat carrier behind her that I realized she must have been babysitting them.

Unfortunately, Myrna didn't turn off her mic, and when Shirley leaned over to whisper something in my mother's ear, the entire audience heard her every word. "Streetman did a little poo-poo near the great lawn but I took care of it. Essie sat still and watched from the carrier."

Then someone shouted, "Dogs aren't allowed on the great lawn," to which someone else replied, "Says who?" That started a back-and-forth banter that didn't end until Paul grabbed the mic and said, "If you're worried about a little dog poop from a six-pound chiweenie, you're really not going to like the transfer station that's headed our way. Not too late to tell the planning commission where to stick it."

Augusta plunked herself in the nearest chair and slapped a hand on her cheek. "This rivals the entertainment from Talking Stick." Then she looked directly at me. "If you plan on making a move, I'd suggest you do it now. If I'm not mistaken, that's Melissa Cookston being escorted to a table near the patio. Bobby Flay and John Markus can't be far behind."

"Send for the militia if I screw things up," I said. "Nate and Marshall are around here somewhere."

Augusta sat up in her seat and looked around. "All I see is that deputy who looks like a giant desert toad. I'm afraid you're on your own."

*Terrific. I'm about to confront a possible murderess and no backup in sight.*

# CHAPTER 39

I lost sight of the ukulele performers when Paul's catastrophic drive-through in the parking lot disrupted the program. Fortunately, only one of them was a tall redhead who could easily be spotted in a crowd. I took a deep breath, counted to ten and proceeded to work the room like a politician in an election year.

It was surprising how many people I recognized. Dog park frequenters, restaurant goers, library patrons, my mother's neighbors, and the book club ladies, who had become my second family. As I maneuvered my way among the tables, I looked without success for Bernice. She wouldn't have left following that last rendition, would she? Not if she and Enid had a surprise waiting for Clinton.

I kept moving, turning my head from left to right and right to left until my neck ached. Suddenly someone tapped me on the shoulder and I jumped. I spun around and was relieved to see it was only Gloria Wong, looking as lovely as she always did with her petite frame, sleek black hair, and flawless skin. Had I not known she was my mother's age, I would have thought she was closer to mine.

"Your mother's doing a fantastic job MC-ing the program," she said. "I only wish Paul would stop talking about fish. Oh my goodness. Would you look over there? It's that horrid cat-hating woman from the planning commission. She's not supposed to be on the patio. She's the second woman who's been out there."

I looked through the closed patio doors and sure enough, it was Enid. Stepping toward the grill to the left with one hand suspiciously behind her back. The teams hadn't yet taken their positions and the ribs were still in the marinades as far as I knew. Still, something was off.

Gloria crossed her arms and huffed. "What's she up to? You know, I heard she was the one in that joint business venture with Cosmo. Kept bankrolling him money until she finally came to her senses and backed out."

Enid didn't budge from where she stood but the very sight of her in front of the grills made me nervous. I turned away for an instant and looked at Gloria. "Where did you hear all of this?"

"From my flower arranging club. One of the women overheard Enid at the beauty parlor telling the stylist that she was done paying Cosmo off and that she doubted she'd see a return on her investment. Do you think that's motive for murder?"

*Lately, anything seems to be a motive for murder.*

"Um, I really don't—" And then, a deafening round of applause as all three judges reached their table.

"Ladies and gentlemen," my mother announced, "our judges have arrived. Myrna will have the honor of introducing them, followed by Paul, who will introduce the competing teams." Then, because she had forgotten to turn off the mic, she said, "Listen, Paul, don't you dare say a darn word about grilling, baking, broiling, filleting, or pickling fish."

I hadn't taken my eyes off Enid and she didn't make any noticeable moves. I couldn't imagine why on earth she'd position herself in front of that grill, but I was certain it meant trouble.

"It was a Sun City beauty parlor," Gloria said. "I suppose Enid didn't want to cough up the Scottsdale prices. Especially if she coughed up enough money to Cosmo. Oh my! Would you look at that? She flew off the patio like a hawk after a mouse."

Sure enough, in the blink of an eye, Enid was out of sight. I mumbled something to Gloria and raced over to the KSCW table, colliding with everyone in my path.

"Mom! Myrna! Stall the competition. Don't let anyone go near those grills. I think Enid might have done something to them."

"Send for the fire department." Thankfully, the mic had been turned off so no one heard Paul's directive. He went on to babble about accelerants but I was no longer listening. Once again, I shoved my way across the room and out the patio doors. The grills had not been lit so there was no immediate danger, and I didn't smell anything that smacked of a chemical accelerant. But I did pick up a familiar aroma—lavender floral.

Bending over the grill, I took a good whiff and recognized it instantly— Dawn dishwashing detergent. Floral lavender scent. The kind I use in my own kitchen. Since the propane hadn't been turned on, I moved my hand across the metal grate, and sure enough, it was slippery and soapy.

*That witch! Sabotaging the competition. But how on earth would she know which grill was Herb's and which grill was Clinton's and Therm's?*

Suddenly Gloria's words came back to me. "She's the second woman who's been out there."

I looked around and Gloria was only a few feet away from the patio, about to take a seat at one of the tables. I all but landed on top of her. "Think fast, Gloria. What did she look like?" I was out of breath and my heart was pounding.

"Enid? You saw her as well as I did. Gray roots on short black hair, pencil-thin to the point of being unattractive—"

"No, no. The other one. The first woman. You said Enid was the second one out on the patio."

"The first one was your classic bleached blonde. If her top and capris were any tighter, they'd split."

"Marianne. It's Marianne."

"Who?"

"Never mind. Thanks, Gloria."

For the first time that I could actually remember, my mother listened to me and stalled the competition. Not only did she have Myrna and Paul introduce the competing teams, but she insisted each team member step up to the mic and say a few words. In doing so, all I could hear were comments like, "What am I supposed to talk about?" "No one told me I needed a resume," and "I'm not telling anyone anything."

I thought the last comment came from Bill but I wasn't sure. It didn't matter. What mattered was that my mother gave me enough time for a second gander on the patio. This time with the other grill. By now my movements came automatically. I don't even remember going outside but sure enough, there I was, leaning over the grill that Enid hadn't approached, so engrossed I hadn't realized Deputy Ranston stood behind me.

"Is there a reason you're inspecting the grill, Miss Kimball? Kimball-Gregory?"

"Enid Flox put dishwashing liquid on the grill to the left."

"And you saw her do that?"

"Sort of. I saw her standing in front of the grill with a hand behind her back. A hand that could have been pouring Dawn on the grate."

"I see. And *this* grill?" He pointed to the only other one on the patio. "Did she pour anything on it?"

"I didn't get a chance to check." I bent down, and sure enough it was a familiar detergent scent. This time Palmolive. The likelihood of Enid and Marianne working in cahoots was slim to none but it was uncanny how alike their diabolical minds were.

Next thing I knew, Ranston took out his phone and texted someone. Within minutes, a man from the rec center was on the radio with the following announcement: "Please hold tight, ladies and gentlemen. We've had a slight technical problem with our propane grills and need to bring in replacements from the great lawn. This should only take a few more minutes. Meantime, get to know who's competing. More introductions on the way."

I eyeballed Ranston. "A technical problem? Really?"

"We've got a huge crowd out there. Can't very well tell them the bloody affair's been tampered with. You know those folks. They go crazy if a restaurant runs out of the sugar substitute they use."

"Um, what happened to having a tight perimeter?"

"That went out the window when that careening golf cart made its entrance."

"So now what?"

"We try to find this Enid Flox and see what her problem is. Good grief. Dishwashing liquid. What next?"

"Um, she's helping out a friend get even for being ditched by her ex-husband."

"Harrumph. They usually go to social media for that. What friend? What do you know?"

"Enid didn't have an issue with Herb or his team. But she's really cozy with my beautician, who happens to be Clinton's ex-wife. Come to think of it, Bernice might have been Enid's former neighbor. I met a lady on her block who mentioned something like that. And as I was saying, I think—"

"Oh, never mind, Miss Kimball. Gregory. This is sounding more and more like one of those never-ending soap operas where it takes a year for the coffee to percolate. I need to find this Enid woman and I can't do it standing around here."

With that, he took off. Still no sighting of Nate or Marshall, but I had a funny feeling they weren't too far away from the KSCW table babysitting the competing teams. I was back to my original plan—getting Bernice to spill the beans.

While a maintenance crew lugged two propane grills to the patio area and moved the existing ones off to the side, I scoured the area for a tall redhead. I found her exiting the ladies' room and clenched my fists as I approached. Other than an elderly man at the drinking fountain, the hallway was empty. If ever I needed to deliver a performance worthy of an Academy Award, this was the moment.

"I know what you did at the railroad tracks," I said, the words sounding oddly familiar. Crap. It was the lead-in to a movie about some maniac who stalks young adults at a beach town.

She brushed a strand of hair from her brow and crinkled her nose. "What are you talking about?"

"Um, first of all, I want to say you're the best hairstylist I've had in a long time and I'm going to hate losing you."

"I don't understand."

"Bernice, I know you were the one who killed Cosmo. He orchestrated the moves your ex-husband did to cheat on you and you never forgave him. I don't blame you. What he did was unforgivable. And to see him with—"

"That bimbo?"

"Um, with Marianne, well, that must have been intolerable."

"It was insufferable. But you can't prove a thing."

"Uh, actually, I don't have to. You see, while this event is going on, a forensic team is at your salon obtaining evidence from that transfer wheelchair of yours. The one that still has the grains of sand and dirt on its wheels. Sand and dirt from the railroad tracks, not the decorative surface stuff they use around here."

"That's impossible."

"They obtained a search warrant and a key from the owner of the strip mall complex. Remember when I told you I worked for Williams Investigations? They're consultants on the case. That's how I found out."

Bernice's ruddy complexion turned ashen but she didn't flinch.

"I like you, Bernice. That's why I thought if I could find you and tell you ahead of time you could approach the deputies and give them your side of the story before they slap handcuffs on you."

"Don't you dare say a word! Don't breathe a single syllable!" It was Enid. The marionette lines around her mouth looking even more pronounced. She rounded the corner of the hallway and thundered toward us.

*An Academy Award? I'll take a daytime Emmy for this performance.*

# CHAPTER 40

" I can't believe you didn't think to hose off the wheels of that collapsible chair," Enid said. She brushed past me and was nose to nose with Bernice.

"I wouldn't've had that chair in my car in the first place if it wasn't for you. It's meant for salon patrons who have trouble walking from their cars. Besides, I thought you were going to loan it to your church for a midweek event and get it back to me. Not use it to, well, you know."

"Move a dead body? Or an almost-dead body?" I asked.

The two women ignored me and kept at each other.

"This is all Neville's fault," Enid said. "He's the one you should be yelling at, not me."

*Neville? What am I missing?*

"And have him go crazy on me like he did with Cosmo?" Bernice's face reddened and she pointed a finger at Enid.

I took a step forward and stretched my arm so that it blocked both women. "Are you trying to say it was Neville who killed Cosmo?"

"It was Neville's clumsiness," Bernice answered. "I don't think it was intentional at the moment."

Enid shot her a look. "Think for yourself. When he found out Cosmo lost all their money on a lousy investment, he went ballistic. Got the word from his broker shortly after they canceled the public hearing. Toxic fumes and all that. Those maintenance departments really need to do a better job."

"Look, right now there's enough evidence to put Bernice in the Fourth Avenue Jail," I said. "Not my favorite Phoenix hot spot. And she won't get out until the weekend's over." *How's that for a command performance?* "Tell the truth. What did Neville do?"

Enid and Bernice looked at each other for what seemed like an eternity. Finally Bernice spoke. "After the sheriff's deputies ascertained it was a dead trout in Cosmo's engine, they wrote it up and left the scene. Neville was still with Cosmo. I know because that was the time I came out of the supermarket and loaded my car. I parked it near Cosmo's. Of course at the time, I had no idea it was Cosmo's car."

"And I had no idea it was Bernice parked by Cosmo's car," Enid said. "I'd left the social hall but got waylaid talking with some former neighbors in the parking lot before I saw Bernice."

"And then what?" By now I was twitchy as ever and afraid I'd lose my momentum.

Bernice clasped her hands together and exhaled. "Cosmo went to open the car's hood again and Neville leaned over. The force of his weight caused the metal bar that holds up the hood to come loose and when it did, the hood slammed against Cosmo's head. Just like that. Boom! Cosmo fell over into the engine and didn't move."

I gulped. "He was dead?"

Again, the women looked at each other. "More or less," Enid said. "His face got wedged into all those nasty car parts under the hood. It was hard to tell. Then Neville spotted me on my way over to Bernice and motioned me over. It was serendipitous really. We looked at each other and knew in that split second we had to do something."

"To save Cosmo?"

"Oh, heck no! He would have ruined everything for us. Like I said, it was serendipitous. It wasn't as if I planned it but Neville said if I didn't help make sure Cosmo wasn't going anywhere, he would tell the authorities I murdered my great-uncle. Couldn't very well have that!"

I widened my eyes. Everything was coming at me all at once. "Did you? Kill your great-uncle?"

"Of course not. It was a threat Cosmo made because he didn't want me to back out of a business deal he and I were in. He must have said something to Neville."

"So you murdered Cosmo?"

Enid looked at Bernice. "Murder is such a strong word. I hastened his departure from this world. Another slam of the hood was all it took."

I tried not to picture it. "Um, let me guess. You and Bernice used the transport wheelchair to get Cosmo into Bernice's car and over to the railroad tracks before dumping him. Am I right?"

"Neville and Bernice did. I stayed back and wiped Cosmo's car clean from the hood all the way down to the interior. Except for the dead fish. I wasn't going near that thing. Then I left and went home. Bernice told me she drove Neville back to the parking lot, put the wheelchair in her car, and went straight home."

"That's the truth," Bernice said. "I even had to throw out some soggy groceries."

I wasn't sure of my next move but it didn't matter. At that very moment I heard Shirley's wail from the other end of the hall.

"Lordy, Phee! I've been looking all over for you! Streetman and Essie are missing. I must not have zipped that carrier up all the way. They're lost somewhere in this social hall. I wondered why they were so quiet. Now I know. Oh, Lordy! We can't let your mother know. Not in the middle of the broadcast. You've got to help me find them!"

I turned to Bernice and Enid, muttered the cliché of all clichés, "It's not over yet," and took Shirley by the arm. "It'll be all right. We'll find them. Streetman is very food-oriented. We just need something to entice him. And from what I've seen, he won't let Essie out of his sight."

As I looked past the social hall to the patio, I saw Herb and his crew standing over one of the replacement grills, while Therm and Clinton were at the other. From a distance, the scene looked idyllic. According to what I had been told, the ribs were parboiled and marinated, allowing the contestants about an hour to complete their grilling.

Meanwhile, I could hear my mother, Myrna, and Paul bantering over the airwaves. Attendees went back and forth to the food trucks while I dove under every single table, chair, and fixed piece of furniture. Shirley went to get Lucinda and Louise's help, insisting they would be discreet. "Forget Cecilia and your aunt," she said. "They'll only start a scene. Best not to get them involved until we're really desperate."

Then, as if I didn't have enough to consume me, Bowman approached. "Lose something?" he asked.

"If you must know, it's my mother's dog. He got loose in here."

"That little snapping turtle? You'll know soon enough. Someone will be screaming."

"Listen, I happen to know who our murderer is. Well, not premeditated murder in the actual sense, but more like a few degrees down. But not manslaughter or accidental death, more like—"

"What? Sorry. Just got a text from your boss. That looney cyber-sleuth of theirs tracked down the money angle. I need to get a judge to issue a search warrant. Then we're on our way to make an arrest."

"Didn't you already make an arrest?" But it was too late. Bowman bolted out of there.

"Don't blame me if Marianne tries to murder Therm," I mumbled under my breath before peering under another table.

The search and rescue for Streetman and Essie continued for another half hour. It was only when I heard my mother announce the judging to begin in ten minutes that my fear had turned to full-blown panic. As I bent under yet another table, I felt a familiar squeeze on my shoulder.

"Marshall. Thank goodness. Streetman is missing. The cat, too."

"I wondered what you and the women were doing. It was like watching a sideshow. Don't worry. We'll find them. Nate's with Bowman and Ranston. Rolo uncovered enough shady stuff to implicate Neville Lindblossom for extortion. That could mean—"

"He did it."

"I know. That's what I started to say."

"No, he really did it. Bernice and Enid were his accomplices. Sort of. Long story, but right now we need to find those animals."

I started to tell him what I had discovered when I heard another announcement. This time Myrna made it. "Contestants, please place your ribs in the bowls and bring them to the judges' table."

"Oh my gosh. This is it. The moment of reckoning," I said. I turned to the patio area when something caught my eye. It was some sort of small greenish box that was tossed in front of the patio doors. Marshall saw it, too. "Look! That's Essie, isn't it? She's batting that little box around."

Before I could answer, Marshall shouted, "Stay seated, everyone!" He moved to the patio doors faster than my aunt Ina to a dessert table. Within seconds he had the little kitten in his hands and, not unexpectedly, the dog at his feet.

"Cut it out, Streetman," everyone heard him say, "your cat's fine."

A bloodcurdling scream followed. "My babies! Mommy's precious little gladiators!" I would have emptied the contents of my stomach right on the spot had it not been for Shirley, who also screamed, "I'm so sorry, Harriet. Lordy, I don't know how they got out."

My mother rushed to the patio doors, snatched Essie from Marshall and then bent down to scoop up Streetman. Louise hurried over with the carrier, and within seconds those two balls of fur were contained once again.

"It's all right, Shirley," my mother said. "Streetman is a notorious escape artist. I should have known better. Next time I'll put on one of those kiddie locks."

As my mother, Shirley, and Louise fussed over the pets, Marshall bent down to retrieve the little greenish box the cat had been playing with. He held it at arm's length and then hurried back to me.

"Take a good look at this. Dancing chickens and all. If I'm not mistaken, this is the avocado recipe box Therm claimed had been stolen from his house." Marshall opened the box and pulled out scraps of paper, including Herb's original recipe, a small key, and a handwritten recipe for Momma Maybelle's toffee cookies. Next thing I knew, he made his way to the judges' table just as Herb and Clinton deposited their bowls of ribs in front of the three connoisseurs.

"We've got some cheating going on," Marshall stated. "And I'm holding the evidence."

A collective groan from the audience filled the room, and in that moment, I knew Herb and his pinochle buddies could kiss their food fortune goodbye.

# CHAPTER 41

Two of the judges stopped sampling the ribs and deposited the bones in the empty plates in front of them. The third judge, Melissa from Memphis BBQ, held a rib to her lips, took a bite and then added it to the bone pile.

It was impossible to hear the conversation, but Marshall must have been convincing because a few moments later one of the judges approached the event announcer, who in turn walked to the front of the room, holding the handheld microphone as if it was a bayonet.

"We have very unfortunate news, ladies and gentlemen," he said. "The Master Grillers competition has been terminated. Please feel free to enjoy the delicacies from the food trucks and, of course, each other's company."

To say the announcement didn't go over well would have been the understatement of the year. Possibly the decade. The shouting, grumbling, table pounding, and overall ruckus turned the fun-filled event into the proverbial storm of discontent.

"We demand to know what's going on!" someone shouted, only to have his comment followed by a dozen more with the same demand.

Lucinda rushed over and shook my arm. "Did someone try to poison the judges? Is that what's going on?"

"Shh! No! Clinton and Therm's team were the ones who stole Herb's original recipe. Marshall is sorting it out right now with the judges and the organizer from the Food Network."

Cecilia pulled at a loose strand on the sleeve of her white blouse. "This is awful. Our community's reputation will be stained forever."

The community's reputation may have been stained, but as far as my mother, Myrna, and Paul were concerned, their moment in the limelight was not to be blemished. All of a sudden, I heard my mother announce, "We at KSCW may not be announcing the Master Grillers winners but we're happy to talk about our favorite cozy mysteries." At which point Paul added, "And fishing spots. I've got a lineup of Arizona lakes, streams, and ponds that every angler and reeler from here to Yuma should know."

I rolled my eyes and cringed as the three of them shouted out a hodgepodge of cozy mysteries and fishing spots. I had no idea which was which and I doubted the audience did either. But that wasn't the worst.

Herb's bellow echoed across the room as he, along with Kevin, Wayne, Kenny, and Bill, marched toward Clinton and Therm, who were now standing a few feet from the judges' table. "You lousy lying cutthroats! You broke into my house, stole my recipe, and took away my chance of winning that spot on the Food Network."

Clinton lifted his head in the air and huffed, "You were never going to win. If anyone should be upset, it's Therm and me. That prize was all ours and now it's gone."

Out of nowhere, I heard sobs. Not little sniffling sobs, but outright gasping, crying sobs as Marianne made her way to Clinton. "Is it true? What the announcer said? The contest was canceled?"

Clinton nodded and went to give her a hug.

"I need time to think things over," she said. "I'll be in touch."

And like that, the woman vanished from the social hall and most likely out of Clinton's life.

With Bowman, Ranston, and Nate off to corral Neville, that left Marshall and a few uniformed assistant deputies to take statements from Clinton, Therm, Enid, Bernice, and Marianne.

Bernice and Enid, although complicit in the disposal of Cosmo's body, were quick to offer up Neville to the deputies in charge. Therm and Clinton admitted to their role in the theft of Herb's recipe, with Clinton admonishing Therm for cleaning up. I could hardly keep a straight face as Clinton pointed a finger at his buddy and groaned, "You just *had* to tidy up the place. Couldn't leave it alone, could you? Didn't I say that was a dead giveaway? Everyone knows what a compulsive germophobe you are."

While the questioning and information gathering continued, I moseyed over to the KSCW table where the program, thankfully, had wound down.

"Can you believe the audacity of some people?" my mother asked.

"Huh? What?"

"I'm talking about Paul. Look over your shoulder. There he is now. He's trying to convince Bobby Flay to have a fish grilling competition."

*Yep. Cecilia's right. This is turning out to be one big blemish on the community.*

"Forget Paul. Thanks to Essie and Streetman, those cheaters were caught. I mean, yeah, I'm sorry Herb lost out, but in the long run, Herb's no worse off."

My mother shook her head. "He could have been *well-off*, but at least my little fur babies were the heroes of the day."

"Um, actually, your daughter is the heroine of the day. I found out who killed Cosmo and the assistant deputies are dealing with it right now. Needless to say, I'm the one who—"

"Honestly, Phee, you're becoming so jealous of the dog, and now the cat of all things."

I tried not to scream and instead bit my lower lip. "Did you hear me? We know who killed Cosmo. It was Neville Lindblossom, the vice chair of the planning commission. Bowman, Ranston, and Nate are at Neville's place right now."

"He killed Cosmo so he could take over the planning commission?"

"No one's that crazy. It was an accident of sorts, although a jury will need to make a determination. I'll explain later."

"Good, because Streetman and Essie are hungry. I've got to get them home. Call me or stop by."

I gave her a hug and walked back to where Marshall and the deputies were still inundated. Thankfully the crowd who came to see the competition finished munching and mingling before leaving peacefully. I spotted Augusta, who gave me a thumbs-up, and Gloria Wong, who waved on her way out the door.

Lyndy and her aunt must have exited at some point because I didn't see them, but my aunt Ina spied me and raced right over. "Phee, I have wonderful news. My Louis has been invited to be a guest food critic on the Food Network. Isn't that marvelous? Look! There he is now chatting with John Markus."

I glanced over to where my uncle stood and nodded. "Wonderful. Simply wonderful."

And while the frenzied atmosphere returned to normalcy, one question remained. How did the evidence of Cosmo's murder wind up on Abigail's Callaway golf club? According to Enid and Bernice, Cosmo hit his head under the hood. Then Neville and Bernice moved him to Bernice's car while Enid wiped everything down.

"Quite the night," Wayne said as he and Bill walked past me. "We're going to wallow in self-pity and beer at Curley's. You and your husband are welcome to join us if he ever gets out of here." Wayne reached into his pocket and pulled out a worn red bandana that he promptly used to wipe the sides of his face and neck. "Air-conditioning my patootie. It's hotter than blazes in here."

Bill slapped him on the shoulder. "An ice-cold beer will take care of that. Come on." Then to me, "Are you in?"

"Um, maybe some other time. I have no idea when we'll get out of here and I'm exhausted. By the way, sorry about that raw deal."

Wayne shrugged. "Clinton and Therm will get what they deserve."

I watched as Wayne put the bandana back in his pocket and ambled out of the room with Bill at his side. Then, something occurred to me. More like a quick memory flash from the time I saw Neville with Cosmo when the social hall had to be evacuated thanks to the unfortunate moose urine incident. At the time, Neville took out a blue bandana to wipe his neck before putting it back in his pocket. He could have easily used that bandana to wipe blood off of the engine parts and later transfer it to Abigail's golf club.

The *why* plagued me until I remembered something Abigail had said. She spurned Neville and maybe, just maybe, the guy was unbalanced enough to get even. It would have been really easy for him to extract Cosmo's keys from his pocket, or the ignition if that's where they were, and hold on to them until later. Once he collected the blood evidence, he could have easily used a solvent or disinfecting wipe to remove any evidence.

Granted, Cosmo's death was weeks ago, but if it was one thing I knew, the laundry habits of single men could be downright chilling. When my cousin Kirk was in college, he boasted about purchasing new briefs rather than bothering to launder the ones he had.

I reached for my cell phone and sent the fastest text on record to Nate: *Search Neville's dirty laundry. Look for a bloodstained blue bandana. The dried blood is Cosmo's.* Then, I hurried off to tell Marshall.

Three hours later we got our answer. Neville broke down and confessed everything. Well, not the murder, but the planting of evidence in Abigail's garage and helping Bernice dump Cosmo's body by the railroad tracks. He insisted it was a freak accident but was afraid no one would believe him.

"Guess we can finally hit the sack," Marshall said. "Bowman and Ranston are on their way to the Fourth Avenue Jail with Neville and they called Abigail to let her know."

As I pulled the covers to my neck, I turned to Marshall. "Who put the dead fish in Cosmo's car? Did they ever figure that out?"

"Aargh. Put it on the list."

# CHAPTER 42

It took the remainder of the weekend for everything else to get sorted out, and by Monday morning Marshall and I were like zombies crawling into work. We drove one car that morning since Marshall didn't have any appointments outside the office.

"Snap out of it, you two," Augusta said when we made our entrance. "Nate's behind closed doors meeting with a new client so I didn't have a chance to grill him. The news said four arrests were made and that details will be available on the noon broadcast. Same for every single channel. I'm not waiting that long. Spill the beans."

Marshall tossed his empty Starbucks cup into the trash and stretched. "Good morning to you, too, Augusta. If you're taking notes, here goes: Therm was arrested for breaking and entering as well as petty theft. Bernice, Enid, and Neville were arrested for unlawful disposal of a dead body, and Neville is facing further charges for murder in the second degree. Which, by the way, may get reduced to manslaughter or some other felony. Hard to say."

He went on to provide the salient details while Augusta took in every word before turning to me. "Aren't you glad you confronted those two biddies?" Then back to Marshall. "If it wasn't for Phee, all of you would still be chasing around."

My face warmed. "Actually, it was Augusta who nudged me. She deserves the credit."

Just then the phone rang and Augusta picked up. "It's Deputy Bowman." She handed the phone to Marshall and widened her eyes. Listening to one-sided conversations is nerve-racking. It's impossible to figure out anything and Marshall's chitchat with Bowman was no exception. All we heard was "Really?" "You don't say?" and "How about that?"

"What?" I asked the minute he hung up.

"We got the answer to your dead fish in the car engine. Bernice put it there. She wasn't exactly truthful when she told you what happened." Then he smiled and started to laugh. "She recognized Cosmo's car when she drove to the supermarket and she told Bowman that her first instinct was to flatten the tires or scrape the paint with her car key. She walked over to the car, and to her surprise it was unlocked. That's when she decided on a more ingenious plan to 'shove it to the man who ruined her marriage.'"

Augusta straightened up in her chair. "Hell hath no fury like a woman scorned."

I rolled my eyes and waited for Marshall to continue.

"Bernice went into the supermarket and purchased a large filleted trout. Fresh, not frozen. She went back to the car, popped the hood, and tucked it in the manifold. She returned to the store, completed her food shopping and, well, you know the rest."

Augusta shuddered. "Got to hand it to the woman. She knew how to get even. Nothing like a rotting fish in a heat wave."

"Good grief," I said. "Here she was, worried about vandalism, when she wound up doing something far worse. Any other tidbits from Bowman?"

"Yep. Case closed on the pinochle cards in the jacket pockets."

I shook my head. "Not Bernice again? She was at the Stardust Theater for the public hearing."

"Nope. Not Bernice this time. Our buddies Therm and Clinton were apparently quite the active duo."

"Huh? How could they? They weren't on the stage with the planning commission."

"No, but they knew who the members were. Really easy to tell from their name tags. Therm and Clinton admitted to mingling around before the hearing got underway and slipping the cards into the pockets of four commission members. You were right about them wanting to set up Herb."

"Aargh. And I suppose they were the ones who gifted Paul with a little dead fish and Herb with a deck of cards?"

"Surprisingly, no."

"But, but—"

"Hang on. I'll get to it. Good thing for Bowman that Therm and Clinton were quite chatty because this one takes the cake—It was Marianne."

"Marianne? Clinton's girlfriend?"

"The very one. Her plan was to unnerve Herb so he'd get careless and lose his concentration when preparing his marinade."

"Heard it all," Augusta chimed in. "But if I'm not mistaken, why involve Paul?"

"From what Bowman was told, Marianne knew Herb and Paul were chummy so she wanted to shake them both up."

I brushed a few strands of hair from my face and stood still.

"You okay, Phee?" Augusta asked.

"Yeah, I'm fine. I mean, I *should* be fine. After all, the culprits were caught and Rolo's figured out that bogus pyramid scheme Cosmo roped Neville into. Guess it will be up to the prosecuting attorney to prove Neville shoved the hood bar or strut on purpose."

Augusta tapped her desk. "Or not. Last time I checked, they've got defense attorneys, too."

Marshall turned and started for his office. "It doesn't matter. Our job's done and we can all rest easy."

"Like hell. That transfer station vote is tonight. If it goes through, the reaction in Sun City West will be worse than the Bolshevik Revolution."

"Sorry, hon. It's out of our hands."

"Don't look at me," Augusta said. "It was never in my hands."

I walked into my office, closed the door, and booted up the computer. "It's you, me, and some invoices," I said to the machine. "At least I'll find some solace in that."

It was surprising that my morning wasn't interrupted by phone calls from my mother but I figured she was busy yakking with the book club ladies, my aunt, and now Gloria Wong, who had become another voice in the rumor mill. Then, at precisely twelve fifteen, the spell was broken.

"Phee," Augusta called out, "your mother's on the line."

I picked up the receiver and held my breath.

"Did you hear the news? It was just on KPHO. Then I turned to FOX 10 to make sure KPHO got it right."

"Got what right?"

"The transfer station vote. It's canceled. Kaput! Over and done with!"

"You mean they're going to reschedule it?"

"No, it's off the table. O-f-f. They couldn't hold the vote. They decided not to pursue the matter any further. Not with Cosmo dead and Neville and Enid arrested. Not to mention Abigail."

"What about Abigail?"

"She resigned from the planning commission. Effective immediately. I've got to call your aunt Ina and let her know before she drives your cousin Kirk crazy. Good thing you have me for a mother and not her."

And with that, the call ended, leaving me holding the receiver in midair.

"Lunch is on me!" I shouted. "Pizza for all of us! We've got some celebrating to do!"

Augusta grabbed the phone and pushed the speed dial number. "I'm getting the meat lovers' before anyone can change their minds. Then you can tell me what we're celebrating."

"Two cancellations—a BBQ competition and a transfer station. It doesn't get any better than that in Sun City West."

# EPILOGUE

Neville's trial was set for late fall but no one paid much attention. Instead, they were all fussing about the results from the Christmas in July calendar contest. It seemed the photo of Streetman with Essie chewing on his costume had appealed to the judges and it became the cover shot for the new calendar.

"That dog better not find anything else to bring home," I said to Lyndy a few weeks later. "I don't think I could stand it."

She splashed a handful of water at me and swam a few feet away. "It's not the dog I'd worry about, it's those murders that keep wafting your way. Maybe it's time you traded your accounting degree for one in criminal investigations."

"Shh! Not so loud! That's how rumors get started."

"So you'll consider it?"

"Absolutely. When Phoenix gets a full foot of snow!"

# About the Author

J. C. Eaton is the pen name of husband-and-wife writing team Ann I. Goldfarb and James E. Clapp.

A New York native, Ann spent most of her life in education, first as a classroom teacher and later as a middle school principal and professional staff developer. Writing as J. C. Eaton, she and James have authored the Sophie Kimball Mysteries, the first book of which, *Booked 4* Murder, took first place in the 2018 New Mexico-Arizona Book Awards in the Cozy Mystery category. They are also the authors of the Wine Trail Mysteries and the Marcie Rayner Mysteries. In addition, Ann has published nine YA time travel mysteries under her own name.

When James E. Clapp retired as the tasting room manager for a large upstate New York winery, he never imagined he'd be co-authoring cozy mysteries with his wife. Nonfiction in the form of informational brochures and workshop materials treating the winery industry were his forte, along with an extensive background and experience in construction that started with his service in the U.S. Navy and included vocational school classroom teaching.

You can visit Ann and James at www.jceatonmysteries.com, www.jceatonauthor.com, www.facebook.com/JCEatonauthor/, and www.timetravelmysteries.com.

Lightning Source UK Ltd.
Milton Keynes UK
UKHW012253081122
411848UK00004B/239